VOODOO PRIEST

N GRAY

By N Gray

Blaire Thorne

Ulysses Exposed

Voodoo Priest

Butterflies and Hurricanes

Salvation

Underworld Legacy

Scout Thorne

The Secret Tomb

Murder of Crows

Shifter Days, Vampire Nights, & Demons in Between

Twisted

Lady Hawk and Her Mountain Man

Hidden Shifter

Wolf

Wolf Retreat

Night Hunter

The Fixer

Kai

Lee

Flynn

Jude

Vinci Books

vinci-books.com

Published by Vinci Books Ltd in 2025

1

Copyright © N Gray 2019

The author has asserted their moral right to be identified as the author of this work in accordance with the Copyright, Designs and Patents Act 1988. This work is a work of fiction. Names, characters, places and incidents are the product of the author's imagination or are used fictitiously. Any resemblance to actual persons, living or dead, places and incidents is entirely coincidental.

All rights reserved. No part of this publication may be copied, reproduced, distributed, stored in any retrieval system, or transmitted in any form or by any means, including photocopying, recording, or other electronic or mechanical methods, nor used as a source for any form of machine learning including AI datasets, without the prior written permission of the publisher.

The publisher and the author have made every effort to obtain permissions for any third party material used in this book and to comply with copyright law. Any queries in this respect should be brought to the attention of the publisher and any omissions will be corrected in future editions.

A CIP catalogue record for this book is available from the British Library.

Paperback ISBN: 9781036702298

The EU GPSR authorised representative is Logos Europe, 9 rue Nicolas Poussion, 17000 La Rochelle, France
contact@logoseurope.eu

"I didn't want to pick up a gun or a blade and kill the monsters. However bad they were, they were still people. I might be able to protect myself if it was self-defense, but I couldn't see myself killing someone on purpose. Could I?"

-Blaire Thorne, Voodoo Priest-

Prologue

Scout was sitting on my lap. She was so small and light that I barely felt her weight as I wiped away her tears. But, instead of tears, it was blood I was smearing all over her face. I saw liquid in her ears, so I cleaned that, too; the tissue covered in the same dark, maroon liquid.

She blew her nose, and that, too, came away bloody.

I had to remain calm. Scout was hemorrhaging everywhere, and I wanted to help her. I was trying to keep her relaxed, but the blood was everywhere.

"Help me, Mommy," she said, another red tear staining her cheek.

I held her small body tightly against mine. I pictured all the whiteness of my healing aura and pushed it into her, the cool, serene force of my power searching for the virus killing her. My strength finally found that hopeful spark and reignited it.

"It burns. You're burning me, Mommy!" Scout cried out, her tiny fingernails digging into my skin.

A dark figure emerged from the shadows and towered over us. His large hands pried their way between our embrace; those dark hands were covered in soot. Black feathers danced in the air all around him and fell over us.

"Mommy, please don't let him take me! I want to stay with you…" she said, her shrill cries echoing off the walls.

"No, you can't take her now. I haven't finished. I was helping her. No, no, please, not yet," I cried.

But my pleas were ignored.

The clandestine figure opened his wings and scooped Scout into his arms.

"I can protect her, Blaire. I'm the only one who can take away her pain."

"Nooo!" I screamed, but my scream was heard by no-one but the four walls of my bedroom.

My chest ached, my breathing was labored, and my tears flowed.

I climbed out of bed, blew my nose, and washed my face in the bathroom.

Heavens, what the hell was that?

In the mirror, I saw a black feather lying atop my shoulder. I stared at the object, frozen by the thought of whoever the figure was still being here. But as I reached my shoulder to remove it, it was gone. I glanced in the mirror again, and it was no longer there.

A noise from my bedroom caught my attention. Something moved in the dark shadows near the curtains. My pulse thundered in my ears. With one hand curled around the doorjamb, I flicked the bedroom light on, but it was only the wind from the open window moving the curtain. I exhaled a shaky breath.

It had only been a dream, but it had felt so real. And

even though it was just a dream, the smell of burned flesh was still wafting in the air.

The feel of my daughter in my arms had been comforting. She must have been six or seven years old in the dream, and my chest began to ache.

I missed her and desperately wanted to see her again.

Chapter One

My hips started burning, my legs were already numb. I was mirroring Seraphine, but where she had had years of training and sitting in the lotus position, I had only had two sessions. We were midway through the second session, and again it only comprised meditation, core strengthening and drinking copious amounts of green tea.

Seraphine's a witch and had agreed to train me in all things spooky. Two months ago, when she had removed the curse that almost killed me—a curse she had placed on her then-boyfriend, Danny—she had metaphysically seen that I had some kind of ability.

Seraphine explained that I had a direct metaphysical connection to the spiritual world; to any mystical world. And, with the right training, I would be able to syphon other powers and store them until I needed to use them. She had also hinted that she had sensed something else within me, but she hadn't been quite sure what it was exactly.

So far, I had no idea how to do any of that, but apparently she was training me. I would have to wait and see.

She uncrossed her legs and stood up gracefully. With silky-smooth chestnut hair that flowed all the way to her knees, she always managed to keep it out of her face without having to tie it up. She was about as tall as me—five foot five—and had the right amount of curves to drive any man crazy. With a thin nose and lips, and sharp features to complete the look, her eyes were the best of all her features.

The eyes revealed so much about a person, giving little clues as to what they liked and what they were thinking. The different shades of the iris were the best part, and some were utterly captivating, like Seraphine's. Hers were the lightest green I had ever seen, almost translucent because there wasn't a dark ring surrounding her iris like almost all green eyes had. And, depending on her mood, they would either lighten or darken. I would say she was the most exotic-looking person I had ever seen.

I uncrossed my legs, straightened them out in front of me and wiggled my toes until I could feel them again. Seraphine was older than me and she made standing up from a seated position look so easy and boneless; yet there were crunching and clicking sounds coming from my hips and knees.

"Don't grow impatient." It sounded like a warning. "We train for years before we can touch any of our spell books. We meditate and read about the differences between good and evil before we can even think about learning any spells," she said, still stretching.

"You are not like us, yet you are. We don't know how to go about doing this without harming your," she added, standing straight. "There's much for us to cover, but I don't want it to be too much, too soon. It will all take time." She ended her dialogue with a smile that didn't reach her eyes.

"I know," I said with a slight groan. The feeling in my legs returned, and stood up slower than I wanted to. "I'm not impatient." I tried sounding pleasant.

Seraphine had invited me here to learn about the potential I was harboring, but she hadn't taught me anything useful yet. I was feeling restless because we hadn't done anything, but I was also excited to learn something no matter how small. Hopefully I wasn't wasting my time and hers.

"Let's have some tea; proper tea, not that green stuff we've been drinking." The humor in her eyes matched her curved mouth, and she started walking toward her spacious kitchen.

I followed her. A kitchen like hers was a chef's dream. My jaw had dropped last month when I first visited, and she had been positively glowing when she told me how much she enjoyed cooking.

She switched the kettle on and grabbed two cups and saucers from the cupboard for the tea.

"I thought we could have tuna mayo sandwiches with our tea today?"

"Sounds lovely," I beamed at her. I didn't mind what she made; her culinary skills were excellent. Last month, we had chicken sandwiches, but it was like nothing I had ever eaten before. I had two sandwiches and didn't eat for the rest of the day.

I came prepared today and skipped breakfast.

We sat at her dining table with our tuna sandwiches on China plates which matched the placemats underneath. She poured tea out of a pot into our gold-rimmed cups. My mouth watered. Now all we needed was the Queen.

Today, she sat next to me; last month, she sat across from me. Now, her place mat was right beside mine. The table was a twelve-seater, and I fought the urge to scoot away from her. But I wouldn't be rude inside her home.

There was a silver cloche covering the food; I waited for Seraphine to remove hers first before I removed mine. My left hand rested comfortably on the table when she grabbed it, making me flinch. I fought not to squeal and yank my hand away.

It wasn't that she held my hand, but she had never touched me before now. She didn't strike me as the touchy-feely type.

I glanced down at our hands then back up to her face. When her gentle touch started warming my hand along with tiny pinpricks forming where she held me, I glanced down again. Then the pinpricks moved up my arm.

My chest tightened and I sucked in a breath.

"Breathe," she said, her eyes were still closed and she held my hand firmly.

I exhaled slowly.

"Tighten your core muscles," she barked like a drill sergeant.

I nodded even though she couldn't see me, then inhaled slowly and exhaled.

"Close your eyes," she said sharply.

As I closed my eyes, the pinpricks mutated into red hot flames and moved higher up my arm. I bit my lip, trying hard not scream.

"Breathe."

"It's hot," I moaned, raising my voice slightly, and fighting the urge not to yell at her.

"Now take it in. Hold in the burn."

The fire moved into my shoulder, crept along my collar

bone, and around my neck. It circled my heart and squeezed it. My breathing came in short, shallow breaths, beads of sweat starting pouring down my face as my clothing clung to my body. My right hand gripped the side of the chair, and that hurt, too.

"Blaire!" she yelled.

"What?" I said through gritted teeth.

The fire was crawling through my veins, near my jaw, in my ear, and right behind my eye socket.

"Aaah! It hurts, Seraphine. It's too much."

I wanted her to let go. I needed her to let go.

The fire she had ignited inside me reached my brain, and my breathing became labored. I pushed air through the circle of my mouth like expectant mothers did when pushing; except I was trying to push the fire out of me, and not a newborn.

She removed her hand off mine and the fire receded, like ice running through my body.

I rubbed my hand where it still hurt.

She turned to face me.

"Now do the same to me." Her pale green eyes had bled to the color of seaweed; a startling difference that made her face appear stern and unapproachable. She opened her hand for me to take and smiled kindly.

I still felt the fire pulsing at my fingertips; it was there for me to use. I did as instructed and took her hand gently in mine, thinking about what she had said; that I needed to take that power and use it on her.

I pictured the fire that had burned through me and how it had hurt throughout my body. Extending my fingertips, I pushed that little spark back into her, then gripped her hand tightly with my nails digging into her skin.

She tried to pull free of my grip, but I held on.

A smile spread across my face; a grin somewhere between smug and pleased.

I let go of her hand and that little spark disappeared, using everything she had pushed inside of me.

A pained expression crossed her face, and when her eyes fluttered open. There was something else present in her stare reminding me of regret.

"Are you okay?" I asked, turning my body to face her.

"It was only a test, but…" She turned her hollow gaze in my direction, and I held my breath. She was quiet for a moment, her haunted eyes flicking away to stare at something behind me. I didn't want to look away. "How were you able to do that?"

I shrugged and stared at my fingertips as I wiggled them.

"I don't know. When you let go of my hand, I could still feel the energy at my fingertips. All I had to do was push it into you the same way you did to me." I shrugged again. "I felt it; how it went into your hand and up your arm. And while that was happening, I thought how I wanted it to hurt you as badly as it hurt me." I sounded sinister or vindictive, and licked dry lips. I reached for my tea cup and enjoyed a sip.

"That was good. You're a fast learner," she said, staring vacantly, as if she was still in shock from my power display.

"I wonder if I was able to do that before—"

"Have any of your memories returned?"

"No," — I shook my head, — "it's all still a blank…" I hesitated, closing my mouth.

"What? What were you going to say?"

To look at her would show too much. I'd been having strange dreams that might be memories, but I wasn't sure what they meant; if anything at all.

"Look at me." Seraphine was nothing if not persistent. "What aren't you telling me?"

"I've been having dreams... Of my daughter," I said, looking into Seraphine's eyes as they returned to their light green hue. "Or they could be memories, but I don't know. I can't be sure."

"It's been two months, Blaire. Your wounds have healed, have they not?" She touched the fine scar above my left eye, a light brush of her fingertips with no magic behind them.

Mel, the were-wolf doctor who treated me after I was attacked by a were-wolf and a were-lion, had done a wonderful job that if you didn't know I had stitches on my face, you wouldn't know the scar was there. The scar on the left side of my abdomen and back was another story altogether; it stretched from my belly button all the way across my body, ending somewhere near my spine. The red welts of the scarring branching off in all different directions looked like a road map, the result of my attackers trying to tear me apart.

"Yes, the wounds have healed."

"But not in here." She pressed a finger lightly to my forehead.

I blinked back tears.

My favorite song started playing, and I knew Ralph was calling.

I mouthed my apologies to Seraphine for interrupting our conversation and fished my cellphone out of my pocket to answer the call.

"What's up?"

"Are you done yet? We have a new contract and I think you should join me on this one."

"I don't know, Ralph..."

After I was attacked, I suffered from short-term amnesia

which had robbed me of my identity. In the weeks that followed, I had slowly learned the truth about myself, and, in all honesty, it wasn't exactly a truth I was thrilled about.

Since the 'new me' still wasn't sure about being an assassin, I had been convalescing on holiday for the past two months, and each time Ralph had received a contract, I had politely declined his offer to join him.

Ralph was my partner in the killing game; we used to scope out targets and kill monsters together. Ordinarily, I was usually the one to do the hit, and I wasn't sure I wanted to keep doing that.

"You can stay in the car, I promise."

I hesitated. I wanted to, but caution told me not to go.

"Are you still there?"

"Yes, I'm here."

"I need to fetch you anyway. You might as well just ride along instead of sulking back at your place."

I rolled my eyes and was glad he couldn't see it.

"Are we done for the day?" I asked Seraphine.

She nodded.

"Okay. You can fetch me now."

Chapter Two

I helped Seraphine clear the table when we were done eating and thanked her for the session. We set a date for next month and agreed that I would bring something sweet for tea. At first, she refused, saying it was her house and that she looked after her guests and not the other way around. Since she wouldn't take money, I told her it was a small gesture to repay her for helping me. She reluctantly agreed. Unfortunately, my baking skills were awful, but I knew a great bakery around the corner from my house.

I crossed my arms over my chest and wrapped my coat tightly around my body. It was only autumn, but the wind had an icy chill to it today.

As I waited outside for Ralph, I thought of my daughter, Scout, and what she was doing. I wondered whether she was outside in the cold like I was, or someplace warmer.

Her father, Mason, had to run away with her to keep her safe. That happened ten years ago, but for me, I relived it again months ago upon hearing about my past.

I heard Ralph's car before I saw it. It seemed everyone

at Ulysses Assassins drove the ugliest and oldest car they could find. Mine was an old blue Honda, which was still being forensically investigated in a warehouse somewhere, after Sebastian and I had found it with a Ulysses employee's torso and severed hand in the trunk. We still didn't know who had killed Shane, but his body had been dismembered in our boss Marcus's house; but he didn't know who was responsible.

Miles and Danny, the two were-animals who had attacked me, had denied killing Shane. And Roland, the vampire who orchestrated my assault, would never get his own hands dirty, so I was fairly certain it wasn't him, either.

Ralph's Land Rover stopped at the curb beside me, a cloud of smoke trailing behind it.

"Geez, Ralph, when are you getting rid of this piece of shit?" I asked as I climbed into it.

"Leave my baby alone." He rubbed the dashboard tenderly.

"Gross." I scrunched my face.

His full lips curved into a smile baring all his teeth. Ralph was handsome in a rugged, outdoorsy kinda way. The first two times I saw him after the attack, he had looked different each time.

The first time he'd been wearing a fishnet shirt with leather pants, sporting a beard and curly hair that fell to his shoulders.

The second time, he came to my house dressed in a business suit and his beard shaved to leave only a mustache.

His hair was still long these days, neatly framing his face. And with the beard gone, I could see the dimple in his chin that softened his face.

Today, his face was cleanly shaven and smelled like aftershave. But he had left the soft brown curls to fall where they wanted to. And beneath the long dark eyelashes, his eyes were the color of the sky just before nightfall.

When Ralph wasn't working, we usually spent time together. And apart from those two occasions where he had dressed up, he usually wore sneakers with jeans, a vest, and a loose shirt to disguise the shoulder holster for his gun.

As I settled into the seat, I could see that Ralph was in recon mode; ready to observe and survey potential targets. Today would be the first time I was tagging along on an actual contract.

In response to the excuses I always had not to go with Ralph, Marcus, our boss at Ulysses Assassins, had said that if I didn't start pulling my weight, he would forfeit my salary. Which I understood; he couldn't keep paying someone who wasn't working. I had enough money to last me a while, but then what? I didn't know what I'd do once the money ran out. Unless I had a stash of cash somewhere and I miraculously remembered where it was, I had to work even if it was sitting in the car and watching someone all day.

When Ralph pulled away from the sidewalk, he had his serious face on.

"Your gun is in the glove compartment," he said sternly.

"Ralph—"

"Don't Ralph me," he said, cutting me off. "You've had time on the range to retrain your eye, so wear it already. Anything could happen, Blaire. You need to carry it with you. Always." That one word a silent warning. "What if that witch had tried to hurt you, but you couldn't protect yourself because you were unarmed?"

I crossed my arms over my chest and pouted.

"Put it on. You know I'm right."

I rolled my eyes, but he couldn't see me. I opened the

glove compartment and took out the shoulder holster, slipping it on over my top and securing the gun—a Glock 19 pistol. I put my coat on over everything, zipped it up to the top, and fastened the seat belt again.

"Are you happy?"

"Yes," he said, but he didn't sound it.

"What's wrong now?"

He looked across at me when we stopped at a red light. There was a somberness in his eyes that couldn't be mistaken.

"I can't lose you again," he said sadly.

My chest tightened and my throat ached. I turned away from the pain in his face because if I kept looking at him, I knew I would cry.

"The light has changed," I said.

He pulled away slowly, and we cruised onward with the rest of the lunch hour traffic.

"So, what's this new job?" Changing the subject was easier and helped me think about something besides the attack and the nightmare that had followed. Ralph was my best friend, there to hold me at night when I cried out and I didn't want to go back to sleep. He had stayed by my side for a month until I had told him to go. He couldn't babysit me forever, and he had his own life to live.

"A suspected murderer," Ralph said, clearing his throat.

I frowned and turned in the seat as far as I could to look at him.

"So why aren't the police arresting him?"

"They don't have enough evidence."

I frowned harder. Either I was slow, or the cops were useless; which was already my opinion, given that I had been left to solve my own mystery around who had attacked me.

"I don't understand, Ralph. Gathering information and getting the bad guy is usually the cops' job. Why are they handing it to us? We usually only get jobs where all that's been done, and all we have to do is pull the trigger."

"When there are jobs the cops can't handle, or because it could cause political uproar, they pass it over to us to handle quietly. This is one of those jobs."

I narrowed my eyes.

"What?" he asked when he saw my face.

"What aren't you telling me?"

"Fine," he said with a heavy sigh. "They arrested him and charged him with the murders, but then there was another murder with the exact same MO as the others. They knew it couldn't have been him because he was in custody when it happened, so they had to release him. They knew he was connected to the murders; they just didn't know how. So, they asked us to figure it out." He hesitated. "To get rid of the problem."

"Shit." I sat straight in my seat and focused on the cars ahead of us. "So, is that where we're going now?"

"Yep."

"How many people has he killed?"

"The folder is on the floor near your feet."

I looked down and saw a thick manila folder and picked it up. I paged through it, glancing over the police reports. There had been seven murders; each similar that they had to be the handiwork of the same person. All the victims were male, six foot two, between two hundred and two-hundred-and-twenty pounds, and Caucasian.

I gasped when I saw the first crime scene photo, closing the folder so quickly that a few of the photos fell to the floor.

Shit, now I had to look at them when I picked them up.

My stomach turned, and I felt dirty, like the pages in the folder were crawling with insects and I didn't want to hold it anymore. I dropped the folder on the floor again and looked up at the traffic.

"Are you okay?"

"You could've warned me," I moaned.

Ralph gave a hearty chuckle, found a parking spot, and cut the engine.

"That's his shop over there." He pointed to the center across the road. All the shops looked ordinary enough; a barber's, a pet shop, a convenience store and then there was the voodoo shop. It looked much the same as all the others in Sterling Meadow.

I wondered how the killer chose his victims and whether he performed rituals or tarot readings.

"Did any of his victims buy anything from him?"

"I don't know. Was it mentioned in the folder?" His eyes flicked to me and then to the folder on the floor by my feet. "Aren't you going to read it?"

"Dammit, Ralph." I picked up the folder. "Can't you just tell me?"

"No, I need your take on it. We're a team, okay? And before you say anything, I know you don't remember, but I know you still have that inquisitive mind. We just need to bring that part of you to the surface again."

I huffed, opened the folder again and read the full reports.

The victims all held very different jobs; there was a magician for kid's parties; a bus boy; a lawyer; a teacher; a data analyst; a cartoonist; and, lastly, a homeless man. Yep, all very different, and, from the looks of it, they all belonged to very different social circles. I couldn't see any connection between them at first glance.

The first victim had been the magician; he had attended a kiddie's party and never came home. His wife had filed a missing person report the next day when she couldn't locate him using an app on her phone. The magician was average looking, with short brown hair, brown eyes, and thin lips.

They eventually found the magician in a field near a school, minus both hands. During the autopsy, the medical examiner had discovered an item sewn into his hollow cavity, in place of his organs. The photo I held was that of a little voodoo doll made from brown material; it had two buttons for eyes, a smile stitched with red cotton, and a little bell sewn to the middle of its body. It would have been a cute little doll if it hadn't been for the bright red blood that had stained it.

The tuna sandwich I had eaten only an hour ago was ready to make a reappearance, but I swallowed hard; I would not throw up today.

The picture of the magician's corpse was in black and white, and I breathed a sigh of relief; I had seen enough red on the doll. The magician's body had been dumped. As in thrown-out-of-a-car-while-it-was-still-moving kind of dumped. His body had come to rest on its side, the arms sprawled in unnatural positions and the legs crossed. The report said his entire body had been covered in dirt, as though he had rolled into that position and collected sand before he had stopped moving.

The other six bodies were found in very similar circumstances, the only differences being the locations, which were scattered all over the city. There was nothing connecting them; nothing about their background, or where they worked, or who they knew was connected. They seemed to be random victims, yet they must have been specifically selected because of their corresponding height and weight.

"How tall is our man and what does he weigh?"

Ralph's smile was a good one. That made me smile because something I said thrilled him. I had said something worthy of that smile.

"I knew you could do it."

"What?"

"Your question. It was perfect. Just the kind of question the old Blaire would have asked."

"Glad I can be of service." My smile mirrored his.

"He is six foot two and weighs two-hundred-and-ten pounds." He removed a piece of paper from his pocket with the information on, unfolded it and handed it to me.

"You were testing me?" I scowled.

"Someone's got to, seeing as though you won't push yourself."

"Fine," I said, placing the piece of paper inside the folder. "What are we going to do now?"

"We wait."

Chapter Three

It was a little after 4pm when the man exited the shop. From where I sat, I could see that he had hair as white as snow, and his skin was morbidly pale. He surveyed the area and then locked his shop. He walked to an old red Chevy truck, climbed in, and drove out of the parking lot.

Once the Chevy had passed us, Ralph started the engine and pulled into the flow of traffic behind a green Ford.

"Is that Ross McNielty?"

"Yep."

"Do you think he saw us?" I asked, keeping my eye on the red Chevy truck.

"Not sure. We'll soon see if he makes any sudden turns. I know his home address, so if he does decide to go on a joy ride, we can wait for him there."

When Ross McNielty stopped at a drive-thru, we parked on the other side of the road as he ordered his dinner. Once he had been handed his food, he drove off in the direction we had just driven, so Ralph had to make a U-turn.

We kept a little distance between us and the red Chevy truck in hopes he couldn't see us tailing him or that was the plan, anyway.

Instead of going back to the shop, McNielty turned left before the center where his shop was, passing a school with kids playing ball, two churches and a mall. After fifteen minutes of driving, he eventually stopped in a driveway.

"Is this his house?"

"Yep," Ralph said, as we slowly drove past his house and parked around the corner, four houses away.

"What now?"

"Now we wait."

"Should I have worn an adult nappy?" I said, rolling my eyes.

"No," — he snorted with laughter, — "I doubt we'll be waiting that long."

"I hope not." I unbuckled the belt and settled lower in the seat until I was comfortable.

Ralph opened his window. The breeze was chilly; I shivered and hugged my body tightly.

More cars parked in the various driveways as people came home from work. It was 4:30pm and the cold was creeping in and the sun hadn't even set yet. We still had an hour and a half left of daylight and it was already chilly, hinting at a freezing winter if autumn was this cool already. I made a mental note to buy a warmer jacket from the outlet mall.

The houses in the neighborhood were typical of suburban life. Some were double story, but regardless of the number of floors, each of them was massive. And they all had immaculate gardens.

"What else does he do at his voodoo shop to be able to afford this place?" I asked while surveying the other houses.

"You tell me. His house is worth at least nine hundred thousand dollars, and I doubt selling shitty trinkets from the shop covers his mortgage."

"What else does McNielty do in his spare time?"

"Apparently he plays poker every Wednesday. He should be leaving around five, which will give us time to look around."

"Do you mean go into his house?" I flashed wide eyes. "As in break in?"

"Uh-huh."

"Shit."

The first stars of the evening were twinkling in the night sky when we entered McNielty's house through the back door. It took Ralph less than a minute to unlock and open the simple lock securing the door.

The kitchen was neat and tidy, with the smell of disinfectant still in the air. There was a kitchen island in the center of the room with a bowl of fruit atop it, and an eight-seater dining table across the room near the door.

Ralph handed me a flashlight and switched his on. We scanned the room looking for anything out of the ordinary. I didn't know what we were looking for but I'd entertain the theory that I did.

"Touch nothing." He warned.

"I know," I replied a little petulantly.

On the far side of the living room stood two cabinets lined with shelves. All were full of jars. The cabinets cordoned off a small section of the room that obscured our view. It was only as we walked farther inside that the smell caught me off guard. I preferred the disinfectant smell at least it was clean and sterilized.

"What's that smell?" I whispered to Ralph, pinching my nose closed.

"I think it's coming from the bottles." He jerked his chin in the cabinets direction.

Each of the jars held different items, immersed in some kind of preserving liquid that was yellow in color at the top and red toward the bottom.

"He has tongues, ears, eyeballs... even a penis in these jars." I pointed to a jar near the floor. I shuddered. "There's even a shrine back here."

Ralph stood beside me, and we stared. It took me a couple of seconds to register what exactly it was we were staring at.

There were dried ears hung from a string that surrounded a number of candles like a curtain, which had been dotted around a framed picture of a woman and an open metal box that had been placed in the middle of the table.

"Jesus, what the fuck is that?"

"I think it's lady parts."

"You're joking?" Ralph's eyes widened.

"Well, what does it look like to you?" I said, pointing to the contents of the metal box.

He looked again, but I didn't think he registered what the object was. His face contorted with disbelief as he concentrated on the item, but his mind seemed to be rejecting the horrific concept behind the display.

The labia and clitoris had been arranged like a flower on a bed of tissue paper inside the metal box. Once Ralph's mind finally accepted the grim truth, he turned away from the table and swallowed hard.

"Let's go see what else there is," he said in a strained voice.

"Agreed." For the second time that day, my lunch almost repeated on me. I hoped that the woman was dead before that had been done to her.

I tried to breathe through my mouth, but the smell from the bottles burned the back of my throat and eyes. I wiped my eyes dry with my hands as we entered the first bedroom.

The bedroom was dark; the light from our torches revealed black walls and drawn black curtains. The silver chains caught my attention first. Connected to the chains were leather straps; the ones used to hold someone against a wall with their arms above their head. In the middle of the room was a large bench connected to a single beam, which was covered with a soft leather cushion.

"What is that for? Is it a seat or something?" I frowned.

Ralph shook his head and said something, but I couldn't quite hear him.

"What? I can't hear you." I approached him and saw that he was pale, his blue eyes dark in comparison to the color of his face. "What is it, Ralph?"

I glanced back at the seat.

"It looks like a Spanish horse, but without the spikes. It was used as a device for torturing women." He looked at me, his eyes drowning in horror. "It's been modified for pleasure."

"What?" I looked at the horse again, frowning, and shone my light onto the legs. There was an ankle strap on each of the legs to keep the woman bound and her legs apart. On the soft leather seat itself were more straps, which would bind her hands in front of her as she lay over the horse, her lady-bits flashing whoever was standing behind her. There was a step on the floor so he could reach her.

"Shit, Ralph. I want to get out of here. I don't like this fucking horror house."

"We still need to check the other two rooms. Then we can go."

I reluctantly nodded in agreement.

The second bedroom was normal by comparison, containing only a bed, a couple side tables, and a cupboard. Thank heavens. I didn't think I could stomach another torture room.

The main bedroom had a huge bed in the center; two king-size beds pushed together, made for an orgy of people. The carpet was white fur; I knelt down, and it was soft to the touch.

The curtains in this room were open, and car headlights suddenly blinded me. As I clambered away from their glare, the car engine died, and someone climbed out of the car.

"Fuck! What do we do?"

"Hide," Ralph instructed.

The front door opened, and Ralph scrambled out of the main bedroom. I fell flat onto the soft white floor and rolled under the bed as the person came through the door of the main bedroom.

Lying on my back and looking up at the bottom of the base of the bed, my fingers held onto the flashlight as it lit up the wood. I hurriedly switched it off as he neared the side under which I was lying.

The person walked around the bed and stood near me, his feet beside my face. He wore black leather dress shoes, and they smelled like polish. Also beside my head was a pack of cards and a roll of token chips. The feet moved, and a hand came under the bed. He was searching for something on the floor.

My heart started beating faster, and I held my breath.

His fingers came near my shoulder. All I could think of was that he was about to look underneath the bed and find me.

The contents of the first bedroom were still fresh in my mind, and I wondered what he'd to me when he saw me. I remembered the shrine and the metal box as his fingers inched closer to my face.

Relying on gut instinct, I gently pushed the cards and chips nearer to his searching fingertips, and he picked them up. I let out a shaky breath as quietly as I could as he went into the bathroom and closed the door. I blinked back tears.

He flushed, left the bedroom, and exited by the front door. The car roared to life and headlights flooded the room again.

I wiped the tears from my face, and lay quietly for a moment, relearning to breathe and blink. When a hand grabbed me I screamed.

"Shh, it's me."

"Dammit, Ralph, you scared the crap out of me." I wanted to laugh, but my heart was still knocking hard against my rib cage. "He almost touched me. He almost found me." I took short, shallow breaths, still clutching the flashlight.

"Let's get the fuck out of here. I think we've seen enough."

I nodded and quickly rolled out from under the bed. I started to walk out of the room when I heard muffled sounds.

"What's that?"

"What?"

"I heard crying… or something."

"I can't hear anything." The lines between his brows furrowed.

"Shh! There it is again." I pointed to the closet against

the far wall of the bedroom, approached and opened all the doors, but they were full of clothing.

Another muffled cry.

I climbed into the closet and knocked on the back panels. They all sounded solid until I reached the one on the far left.

"There's a door here. Help me open it."

"We shouldn't be doing this. He could come home again," Ralph said nervously. "Let's get out of here."

There was a click, and the wall gave way. I opened the hidden door to reveal a set of steps leading downward. I felt for a light switch and, finding it on the right, flicked it on.

Ralph closed the hidden door behind us and followed me down the stairs.

We reached a corridor that veered to the right then stopped by a locked metal door.

I moved the slider to reveal a window in the middle of the door, and saw someone lying in the middle of the room.

"It's a woman," I said, shocked at our discovery. "Let's get her out." I glanced around. "You're tall, can you see a key anywhere?"

Ralph brushed past me and ran his fingers above the top of the doorframe, coming away with a key in his hand. He unlocked and opened the door.

The woman stared at us with eyes as black as a starless night. Her mouth opened as she screamed, but there was no sound.

I shone the flashlight on her face; the beam landed on the torn fleshy bits where her tongue was meant to be. And her hair was cut so short I could see her hacked off ears.

"Fuck, he's done a number on her," I said as we approached slowly.

The woman rose from the floor like a zombie, then

darted for Ralph. Her blood-soaked arms stretched out in front of her, trying for his neck. She jerked backwards when the restraints stopped her an inch from pulling out his throat.

Ralph hurried away from her.

The woman's head pulled backward, the restraints around her neck and waist keeping her prisoner.

With the flashlights still on her, we could see clearly. There were bloodstains on her white dress near her crotch. I looked from her to Ralph and noticed he saw it, too.

"How can she still be walking around?"

"Look at her eyes."

Her black soulless eyes stared at us, through us, like she wasn't seeing anything at all. Her lips moved as if she was talking, but there was no sound. Her brown pixie hair looked like it hadn't been washed for weeks, and her fingernails and toenails had been ripped off. She smelled of feces, and her arms were caked with it.

There was nothing else in the room except for her, a cot in the corner, and dirt.

"Let's go," Ralph said, backing away. "If we don't know what he did to her, then we don't know what she can do to us. She should be dead if it's her parts in that metal box." His eyes stayed on the woman as he reached the door.

I nodded in agreement and followed him.

We closed the door and locked it. Ralph placed the key back where he had found it and closed the latch. We darted up the stairs and I never wanted to return.

Chapter Four

"We have to tell your cop friend, Ralph," I moaned. "The police have to know what McNielty did to that woman in the basement." I was hugging my knees, rocking in the car seat.

"How do we explain how we ended up inside McNielty's house?" All his concentration was on the road, his eyes blinking at the oncoming car lights.

"I don't care, but we have to do something. He hurt that girl. You were there, you saw what she looked like. And the way she behaved I don't think she felt a fucking thing," I said, shaking my head as visions of that poor girl flashed before me again; all that blood. "And the way she tried to rip out your throat. Her eyes seemed soulless."

"You're right," Ralph sighed. "I'll call Martin after I've dropped you off. He needs to know about her."

"Thank you." It relieved me but something still didn't sit right. Whatever it was, I was sure Martin would take care of it.

Then another thought crossed my mind; that I'd be

alone tonight. Shit. I shook my head; I wouldn't ask Ralph to stay over again. He'd stayed over enough evenings and I needed to get over my fears of being alone. I was supposed to be this kick-ass assassin; but I sure as hell didn't feel like one.

The ride back to my house was quick; too quick. I wasn't ready to get out of Ralph's car and enter my house alone.

Ralph pulled up to the curb and, for a moment, I sat still and stared at my house; the darkness surrounding it, and the emptiness of it all. I hugged my knees tighter.

I exhaled a frightened breath and shook out my arms. I stretched out my legs, and unbuckled the seat belt.

"Thanks for fucking up my Wednesday," I grumbled as I opened the door and climbed out, taking the folder with me. "I want to have another look at this, if you don't mind," I said, shaking the file in my right hand.

He leaned over the seat and peered up at me.

"Knock yourself out. You going to be okay alone?"

"I'll be fine," I said, my smile shaking at the corners, but I hoped he couldn't see it.

"You sure? I can stay with you again, if you want? You know I don't mind."

I considered his offer, but, as much as I desperately wanted him by my side, especially after what we'd seen at the McNielty residence, I told myself to get a grip.

"No, I'll be okay," I said, sounding confident. "What are you doing for the rest of the evening?"

"I'll probably grab dinner and have a few beers. You want to join me?"

I was tempted, it sounds like a fun evening doing nothing, but I wanted to go over the case file.

"No, thanks. I'll just order in. Have a good night." I

turned and went up the footpath. As I reached the front door I opened my mouth to ask Ralph if this was from him but he drove away.

On my porch was a brown package. I scanned the neighborhood but couldn't see anyone suspicious lurking around the corner.

I unlocked and opened the front door and switched on the lights for the porch and the lounge. With my foot, I softly tapped the package. If it was a bomb, I would have been dead, but nothing clicked and there were no ticking sounds after I touched it. When I picked it up, there was another package the size of an A4 envelope beneath it. I scooped that up as well and went inside, dead-bolting the door.

Setting both packages on the kitchen island, I grabbed a pair of scissors and opened the envelope first. Inside was a smaller white envelope that was smooth and silky to the touch. It had raised engravings on the outer edges of the envelope, and tracing the golden pattern with my finger, even the fine etching was soft.

I opened the envelope and removed the note within, when a ticket fell out and onto the counter. The white note had similar engravings on its edges and was just as silky as the envelope.

The note was beautifully handwritten:

Dearest Blaire,
I have stood back and waited. And now two months have passed.
I can't wait any longer.
I miss you.
Allow me the chance to show you all of who I am.
Enclosed with this letter is a ticket to tonight's show.
Please join me.

S

Dammit! It was almost as if Sebastian had read my mind. I narrowed my eyes at his letter, willing him to see me through the page, even though I knew he couldn't.

I opened the second package and removed a black box from the courier company lining. The plain black box had a white bow wrapped around it. I pulled on the bow and it unraveled. Opening the lid slowly, a chuckle escaped my lips, and once I had removed the lid completely. I smiled. Inside was a plush hedgehog.

There was another handwritten note underneath the plush toy, this one written by another hand:

Dear Blaire,
As promised, something adorable and soft for you to cuddle at night.
Best wishes,
Léon

I hugged the plush toy tightly against my chest. The faint smell of spice, wood, and the ocean permeated the air.

Léon had read my mind once. It happened when I was a little scared and overwhelmed, and wanted nothing more than to hold on to a soft toy. He had promised not to read my mind again. He did say he would try to get me a plush toy.

I thought it strange that both men sent me something after two long months. What intrigued me the most was why Léon sent the plush toy on the same day as Sebastian asking me out on a date.

I had been a bad human servant to Sebastian. While Sebastian had been a good master in that he had given me the time I needed to figure my shit out. The problem was I still hadn't managed it. It's hard when you don't know where to start and the person you were was so good at hiding secrets.

Sebastian had called many times and left messages, but I never answered. I never called back. I was too scared.

I stared at the invitation from Sebastian. There were choices to be made for the evening; I could either stay at home, read through the case file, and order takeout; alone, and for the third night in a row, or I could go on a date with Sebastian.

I glanced at the ticket. It granted entry to a concert for one of my favorite bands, Envision. Even the new me liked the old me's taste in music.

Dammit, I wanted to see them live, and here I was provided with an opportunity to see them. I had just over an hour left to get there.

The shower was quick but getting dressed took longer than I wanted; trying on three different outfits only confused me more. Eventually, I ended up with black leggings, black heeled boots that stopped before my knees, a pair of black tailored shorts and an old black Envision t-shirt with a leather jacket over it. After I added a little make-up to brighten my eyes, for once I didn't look as tired as I felt.

I grabbed my phone and hovered over Sebastian's name. I closed down the contacts list and searched for the app that notified a driver to fetch me. I loved technology when there was an app for every need.

Fifteen minutes later, the driver was outside my house. I grabbed the ticket and my bag and locked the front door.

Once we reached the venue, I thanked the driver, climbed out, and gave him a five-star review. I always tried to be friendly, especially if they deserved those five stars.

I stood on the curb and watched the masses of people moving through Security. The time on my phone showed I had fifteen minutes to spare before the concert would start.

With the ticket in hand, I stood outside the gates. The note from Sebastian didn't mention where to meet him, and the ticket didn't include a seat number.

I nervously watched the mass of people pass me by.

"You look lost," someone behind me said.

I turned slowly to see who it was; the voice was deeper than I remembered, so I couldn't be sure.

Sebastian flashed his teeth, revealing a slight hint of vampire fangs.

"You sounded different." I smiled up at him.

I noticed his mouth first, those soft full lips, and then his eyes; strikingly grass green with slivers of gold running through them. He was a were-leopard, a black leopard, but I had yet to see him in his full fur form. I wondered whether his eyes stayed green, and how much bigger would he be in his leopard form, compared to his human form.

Sebastian was about six foot two and I only came up to his chest, so he would have to bend down if he wanted to kiss me. His blond hair had grown out a bit since I had last seen him, and it had started to curl at the ends; I wanted to touch those soft curls and twirl them around my finger.

He was wearing black boots, black jeans, and a black Envision shirt similar to my own, except that his appeared to be much older and the print had faded.

"I wanted you to turn around." He cupped my face in his hands and kissed me; soft and quick, taking my breath away. "Come on, it's about to start." He offered me his hand, and I took it.

We went through a separate section of Security. It wasn't as invasive as the general entrance; there was no patting down of the front of my body, ass or down my legs. After a few bomb scares, security at events such as this usually got a bit touchy-feely.

Once we had been cleared for entry, I saw that someone wearing all black was waiting for us on the other side. He looked like he could be one of the bodyguards that Sebastian and Léon always had around their properties. We followed him to one of the private viewing rooms, and my mouth fell open when we entered. We were so close to the stage that I could see the band's instruments clearly. Even though there were monitors in the room, we wouldn't need them to see the band once the concert started.

"Wow, Sebastian! This is amazing. How did you know I love this band?" I narrowed my eyes, but a smile still played on my lips.

"I didn't know, I swear. They're one of my favorite bands, and I wanted to share this with you."

"I'm sorry I didn't return any of your calls," I said, staring at my hands.

"I understand you needed time to sort some things out. But we can talk about that later. Let's enjoy tonight." He smiled, hugged me with one arm, and turned me around so that I faced the stage. "They're about to start."

Standing in the circle of his embrace, his touch caused my body to vibrate, like an electric current had passed through him and into me. I didn't want him to stop touching me for fear of losing that feeling.

His smell was also familiar. It was comforting. The hint of ocean and citrus, and mixed in there was him, his leopard; wet leaves after a summer rain and dry grass. I closed my eyes, rested my head against his chest, and breathed him in.

Sebastian had saved my life the night I was attacked. He

had picked me up from the alley I was dying in and had carried me to his home.

In order to keep me alive, he had marked me, making me his human servant. The complete process of marking required two marks to be placed upon the human, but Sebastian had stayed his hand after the first. He didn't want to perform the second mark, unless it was something I wanted him to do. Which, I didn't.

Léon, his vampire brother and Master of Sterling Meadow, had tried to mark me first, but it hadn't worked. But because I had been attacked by two different were-animals, I had been infected with both of their viral strains, and it had taken Sebastian, as both vampire and were-leopard, to successfully counteract it. As he was a different were-animal, the conflicting strains had somehow cancelled one another out, and Sebastian had been able to share his vampiric life essence with me, which was enough to keep me from death.

Not answering his phone calls made me seem ungrateful, particularly as he had granted me the space I needed to piece together my returning memories. But truthfully, despite spending the last two months trying to figure out who I was, so far I'd found nothing that I didn't already know.

One thing I did know, though, was that, in that moment where I found myself huddled in Sebastian's arms, it felt right, like I was meant to be there with him.

The tension I was holding onto dissolve from my shoulders.

Strangely, I hadn't missed him these last two months. I had thought of him, but I didn't miss him. There had been no yearning for him, and me doing my own thing and trying to figure things out had been just fine.

But standing with him now began to feel as though I had been missing out on so much. A tinge of regret washed over me.

I turned around in the circle of his arm so I could hug him, wrapping my arms around his body and his around mine. He came down toward me and stopped with his face close to mine, hesitating.

Rocking onto my tiptoes, I met his lips with mine. We kissed gently at first, then a little harder and with longing desire. Our hands explored each other's bodies, and the feel of him so close to me reignited things down below that I hadn't felt since the last time we'd been together.

The music started, and it was one of Envision's best songs.

"Let's watch," he said, ending our kiss prematurely.

We sat on the couch, his arm around my shoulders. The waiting staff brought in food, a few cold drinks, and a bottle of bubbly. We ate, sipped on French champagne, and watched the crowd dance and sing along to all the songs. I knew the lyrics, but I didn't join them.

Those two hours flew by. The concert was an electrifying masterpiece of lasers, lights, guitar work, and singing, complete with a large inflatable vampire that emerged from the stage and tried to attack the band. It was awesome.

After they sang their last song, Heath, the lead singer, spoke to the crowd. "We saved our best song for last. This is for one of our very good friends who wants Blaire to know that he never stopped thinking about her these last two months, and that he's glad she could make it tonight." Then Heath started singing.

"Was that for me?" I asked, clearing my throat, not quite believing my perfect evening.

"I sure hope so, unless there is another Blaire out there I don't know about." He squeezed my shoulder.

"How do you know them?" I asked. "They're from England."

"You know they're vampires, don't you?"

Shit, no, I didn't know. It never occurred to me. With all the different mystical people integrating into society, things like that didn't bother me, and I wasn't sure if it did before, either.

"My family didn't start out in America. Salvador originates from Romania," — he paused for a heartbeat as I remembered that that was where the first vampires had become legal all those years ago. Somehow I could remember all this other stuff just fine, yet it was the stuff directly related to me I couldn't figure out, — "but he moved to France when more and more countries started to accept our kind, and that's where Léon and I were born. We moved around a lot, and we stayed in England for many years. That's when I met the band members, long before they became the popular band they are today."

"If you are about eight hundred years old, how old is Salvador?"

"He's over a thousand."

"Wow."

We watched the last bit of the concert in silence, and when they finished, I pecked his cheek.

"Sorry, I'm slow tonight." I smiled kindly. "Thanks for the dedication. It was thoughtful."

Sebastian pulled me in closer to his body and I wrapped my arm around his waist, nestling my head in the nook of his shoulder.

The band left the stage, and the crowd chanted for them

to come back and sing one more song, but they didn't go back out.

After a few minutes, there was a knock on the door. Sebastian said, 'Enter,' and the same guard from earlier asked whether he could let our visitors in.

"Yes," Sebastian said, rising to greet them.

I turned toward the door and there they were, my favorite band in the world. They were here, as close as they ever would be. My cheeks flush, and I had an urge to hide.

"Blaire, come say hi."

Shit. I stood and walked over to Sebastian.

Heath, the main singer and guitarist of the group, was as tall as I was, which was short for a guy. He looked like your typical alternative rock band member with his short blond hair that was gelled into spikes, the ends of which were colored red.

When one thought of a vampire, one typically imagined beautiful creatures of the night. Not Heath, his entire face seemed crooked, from his nose to the slight dimple in his chin, like he was hit in the face and the bones had grown back skew.

"So, this is the woman?" Heath said, holding out his hand for mine. I placed my hand in his, and as he kissed my knuckles, his beady blue eyes stared up at me, sending shivers down my spine. His thin lips were surprisingly warm.

"Yes," Sebastian said, putting his arm around my shoulder and pulled me in closer.

I didn't have to turn to look at him to know he was smiling.

"I can't believe I'm meeting you! I absolutely love your music." I sounded exactly like a groupie and desperately wished I didn't. My face heated.

Kris, the bass guitarist and backup singer, glanced at me with large chocolate-colored eyes. His dark brown hair was long over his ears and styled into his eyes on purpose. I'd be irritated with hair in my face but he seemed unperturbed.

Kris grinned like he was hiding a secret. He was six foot something, but not as tall as Sebastian. There was something about him I couldn't place, though. Something felt strangely familiar.

Steven, the drummer, had blond hair and glacial-colored blue eyes. His features looked soft and delicate, like he had died soon after his twentieth birthday.

They each shook my hand confidently, but it was Steven whose eyes lingered on mine and kept my hand in his. I tried pulling my hand free, but he held on tightly.

"Anyone who is a friend of Sebastian is a friend of ours." He smiled, showing fangs, and then he let go of my hand.

I put my arm around Sebastian's waist, hesitated when I touched his holster, then moved my hand lower. He placed his hand over mine and squeezed.

"Make yourself comfortable, guys," Sebastian said, and the band came farther inside the room.

"I hope you don't mind, but we brought our own food," Heath said, holding his hand out. Three women entered behind them, holding each other's hands. The women slithered in, one after the other, like a long snake. They looked like the main course and dessert all in one. The three ladies had long blonde hair and wore tight dresses with stiletto heels.

The one bringing up the rear leered down at me before her eyes flicked to Sebastian, and her lips curled upward.

"Hi, Sebastian," she purred.

"Tiffany." Sebastian squeezed my hand again. I wanted

to let go of him and move away, but he held on and tightened his grip on my shoulder.

I knew he had had a life before marking me, but someone like her staring at him so seductively and giving me death-ray-glares rubbed me up the wrong way.

"Give me ten minutes of pleasantries and then I'll take you home," he said, leaning in close to my ear.

I nodded.

Chapter Five

Sebastian let go of my shoulder but kept my hand in his, pulling me with him until we stood off to one side while the band sat on the couch with their dinner dates.

Tiffany sat beside Heath, but he had done nothing with his date as yet. He was too busy watching Sebastian.

"Has your diet changed, Sebastian?" Heath asked, and his eyes flicked toward me.

"I like a variety of food, Heath, as well you know."

"That you do, my old friend. However, I was most surprised to hear that you rejected Galina." Again, a flick of eyes to me and then back to Sebastian.

Something about the conversation between them seemed personal, and I wanted to shy away from it. But Sebastian put his arm around me, pulling me in closer to him, his body warm against mine. I slipped my hand around his waist, but when I couldn't find anything to hold on to, I moved my hand under his shirt and tucked my thumb into his pants. He glanced down at me in surprise. A good surprise.

But when he spoke, it was as though Sebastian's entire focus was on the conversation, and not on me.

"Your sister is obsessed, Heath, and you know it," Sebastian said. "She has always been besotted, but when she found out about Blaire, she overstepped the boundaries, don't you agree?"

Shit. Galina was Heath's sister.

I wanted to leave before this conversation turned ugly.

"Agreed," Heath said, bowing his head slowly. "But what should I do with her now, Sebastian? She is sullen."

"Not my problem," Sebastian said, and it didn't seem like he was going to back down.

"She's a grown-ass woman, Heath," Kris said, arching an eyebrow. "Just because they dated years ago, doesn't mean you can keep holding Sebastian accountable every time she loses her shit. She can fight her own battles." His tone harsh.

Kris seemed irritated by the conversation like they'd had it before. He visibly relaxed when his date mumbled something unintelligibly, holding his attention. She looked like a sleeping doll with her back resting against his chest, and blood drops pooling at the two puncture marks on her neck. He licked them hungrily, savoring the taste in his mouth, then kissed her neck gently.

Steven's date was sitting on the floor between his legs, watching everyone. Her legs were bent to one side, but she sat in such a way so as not to flash anyone.

Steven cradled her chest, nudging her head to one side with his nose, leaving her neck exposed. He kissed her softly on the spot where her pulse readied for his plunge. He licked the spot first, then bit down. One of his hands snaked around her chest and the other grabbed her jaw, keeping her head to the side. Her eyes fluttered shut, her mouth opened in a surprised '*O*', and her arms went limp in her lap.

"Blaire," Heath said, bringing me out of my trance. "Have you ever offered yourself to a vampire before?" Heath asked while staring at Steven and his date.

"No, I don't remember ever offering my neck to a vampire, but two have forced themselves on me," I said, staring at Heath and wondering why it mattered.

The two vampires were Ian and Esther. They had tried to drain me as a result of Esther's jealousy. They were both currently locked in their own cross-wrapped coffins, with a year or so of their sentence still to go.

"What do you mean?" Heath said.

"The evening I was attacked, my head hit the concrete so hard that I couldn't remember much from before that night. So, I don't fully know whether I have ever offered my neck to a vampire, willingly or not."

"You should let Sebastian taste you. I hear his bite is to die for." He regarded Tiffany, and she blushed.

I glanced at Sebastian, but he was leering at Heath. A trickle of pinpricks washed over my arm, and I let go of him. Sebastian noticed and the pinpricks receded as he took my hand in his again.

"We need to leave," Sebastian said, holding his free hand out to Heath, who stared at it before eventually shaking it. "Will you be in town long enough to visit Léon and Salvador?"

"We might stop by, but we'll ring before we do."

"I'll let them know."

Sebastian shook the other two men's hands. While I said goodbye. We left them to enjoy the rest of their dinner.

The bodyguard was waiting for us outside the room. He nodded at Sebastian and walked ahead of us.

There were so many people trying to leave the concert that the exits were blocked with moving bodies. I huddled into Sebastian's side as we strolled.

A cool breeze blew in through the exit doors and shivered. The security that had checked the crowd before the concert started had already left, and all the doors were open.

I stopped and stared at the people as they pushed past us to get through the exits. The hairs on my neck stood on end. I felt the weight of someone staring at me. Perhaps they were waiting for me to find them. Them watching me intensified and goosebumps rose all over my body.

Sebastian stopped and called out to his bodyguard, Rory, to wait for us.

"What's wrong?" Sebastian asked.

"I don't know." I glanced over my shoulder, but there was nothing; just people walking by.

Scanning the large foyer, Rory came to stand beside us, and began scrutinizing everybody near us.

Sebastian touched my arm, and I jumped.

"Are you okay?" he asked.

"It's fine. Let's go." I took his hand, and we continued wading through the crowd.

I just relaxed when hairs rose on the back of my neck again, sending shivers down my spine and blood draining from my face. The white hair and eyebrows were unmistakable. He was a few feet in front of me, just standing there, staring at me.

I stopped dead, pulling on Sebastian's hand. He stopped beside me, following my gaze.

"Who is that?"

"You see him, too?" I wasn't sure if my mind was

playing tricks on me, or if I was really seeing Ross McNielty.

"Sure, I see him; the guy with the white hair."

I blinked slowly, and he was gone.

"Shit! Where did he go?" I asked, looking around. "One moment he was there, and now he's gone."

"Sir,"— Rory stepped closer, — "I sense magic. Black magic." His brown eyes widened, and he licked his lips.

"Who was that?" Sebastian repeated.

I studied Sebastian's face. He was hiding his true feelings behind his blank expression.

My eyes widened as I remembered that woman in McNielty's secret room. Then images flashed in my mind's eye of those glass bottles on the shelves, and the shrine made up of a woman's severed private parts.

I couldn't understand how McNielty knew who I was or that I was here.

"I want to get leave," I said, blinking back tears.

When we reached the Jeep, Rory climbed into the driver's seat while Sebastian and I clambered into the backseat. I held onto his hand even while buckling myself in.

"Okay, talk to me. Who was that?" Sebastian's voice was calm and soothing, and I wanted to wrap the safety net of his body around mine.

"I have to phone Ralph. I have to tell him I saw him."

"Who, Blaire? You aren't making any sense." He moved hair out of my face.

I flinched as though his touch burned my skin.

"What's going on?" he asked, concern evident in his tone.

"I went with Ralph to scope out a new contract earlier. We were only watching the guy; we wanted to see if we could connected him to the murders that's happening around town." I swallowed hard.

Sebastian placed my hand in his lap and covered it with both of his. He was warm. He was safe.

I inhaled and exhaled deeply, and my voice sounded strained when I spoke.

"He's a voodoo priest. He owns a shop in one of the centers. We had a look around his home," — the glow of passing streetlights moved across Sebastian's face and, momentarily, I could see the concern in his eyes before the darkness returned, — "he has body parts in jars," I said, carefully drying my eyes without ruining the little bit of makeup I had on.

"And there was a severed vagina in a metal box on a table surrounded by candles and ears on a string like a fucking shrine. And we found his secret room where a badly cut woman was chained up. She was there, but not really there," — I tapped the side of my head, — "her eyes were black, and she was covered in blood and shit. Her tongue and ears had been removed. It was horrible."

The light from the street moved over Sebastian's face again, and a hint of unease flashed in his green eyes.

"Was that the man? The one with the white hair?" He asked carefully, like he was trying not to frighten me.

I nodded, moving as close to him as the seat belt allowed, but it wasn't close enough; I couldn't feel his warmth.

"You're shaking." He unbuckled his seat belt and sat as close to me as he could. Our bodies were touching from hip to shoulder, and he held me tightly.

"Sir, are we dropping her off at her place or are we going straight to the Labyrinth?"

The Labyrinth. So that's what the monstrous warehouse with the moving walls was called. Very fitting.

"Let's go to the Labyrinth. If this guy is out there and knows who she is, it's not safe for her to go back to her place tonight."

"Can we stop by anyway?" I asked. "Ralph gave me a dossier full of info on the guy. I need to fetch the folder and some clothes."

"I really don't think it's safe..."

"Please."

"Fine. Rory, go to her place first."

I grabbed the folder from the kitchen counter and some clothing from my closet and stuffed it in an overnight bag. When I entered the open-plan kitchen, Sebastian was reading the card that came with Léon's gift. His jaw muscles flexed, and his free hand bunched into a fist.

"When did you get this?"

"Today. When I got home, both packages were on my porch."

"*As promised, something adorable for you to hold at night. Best wishes, Léon*. What does that mean?" he asked with an edge of suspicion, holding up the hedgehog.

I felt self-conscious and wanted to leave the room, but knew I had to answer his questions truthfully. "It goes back to when I was staying with you guys. The evening after we found my car, Léon was sitting on the bed when I woke up, and I was so stressed I thought of—"

"He read your mind?" Sebastian interrupted.

I nodded.

"What were you thinking about?"

"That I needed a soft toy to cuddle." My cheeks heated.

He handed me the toy, but I placed it on the counter and held my hand out to him. He took it, but I immediately sensed he didn't want to hold my hand. Sometimes a man's heart bruised as easily as a woman's. I didn't know what we were to each other—apart from master and human servant—but I felt guilty, and I shouldn't. I did nothing wrong. We needed to discuss this, but now wasn't the right time. I needed to see if Ralph was all right.

"I want to phone Ralph before we go."

Sebastian didn't look happy, but he let go of my hand and went to stand outside.

I took my cellphone out of my purse and saw I had six missed calls from Ralph. I hit the green phone on the screen.

"Are you okay?" Ralph asked, answering on the second ring.

"Did you see him as well?" I asked.

"Yeah, the fucker was standing behind me in the John. But when I looked up again, he'd disappeared. It's like he was there, but not really there, if that makes any sense?"

"Yes, it makes sense; it was the same for me." I nodded, even though he couldn't see me. "I was at a concert with Sebastian, and we saw him in the crowd."

"I'm glad you finally went out with him. Sorry the voodoo priest ruined your date."

At first, Ralph hadn't been too trusting of Sebastian, but as we got to know him and Léon, Ralph seemed to have warmed to them. I suspected that the two of them doing all they could to protect me had helped earn his trust. Also, Ralph said I had been alone long enough, and I should see where things went with Sebastian.

"Someone else ruined it first," I said, thinking of Envision's dinner dates, and in particular, Tiffany.

"What?"

"Never mind. Where are you now?"

"Safe at home. Where are you staying tonight?"

"Sebastian said I should stay with him."

"Good, I'll call you in the morning after I've spoken to Martin."

"Okay, good. Let me know what he says." Hopefully the detective would be able to shed some light on what was going on.

"Sure." He hung up without saying goodbye.

The automatic lights flickered on the moment we parked inside the garage of the Labyrinth. It felt good to finally be able to put a name to the place. Calling it a warehouse didn't do it justice with all the security, moving walls and rooms. The complex felt like a jigsaw puzzle with a mind of its own.

Rory opened the car door for me and I climbed out, with Sebastian behind me.

We walked through the corridors, turning left here and right there. I didn't bother trying to memorize the place because I knew that it would change again, and I would only get confused.

"How do you know where to go if the walls keep changing?" I asked Sebastian.

"Those of us who live here know the changes, and they happen rotationally so we know how it will change on a specific day."

"Goodnight, sir," Rory said, walking off in the opposite direction to where we were going.

"'Night, Rory."

"Where is he going?"

"Were-wolves need to sleep, too, you know." He smiled mockingly.

"I know that," — I smacked his chest softly, — "but don't you always have a guard watching you?"

"No, not when I'm home. And besides, he was more for your protection than mine. I can protect myself, but I can't protect you if I need to fight."

"Oh, and why did you think there would be any kind of threat?"

"Just in case, Blaire. Just in case." He rubbed my arm, then his fingers trailed downward until he found my hand and our fingers entwined.

We stopped outside a door. Sebastian opened it, revealing his room; which appeared to be the same as the last time I was here.

"Can you stay here a moment? I want to have a quick word with Léon."

"Sure." I let go of his hand and he left, closing the door behind him.

I placed my bag on his bed, removed the police file, and started reading. I browsed through the victim's names and their biographical summaries but studied the actual crime reports; each crime scene depicted the same M.O.

Their hands were cleanly removed with a sharp object. The coroner suspected a scalpel was used to cut through the tissue, followed by a motorized cutting tool or a very large sharp knife for the bone.

All the organs were removed; the heart; the liver; both kidneys; the lungs; and the stomach. In each instance, a little brown voodoo doll had been left inside their neatly stitched abdominal cavities.

Each of the seven men had been found in open areas, but never the same area twice. Two men had brown colored eyes, two had blue, and two had green eyes. Only the homeless man had had gray eyes. I wondered whether McNielty would kill another gray-eyed man to make it an even eight.

And they all stood at six feet two inches tall and weighed between two hundred and two-hundred-and-twenty pounds.

I read the gray-eyed man's report word-for-word, finding I had missed something the first time I had read it. He had been the only victim to have his private parts removed. The killer had taken everything, balls included.

McNielty was one sick cookie. He had to be medaling in some pretty bad voodoo shit with all these organs he was holding onto.

Glancing at my phone, I yawned. It was early morning, and I needed to sleep. Since I had showered before the concert, I slipped on my pajamas from my bag, used the bathroom, and brushed my teeth.

When I opened the door, Sebastian was back in the room. He slipped his shirt off and threw it into the laundry basket in the corner. All those muscles moved with such flexibility and ease, like liquid mercury.

Shadows played along his high cheekbones and square jaw. I wanted to reach out, touch his face, and chase the shadows away by kissing the line of his jaw and the soft skin of his neck.

He was good-looking but didn't flaunt it like others would. He didn't care for that kind of attention. My heart sped up a few beats watching him, and I lost a few I.Q. points.

Sebastian was a were-leopard and a vampire, which meant he had all the strength and speed that went with that combination. He had the best of both worlds.

From what I'd read, when a human shape-shifted into their were-animal, they could become as big as a small pony. I wondered how big Sebastian became when he shifted, given that he was already so tall and burly in human form. He wasn't big like body builders were; his muscles were toned and well defined and fit his frame well. But being a were-leopard and a vampire meant he could bench press a minivan and feel no pain, so lifting weights would be easy for him.

Whenever I was with him, the first thing I noticed was the color of his eyes; that striking feline dark green with the slivers of gold running through them.

A hand waved in front of my face, and I blinked.

Shit, had he been talking to me all this time while I did nothing but gawk at him?

My cheeks warming in embarrassment as I glanced at him. The smile on his face told me he knew I had been staring, and that, possibly, he enjoyed it.

The look in his eye held heat, and it was hot enough that it swirled around my neck with the promise of a kiss and more.

He was down to his boxers now, but I kept my eyes above his waist.

"Are you ready to sleep, or are you still going through the file?" He pointed to the photos and pieces of paper that were spread all over the bed.

"Sleep. I definitely need sleep."

I pushed all the papers into the folder and placed it in my bag as Sebastian moved to the left side of the bed.

That's how we had slept two months ago, with him on the left.

He switched off the lights but kept the lamp on.

I climbed under the covers, leaving my arms exposed. I turned onto my side and watched him climb into bed. Once he was lying down, he sighed.

"What's wrong?" I asked.

He turned onto his side to face me and stared.

"There have been things I've wanted to say to you these last two months," he said sadly. "And now that you're here with me, I can't think of one thing to say to you." He smiled but it didn't reach his eyes.

"I don't know what to say, either." My pulse sped up, and I swallowed hard.

What I wanted to say was I felt like a teenager with a crush.

Before today, I would only wonder how he was, or how his day was going. But now that I was so close to him, I wanted more. I wanted to touch him. I wanted to put my hands on his chest and do things with my mouth.

Staring at him only made me feel worse; more nervous.

I closed my eyes and said, "I like you and you like me, and it feels so good when we're together. And, honestly, I want to run my hands over your body and kiss you. But I can't decide whether this attraction is real or if it's because of the mark you gave me."

"Is that why you needed time?" I said, opening my eyes. His stare was penetrating.

"That was part of it, I guess. Mostly, I needed to find out who I really was. But so far, I was a ghost; from the records we could access, the trail only started when I was fifteen. Before then, there's nothing. Whatever my name was prior to then, we couldn't find it. It's hidden very well." I sighed.

"Have you tried the police?"

"Yes, but they only have the same records we do. It's like someone erased me, and there is no way of seeing who my parents were."

He frowned.

"What? Have you thought of something?"

"No, it's just odd."

"What is?"

"That they erased your records like that. Unless—"

"Unless, what?"

"I don't know," he said, shaking his head. "I'm just thinking out loud. Perhaps a vampire could've used their wiles to manipulate someone to delete it?"

"That means a vampire knows me and did that for me." I frowned.

"Exactly."

"But who? And why haven't they come forward to help me again?"

"That's what you need to find out."

"Now I have more questions than answers. Thanks for nothing. You've been no help." I teased through the truth.

A faint smile played on his lips, but it didn't match the seriousness of his face.

The green of his irises darkened.

The silence between us was gentle and comfortable.

As I lay there beside him, it hurt to think that I'd been depriving myself of this. As much as I needed to unlock the secrets of my identity, I now realized I had spent much of the last two months ignoring what made me happy. The problem was I still wasn't able to define exactly what that was.

Whatever we were to each other—whatever we were meant to be—would reveal itself with time. Time could be our friend or our enemy, and it was up to us to decide which of those it would be.

As we stared at each other in the lamplight, it was as if we both understood. We knew, through the mark that Sebastian had made, that the attraction could be real, and even if it wasn't, it shouldn't stop us from trying.

In that moment, I understood. Even though I wasn't the same person I was two months ago before the amnesia, I knew who I was today. I couldn't change the past, but I could control what I did in my future.

My smile reach my eyes. I was glad I had accepted his invitation; glad to be near him; glad that my future was mine.

Sebastian tucked one hand under the pillow to lift his head up slightly. His shoulders relaxed, and he gave me a look that was pleasant and easygoing. A mischievous smile crossed his face, and I frowned at him. Something was up.

"I want you to come with me tomorrow."

"Where?"

"To my leap. I want you to meet Anne and the rest of them."

My stomach did back-flips as I fought not to squirm.

"Who is Anne?" I asked suspiciously. If she was anything like the women who hung out at the Labyrinth during feeding times, then I definitely didn't want to meet her.

"Anne is our alpha female," he said. His mouth curving upward. "She took over from Rick, her husband, after he died."

"Did someone challenge him?"

"No, he was murdered. It's still an unsolved case."

"I'm sorry."

"Don't be. It happened about ten or eleven years ago."

"Why do you want me to meet them? You and I have only just started seeing each other again."

"We have one of our monthly meetings tomorrow night before the full blue moon, and I would like you to come. It's days before the moon is full, so you don't have to worry about anyone shifting near you."

"I don't know, Sebastian."

"I want you to get to know me, and this is part of who I am. I turn into a leopard once a month, and these are the people I hunt with."

I opened my mouth to say 'no' but closed it. Lying there with him felt good, and I didn't want it to come crashing down by denying him his request. He was opening up to me, and I was pushing him away; pushing myself away from him. If this was what the old Blaire used to do then I didn't want to do it either.

I closed my eyes and tucked my hands under the pillow, nestling it under my head. The pillowcase smelled like him; the French soap he favored, a hint of citrus and the musk of a leopard. I breathed it all in, and my tension ebbed away.

"It's so calming to watch you do that."

"What do you mean?" My eyes flittered open.

"It's like you're thinking about something and meditating at the same time. It's peaceful. I like it."

"I can smell you on the pillowcase." I smiled. "It relaxes me." There, some truth; I missed him these last two months. And I missed the smell of him, the feel of him, his touch and his kisses.

If I had to think about it, it didn't matter whether the mark he gave me drew me to him. It was strange, but I wanted to give in to the feeling.

His lips touched mine and I kissed him back. Then he pulled away, leaned on his elbow, and stared lovingly at me.

"Let's shake the nervousness away and take it slow. Whether it's the mark that attracts us to each other or not, it doesn't matter. I want to get to know you," — he pointed a finger at me, — "we can date... and do other things." His smile widened and his green eyes sparkled. "And whatever those other things are, I will take your lead. There's no pressure."

It was like he had read my mind.

"Deal," I said. "I want to get to know everything about you. All that other stuff can just take its course. And, yes, I will go with you tomorrow night. Take me to see your world; all of it. I want to know everything about you."

"Before we go to the leap tomorrow, there is one thing we have to discuss—"

"Not now," I said, cutting him off. "Tell me later. Kiss me." Sebastian's expression had gone all serious on me, and I didn't like it. Our conversation was light and fluffy a moment ago, and thought it fitting to end our first date with a kiss, rather than something inconsequential. Whatever it was, he could tell me tomorrow.

He hesitated as though the words continued burning his lips, but he moved forward and did as I asked.

I curled in his arms and fell asleep immediately.

Chapter Six

The tune from my cellphone was loud. I reached for it on the side table next to me and answered the incoming call.

"Blaire, are you ready?"

"Morning, Ralph. What time is it?"

"It's 9am. I'll be there in twenty minutes."

"Okay, I'll see you then." Before I could say bye, he hung up.

For the first time since the attack, there had been no nightmares. I had slept soundly, comforted by the warmth of my protector. I wanted to stay in bed with Sebastian, but I had to work. I needed to earn my salary and get Marcus off my case. There was also a voodoo man who knew who we were, and we needed to see what we could do about that.

I stretched and begrudgingly climbed out of bed. If Ralph would be here in twenty minutes, I had to rush. I glanced once more at Sebastian who smiled warmly and climbed out of bed to dress, too.

I dressed in the bathroom and was ready by the time

Ralph phoned again to let me know he was waiting for me outside.

I packed all my belongings, and Sebastian walked me through the changed walls of the Labyrinth toward the street Ralph said he had parked on.

We kissed goodbye and held each other for at least ten seconds, which was more than enough time to get the endorphins working.

When I climbed into Ralph's car, I still smelled Sebastian on my clothing. There's just something wonderful about smelling someone you like on your clothes. It's like they would be with you all day.

We planned to see each other that evening at his leap where I'd meet everyone. I wasn't sure about going, but I had already said I would. If I wanted to see whether my feelings for him were genuine or just a byproduct of the mark between us, I had to know everything about him.

I had a few hours to kill before Sebastian fetched me. It relieved me that it wasn't a full moon, where I'd be forced to witness the leap shifting into their animal forms. Not that I didn't want to see Sebastian shift; I just wasn't ready for it yet.

"So how are the love birds doing?" Ralph said teasingly, and wiggled his eyebrows.

"Shut up." My cheeks heated, but I still smiled. "We're spending the evening together again tonight, so you can drop me off at my place when we're done."

"Sure."

"How was the rest of your evening? Did you see the voodoo priest again?"

"No, thank heavens. But I do want to find out how he found us, though," Ralph said. "I've organized for us to check in with Désiré this morning, and then we have a meeting with Martin at the police station."

Désiré, a surgeon at the local hospital, was one of the witches who regularly helped us. She also saw me once a month to help me train the power she and Seraphine saw in me. So far, our sessions had been just as boring as those with Seraphine, but I couldn't wait to tell her about my last session and how I had been able to use Seraphine's power against her.

Ralph pulled into one of the parking spots near the entrance to the General Hospital, and we waited for Désiré in the coffee shop. I ordered a full breakfast and a bitter black coffee. Ralph liked his coffee milky and sweet.

I had just finished breakfast by the time Désiré came around the corner, still in her scrubs.

"Sorry, one of my patients suffered some complications." She pulled a chair out and sat down. "What's up? Your message said it was urgent."

I gave her a quick overview of our voodoo priest and some detail around what we had found at his house, explaining that he had somehow found both of us, and that, strangely enough, we had both seen him at the same time.

She did one of her trademark slow blinks as though she was processing what I had said and was thinking about how she could answer.

"It sounds like he can project himself metaphysically. Did he look straight at you?"

We both nodded.

"He sounds powerful. Maybe if I had a name, I could give you some specific information."

I wondered whether we could share that with her, but before I could ask, Ralph answered.

"Ross McNielty. Do you know him?"

"Ross McNielty?" Her voice became tremulous. "He has white hair and eyebrows?"

We nodded.

"Shit, guys. You are messing with the wrong voodoo man. He is one of the highest priests in voodoo, and his power is formidable. I don't know anyone personally who has done this, but those who are powerful enough can track you by what you leave behind. So maybe when you were in his house, he found traces of you and was able to track you that way."

Ice filled my veins. I glanced at Ralph, and he paled.

"What should we do?" I asked.

"Avoid being alone. Stay with a friend, with each other or whatever, but don't be alone where he can find you."

"Can he find our addresses that way, or can he only see us in the place we are at the moment he's looking?" I asked.

"I don't know." She shrugged.

"What do you know about him?" Ralph said, clearing his throat like it hurt.

"He's a legend mentioned in our books. He was born into the priesthood. Everyone in his family practices, and his ancestors originally came from Haiti before they settled down in New Orleans. Apparently his great-great-grandfather is still alive; I seriously doubt it, though," — she shrugged again, — "but then, with these guys, anything is possible."

I shifted uncomfortably in my seat, glancing at the entrance and the rest of the people in the coffee shop.

"Does he have any family around here, or are they still in New Orleans?" I asked, not seeing any threat inside the shop.

"Not sure. He disappeared for a few years, and some think he went back to Haiti to find the rest of his ancestors.

Somehow, he ended up here, and I don't think he has been back to New Orleans since."

Someone over the intercom requested for Dr. Désiré Saunders to go to the O.R. room.

"Sorry, duty calls." She stood. "I'll phone around when I get a chance and get back to you. But I have to go," she said, and she left the same way she came.

As soon as it was just the two of us again, I exploded. "What have you gotten us into, Ralph? Did the police know this about him?" I sounded as angry as I felt, and I crossed my arms over my chest and sat back in the chair. Heat stirred within me and knew the look I was giving Ralph was not a friendly one. I was pissed, and now both of us were knee-deep in voodoo shit.

"I didn't know either. I thought we knew who all the bad voodoo priests were, but this guy wasn't listed on the search engine when I checked his background. I didn't pick up where he originated from, or if he had ties to anyone else. There was nothing, I swear," he apologized. "I should have known better." He shook his head, and a dark look crossed his features. "Martin handed this over to me too easily. I mean, he is good at his job and his team should have closed this quickly, but now I'm starting to understand."

"What time are we seeing Martin?"

"In forty minutes," he said, raising his arm to check his watch. "Let's go."

We paid and left.

The drive to the District Police Station on 63rd Street was quick. Then we waited in the car until it was the agreed time before heading inside to see Detective Martin Everett. Ralph knew him from when he had been a Marine, but that was all he told me about the man. I guess he had secrets he didn't want to or couldn't share with me. The difference was, I couldn't remember.

The officer at the front desk rang for the detective while we waited in the newly built reception area with its high ceilings. The tiles were white, and there were long colorful wavy patterns along the reception desk. The chairs were neatly arranged into rows.

We sat in the last row with our backs to the wall, where we could see both the public entrance and the internal door from which the cops emerged. If anyone wanted to get to us, it would be through the window at our sides. Anyone crashing through would give Ralph enough time to go for his gun. Because of last night's date, I had left my gun at home.

After a few minutes, Martin came to greet us. He was taller than Ralph, with broader shoulders, deep-set brown eyes, and brown skin. His black hair was shaved close to the skin at the sides and curly on top, with gray highlights. We followed him into a room, where he offered us coffee.

"So, Blaire," Martin said, leaning against the far wall across from us. "Ralph told me about your attack. It sounded awful. How are you holding up?"

"I still can't remember much."

"Do you remember me at all?"

"I'm sorry, but I don't, Martin." I said, shaking my head.

"I suppose that's a good thing. You and I have gone head-to-head a fair few times in the past." His laughter was like rumbling lightning on a stormy night.

It seemed to be a joke we all shared, except me. Even Ralph was laughing, although his laugh was not as deep as Martin's. I smiled pleasantly. It was a smile that said I was trying not to get angry, even though they were laughing at my expense. We were in a police station. I could remain calm.

Our coffees arrived and saved me from further banter. Martin closed the door and sat across from Ralph, holding a personal mug that read 'World's Best Dad'.

"Okay, talk to me, Ralph." Martin's voice held an air of authority. From just those few words, the air felt tighter with the weight of the situation. He must have been scary as hell to all the new recruits; to have to look up at this man with such a deep voice and a large body looming over them. I would have been afraid if I was them.

"The priest," Ralph said gravely. "He knows who we are, and did his voodoo hoodoo on us last night."

"Go back, Ralph. What exactly happened?"

"We were following him, and then when he left to play poker, like he does every Wednesday, we had a look."

Ralph said the word, 'look' slowly and did something that I couldn't see, but Martin understood. They shared a silent agreement that Martin knew we had entered a suspect's house without the owner being present. But Ralph couldn't exactly come out and say it, not in a police station filled with cops. I wouldn't have said anything at all, but that's just me.

"He has some freaky shit in that house, Martin. And," Ralph whispered, "he has a secret room where he's keeping a woman chained. She was bleeding everywhere, and it looked like she was missing her tongue and ears."

Those dark, deep-set brown eyes stared at Ralph. His cop face was impressively blank. I wouldn't play poker with Martin. He had no telltale signs.

"You knew?" Ralph made it a question.

Martin flinched, then corrected himself; back to showing his cop face.

Voodoo Priest

"You ass, I saw that. How could you give us this contract knowing what he's into?"

"That's why I passed it on to you guys; you would know what to do with it. We couldn't find anything on this guy. We followed him for weeks and we came up with nothing, yet the murders kept happening. We need to know how he's been doing it, Ralph."

"Didn't you see the bottles in his house?"

"No, there was nothing in his house when we executed the search warrant. There was no woman, no bottles, and no evidence linking him to the murders."

"Are you sure it's even him?"

"Very sure." He looked down at Ralph.

"How?"

"Red."

"Fuck." Ralph leaned back in his chair and let out a deep sigh.

"What's red?"

"It's not a what, but a who," Ralph said to me. "He's a clairvoyant the cops use when a case relates to vampires, witches or any otherworldly creature. He's one of the best there is. Red points them, even us, sometimes, in the right direction."

"And you're sure Red pointed McNielty out?"

"Yes." Martin gave one slow nod and coughed into his hand.

"What can we do if he comes after us? He's already used his magic to see our faces. Who knows what he will do next?"

"You know the law, Ralph. You know what to do if that happens."

The conversation died down after Martin implied we could kill McNielty if he attacked us first.

The law protected humans should any monster attack them first, be that vampire, witch, were-animal, or any otherworldly creature. We could kill them in self-defense. Shoot first, ask questions later. That was the only way we could protect ourselves against them.

Humans only had weapons at their disposal; guns with silver bullets, holy water, silver knives or poison-tipped crossbows. When we were up against so many different kinds of monsters, with none of the powers that they had, we had to use what we could.

"I don't like your friend, Ralph," I said as we climbed back into the car.

"You never liked him," Ralph said as he started the engine and drove into the flow of traffic.

"Somehow I don't think it's just me who feels that way."

"No, it's not." He made eye contact when we stopped at a red light. "Please could you wear your gun and your knives?"

"I will." They were at home. I kept forgetting to put them on.

The car moved forward when the light turned green.

"Here's what I think we need to do. We check in with Marcus first, and then we need to see where our friend is."

"Are you serious?"

"Absolutely, it's still a contract, and it's money."

"Careful, Ralph. You almost sound like Marcus."

Chapter Seven

Marcus met us in one of the restaurants near the same center as the voodoo shop. It wasn't the wisest decision, but Marcus was already in the area, and as Ralph was driving, they outvoted me.

We sat in one of the red booths facing the entrance, our backs to the wall. At least we had a good view of the voodoo shop.

The restaurant had a variety of clocks on the walls; digital, analogue, big ones, small ones; all set at different times for various countries. Under each clock was the name of the country the time was set to.

The name of the restaurant was Betty's Burgers, and it reminded me of a sixties burger joint where they served your food on a tray which you hooked onto the side of your car door with the window open.

The walls were pastel teal, and there was a red jukebox near the entrance to the bathrooms, which were marked *John* and *Jane*.

Even the waitresses wore a sixties uniform, which

comprised of either a teal or lavender dress that stopped by their knees and a black-and-white striped apron. Our waitress wore teal, and her name badge declared that her name was Doris. Her smile never seemed to falter, and as she moved around the diner, it was obvious that she was always friendly to the customers. She had to be medicated; no one was that happy all the time.

After a brief wait, Doris stood before us with her little white notebook and pencil in hand, ready to take our orders. Ralph and Marcus ordered hamburgers and fries, and I asked for a black coffee.

When she left, we gave Marcus the short version of what had happened with McNielty and what Martin had said earlier. Little red blotches started to spread from Marcus's chest all the way up his neck.

Doris was back with their meals and my coffee. The burgers were double-decker patties and cheese, with relish and garnish, on a fresh bun. My mouth started to water. I called Doris back and ordered one for myself.

"You guys know I hate taking contracts from Martin," Marcus said when Doris left. "I will gladly take a contract from any other cop, but him..." Marcus shook his head. "I don't trust the man."

Ralph bit into his burger and glared at our boss.

"What about you, Blaire? What did you think of him?" he asked, glancing at me as he ate a few fries.

"I don't like him. He gives off a bad vibe. I don't know how to explain it, but he does." I shuddered at the mere mention of him.

"You see," — Marcus pointed a finger at me, — "you see, Ralph," — he pointed at Ralph, — "I'm not the only one who doesn't like him. I know he's your buddy from your Marine days, but shit, man, he gives us all the creeps."

"Okay," Ralph said, with a mouth full of food. "I get it." He swallowed and took a sip of his soda.

"No more contracts from him," Marcus declared decisively. "Actually, no more from anyone who works at that police station."

"No more," Ralph said with a nod.

"Promise."

"Uh-huh," Ralph said. "This is the last one."

"I can't believe you want to stay on this," Marcus said with a frown carved into his forehead.

"It's a large contract, Marcus. Do you want the money or not?"

The red blotches that had started on Marcus's neck had spread to his cheeks. "How much are we talking about here?"

"A lot. Look at it this way; all three of us can buy new vehicles out of it."

Marcus thought it over.

"Dammit!" Marcus hit the table with his fists. "No one get dead, all right? I can't afford to lose another one." Even though his eyes were small, I could usually see that they were the color of winter skies, but not now; now they were dark gray. The color of storm clouds.

One thing about Marcus was that he loved wearing tailored suits. In many ways, he reminded me of executives in their prime. When he was nervous, like now, he rubbed his clothing between the index finger and the thumb of his left hand; the hand with two digits missing from gangrene.

Marcus was a were-lion, and tough as fucking nails. But two months ago, while we investigated Léon, Ralph and I had found Marcus in an alley after his then-girlfriend, Melinda Cromwell, had injected him with her so-called cure; she had been trying to eradicate his inner animal, to leave only the man behind. But it hadn't worked, and he had almost died. Whatever was in that solution had made him too ill to shift into his lion form, and he had ended up losing two fingers as a result.

And since then, I had come to learn that we always had disagreements, but we were like a family. We were closer than your average company.

When I was attacked and left for dead, one of our colleagues, Shane, had been killed. It had been a hard blow for us. Marcus was still trying to piece Shane's murder together. We didn't know who had torn his limbs apart, dumped his torso in the trunk of my car, and left his limbs in Marcus's bathtub. We didn't know why he was killed or who did it. At first, we had thought it was Roland or Miles, but they denied it every time. So, we—or rather, Marcus—really couldn't afford to lose anyone else.

When my burger arrived we ate our meals in silence. While Ralph and I took turns watching the voodoo shop in between bites.

"I hired someone," Marcus said after the waitress had removed the plates.

Ralph and I glanced at him at the same time.

"Who?" Ralph asked, wiping his mouth with a paper napkin.

Marcus hesitated. His eyes flicked from Ralph to me, then back to Ralph.

"Someone we need," he said.

"What does that mean?" I asked.

"He's a witch, or a warlock, or whatever they're called. He is very young, but very powerful. I've asked him to come here at 3pm."

Marcus glanced at his watch; I could see the face, and it was almost three now.

"There he is." Marcus stood and waved at someone as they entered the restaurant. I turned to see who it was. My mouth opened a little.

"Fuck, Marcus, he isn't just young, he's still a baby," I whispered.

"You were young when I recruited you, Blaire. Besides, he's fuckin' good, and we need him on our side."

"Wait, what? How old was I when I started working for you?"

"Uh," — Marcus hesitated, — "about fifteen."

"You never told me."

"You never asked." He shrugged.

He had me there. I had never asked, but I frowned at him anyway. He knew my memory was sketchy, but he seemed to be keeping information to himself. He wasn't paying me any attention, so I relaxed in my seat; it was a waste of time being mad at him.

Movement caught my eye, and the boy was suddenly standing beside our table. He reached over and shook Marcus's hand.

"Everybody, this is Devan. Devan, this is Ralph," — Marcus pointed to Ralph and then to me, — "and that's Blaire."

Devan's skin was the color of milk and littered with freckles. He had short, straight strawberry blond hair that had grown out over his ears. I found it amazing that people with red or strawberry blond hair almost always had green eyes.

After Devan shook Ralph's hand, he shook mine, and I noticed that both of his eyes were pale, but one was green and the other was blue. They were both strikingly clear and distracting at the same time. At first glance, I noticed the blue eye because it had a dark ring around the iris, reminding me of the eyes of a husky, and then the other eye, with its pale green color that seemed to bleed into the white of his eye.

The rest of his face was young and pretty; he had sharp features beneath the baby look that he still needed to grow out of. He was tall and as thin as a rake.

When he took my hand, it was with a good, clean, and strong shake; I smelled the soap he used to wash his hands with, and they were nice and dry.

Ever since my attack, my senses had improved, and I was able to smell and hear things much more acutely.

"Sit," I said, moving up to make room for him.

"How old are you, son?" Ralph asked, giving the boy a serious look that said everything and nothing all at once.

"Nineteen."

He looked younger than that; maybe even as young as seventeen. That explained the baby-face and the missing hair from his chin.

"I hope I'm not being too personal," Devan said, looking at me, "but there is something about you. You have a gift of sorts."

"What are you talking about?" Marcus asked, leaning on his arms on the table.

Devan closed his eyes. "She was born with a gift." He opened his eyes and stared at me. The colors of both eyes darkened. "Your white spirit is bright and very open, but your mind is locked."

My jaw dropped a little. I closed it and swallowed hard. I blinked slowly while I tried to think of what to say next.

"I'm guessing you're a clairvoyant?" I said.

"Yes, I'm called that sometimes. And there are other things I can do, but it only works on those of a similar calling to mine."

"Since when are you a witch, Blaire?"

"I'm not a witch, Marcus," I said, sounding defensive. "But I have something. It's all new to me. I'm still trying to figure shit out."

Devan lifted his right hand to touch me, but the look on my face must have shown how I felt, and it was a *'do not touch me'* look. If he was a powerful clairvoyant, then he could see more than just what was visible on the surface, and the shake of my hand had most probably given him more than just a glimpse of me. He lowered his hand and left it in his lap, but his eyes watched me carefully.

"What was that, you two?" Ralph asked.

Devan continued staring at me.

"Sorry," Devan said. The full weight of his apology was not lost on me; somehow, he made that one word mean so much more.

"It's all right. Just don't touch me again."

"Anyway," Marcus said, breaking the silence. "As I started telling you over the phone, Devan, I need you to help these two with their current assignment."

"The voodoo priest?"

Marcus nodded.

"Yes, I know of him. Do you have any items that belong to him?" he asked me.

"We didn't take anything," I said, shifting in the chair. "But I don't know if the police did. Ralph?" I turned out of Devan's gaze and looked to Ralph.

"Martin gave me a bag of his possessions. We can fetch it from my place later. Blaire has the case file, if you want to read through it."

"I don't need the case file, just the items."

"You're that good, huh?" Ralph seemed unconvinced.

"Yes, he's that good," Marcus said, a little defensively.

He lifted his arm to call the waitress over. "Do you want anything to eat or drink, or should I get the bill?"

"No, thanks," Devan said, looking outside. "Is that his shop?"

We glanced at the window.

"Yes," Ralph and I said at the same time.

Devan rose.

"Where are you going?" Marcus asked.

"To look around."

"You can't go in there." Ralph's eyes widened.

"Why not? He doesn't know me, and I'm a paying customer." He smiled, showing perfectly straight teeth. "Give me twenty minutes."

Thirty minutes had passed when Devan eventually crossed the road. He headed for the restaurant and was briefly out of view, until something caught my eye from the kitchen side of the restaurant; it was Devan, heading casually toward Ralph's car.

The kid was smart; he didn't want to risk walking directly toward us. Instead, he had taken a detour around the restaurant, and because we had parked the car between several trucks, it was obscured from view in the shop.

Devan knocked on the car window, Ralph unlocked the doors, and he climbed into the backseat behind me.

"Where's Marcus?"

"He had other stuff to do," Ralph said, turning to face Devan. "Now tell us, kid. What did you see?"

I pulled the sun visor down so I could see Devan in the mirror behind me without having to turn around.

Devan's pale eyes darkened as he spoke. "He sells the

usual knick-knacks: books; candles; dolls; masks; incense; bottles filled with potions. He even has kits for vampire hunters and aspiring witches, although none of it's real, luckily. I sensed he has the real stuff out back, though. But that is his stuff; he doesn't sell any of it. Whatever he does back there is dark magic. I've never felt anything so sinister."

"Do you know how it was possible for him to see Ralph and I last night?"

"I know the spell," — Devan turned those dark eyes on me, — "it's just a projection. He doesn't know who you are or where you live. He could only see a glimpse of your face, nothing more."

"Are you sure?"

He nodded.

"How did he do it?"

"I suspect he felt your presence in his house and performed the spell to confirm his suspicions. It conjures an image of the person who was last there and projects a similar image of the enchanter into that person's view so he could see who it was."

"Jesus." I turned to Ralph. "He must have realized when he returned to fetch his things and I was under the bed."

"Would he be able to recognize us again if he saw us in the street?" I asked Devan, glancing in the mirror.

"Absolutely. I would stay away from him if I were you. Particularly you, Blaire."

"Why me?" I asked.

Devan's green eye had bled back to its pale shade, but the blue eye was still dark. It was an unnerving look.

"Has anyone ever told you about your aura?"

"Yes, I've heard it's white."

"It burns bright, Blaire. You are like a star in the night sky, which, unfortunately, makes you easy to find. Most human auras burn a different color or change with their moods. Some are even made up of a combination of colors. Not yours. You are like a source of energy so white that if anyone touched you, they would perish. Your flame is attractive, but anyone wise enough would know not to leap, because you would consume them. Not just witches, but vampires, faeries, were-animals—all of them. You could consume us all. And he knows what you are. If what I sensed is correct, then I'm sure of it."

He held my gaze, his blue eye bleeding back to its prettier shade of sky blue. The heaviness and intensity of his stare made my stomach tighten.

Ralph touched my arm, and I jerked back in the seat. My heart pounded loudly in my ears, and I had to remind myself to breathe.

"What do I do?" I cleared my throat.

"Don't go near him, and don't ever touch him." He no longer looked like the young nineteen-year-old I had just met. His eyes implied an age that was way beyond my years; perhaps even beyond Ralph's, too. The years he had lived did not match the wisdom and experience reflected in his stare.

"So, what should we do for the rest of the afternoon?" Ralph thumbed the air behind him. "Should we carry on watching him?"

"It won't matter; he won't be doing anything of importance today."

"How can you be so sure?" Ralph asked, frowning.

At least one of us was thinking clearly enough to ask questions. All I thought about was if the voodoo priest got hold of me, I hoped I could use the force of his power against him. I had managed it with Seraphine, but that was something small; it was practically pins and needles. With a man hooked on the voodoo arts, who knew what dark magic he could unleash on me. I shuddered at the possibilities.

"I'm sure. I know you don't believe me, Ralph, and I don't blame you. I still need to earn your trust. But this voodoo priest sees clients in a room out the back and is booked up till late tonight. And besides, if you consider his M.O., the murders typically happen on a Friday evening. It's tomorrow night we need to be tailing him."

"How could we miss that, Ralph? He kills them on a Friday, and their bodies are discovered on either a Saturday morning or afternoon."

The smile on Devan's face grew to light up his eyes. He looked young once again; a relaxed, playful nineteen-year-old who wanted to spread the joy he felt with others around him. It made me smile.

"All right then. Tomorrow it is, I guess," Ralph said.

"Are you here with your own car, Devan?" I said, still looking in the little mirror.

"I don't drive."

"Of course you don't," Ralph mumbled to himself, smiling cynically. Turning to Devan, he added, "Can we drop you off somewhere? I need to take Snow White here home so she can wait for Prince Charming to fetch her."

I gave Ralph the look he deserved and rolled my eyes.

"Prince Charming was in Cinderella, genius."

"It's fine. I'll take the bus home." Devan climbed out of the car and, before he closed the door, said, "Come back here tomorrow around 7pm." He closed the door and left.

"Where did he go?" I turned in the chair to watch him leave but he disappeared around the corner.

"That kid is spooky," Ralph said, starting the engine. "Okay, so should I call you Snow White or Glow White?"

"Shut up."

"Home?" Ralph elbowed me lightheartedly in the shoulder.

"Yes, please," I said, laughing.

Chapter Eight

Ralph parked outside my house and cut the engine. The sun had only just started to set, filling the sky with a warm golden glow.

"What time is Charming fetching you?"

"Ugh, stop calling him that. I have just enough time for a quick shower."

"Have you seen him shift yet?"

"You know that last night was the first time I'd seen him in two months." I frowned. "Why'd you ask?"

"I didn't want to say anything before, but the old Blaire didn't care much for shifters. It'll be interesting to know how you handle Sebastian when he goes all furry on you."

"Are you messing with me, Ralph?" I narrowed my eyes.

"No, I swear."

"Why are you only telling me this now?"

"Honestly, I don't know." He gazed out of the window deep in thought. "I'm glad you're getting out there and finally seeing someone, but I just don't want to see you get hurt. I know, I know!" He turned to face me again. "He only marked you to save your life, and I'm just as grateful as you are for what he and Léon did. But your memory hasn't come back yet. It's just… you swore you wouldn't date monsters, and here you are forever tied to one, and dating him to boot."

I couldn't fathom why I hadn't liked shifters; I'd never felt that way when in Sebastian's company. I had to find out more.

"Do you know why I used to feel that way?"

"Forget I said anything."

"No, you brought it up; now you have to answer me. Please."

"I don't know the reason. But whenever we've been on jobs where shifters were the target, each time you'd mention how much you hated them. I just assumed it had something to do with your past. We never asked personal questions. Everything we knew about each other was offered willingly."

I folded my arms across my chest and stared at the road ahead of me.

"We started out as colleagues, and it's only these last couple of years we've become really good friends."

I knew that, for a time, we had been more than friends, but that had run its course. These past two months, we had rarely delved into the deep personal stuff. We carried on like we were friends, and I tagged along whenever he went to the gym or wanted to show me a place that he thought might jog my memory. Otherwise I stayed at home, hiding or rummaging through my cupboards to see if I had missed any other important information.

He didn't know why I had disliked shifters, so it wasn't worthwhile asking him again.

I'd never thought to ask Ralph how dangerous I was, if

at all. All I had to confirm it was the word of Kit, the private investigator Léon had hired to look into my background, who had told me my name for the first time after the amnesia had taken hold.

"How badass was I, back then?"

"Pretty badass." He flashed a grin. "You were scarily good. Even I feared you sometimes. You never hesitated."

"And now?" I asked, blinking slowly.

"Now? Now, you're tame, like your wings have been clipped."

"What's that supposed to mean?" My frown was back.

"It means you're different. Soft around the edges. The complete opposite of who you used to be."

"Which is better? Who I am now, or who I was?"

Ralph opened his mouth to say something, but stopped himself. He took a few seconds to think about it before proceeding.

"I miss the old you. You were my buddy. My best friend. Now I feel I need to protect you all the time," he said the last part in a whisper.

I didn't know what to say. I was a liability. And my amnesia was putting our lives at risk. I didn't want to pick up a gun or a blade and kill the monsters. However bad they were, they were still people. I might be able to protect myself if it was self-defense, but I couldn't see myself killing someone on purpose.

Maybe.

My lip was hurting from biting down on it.

"I'm sorry. I wish the old me could come back, but I like who I am now, too. I don't know. It's hard to describe." I shrugged and loosened the seat belt. "All I can promise is that I will train harder so that I don't endanger your life or mine. I will try harder and we can still work together, but you'll have to kill the monsters."

"I know. I'm happy to. Just remember that soon you might not have a choice." His voice trailed off. The pointedness of the last thing he'd said hung between us for a moment, but I couldn't argue with it. He did have a point. Suddenly he started speaking again. "Anyway, you need to go. Where do you want me to pick you up tomorrow morning?"

He'd changed the subject too quickly for my liking. I didn't think he wanted to talk about it anymore, but if he could move on, then so could I.

"Well, I'm packing an overnight bag, so I guess I'll be at the Labyrinth. What about you? You got company?"

"I have someone."

"Who?"

"You don't know her. Maybe the four of us can double-date sometime?" He laughed, but it sounded forced and empty.

"Yeah, maybe." I smiled, but it didn't reach my eyes. It must have looked as forced as it felt.

I couldn't help Ralph until I helped myself, and, from the looks of it, I had a long way to go.

I grabbed my bag from the back seat, opened the door, and climbed out.

"What time are you fetching me tomorrow?"

"Around nine."

"Great. See you then."

The house was quiet and dark when I opened the front door. I flicked on the light switch for the lounge and kitchen and closed the door behind me, locking it with the deadbolt and the chain.

The wood creaked beneath my feet as I walked to my bedroom, where I emptied the dirty clothing from my overnight bag and packed fresh ones for tomorrow.

I undressed and showered, washing my hair and scrubbing my body with the new scrub I'd picked up that was supposed to help with scarring. As the suds gathered around it, I touched the raised scar that ran from my bellybutton to my spine; the skin around it was the color of rose petals. I rinsed off under hot water.

In the bedroom, I dried my hair and kept the bath sheet wrapped tightly around my body. I sat on the bed and listened to the sound of the ticking clock on the shelf, the humming of the light switch above me, and the wind blowing through the trees.

Normally around this time of the evening, I'd be hearing kids playing in the street, but not tonight. There were no sounds coming from the neighbor's televisions. No sounds from anyone else. The neighborhood was safe; I didn't have to worry about gun fights in the street.

The house was big; a husband and wife with their two-point-five children should be living here.

I shivered.

An emptiness I hadn't felt before had materialized, and for the first time in two months, I felt alone.

My home was eerily quiet.

The walls crept closer. The room grew darker as the shadows from the corners reached out to me.

Standing up from the bed, I moved into the light cascading from the hallway. My chest rose and fell as deep breaths came in quick and heavy. I wiped beads of sweat from my forehead as I searched the room; unsure of what exactly I was looking for, but something was here. The lights were on, but they were dim. Too dim. The shadows were growing, and the light was shrinking.

I wanted to get out of the bedroom. I needed to get out. I turned and ran down the hallway into the lounge where the lights glowed brighter.

I sat on the couch in the lounge and hugged my knees. My jaw was clenched, my hands were shaking, and my skin was cold to the touch. I flinched when there was a knock on the door.

"Who is it?"

"It's Sebastian."

Shit, so much time had passed while sitting here. I rose from the couch, pulled the bath sheet tighter against my body, and opened the door.

"Are you all right?" Sebastian said as he entered. He rubbed my bare shoulders. "What's wrong? You're freezing."

I shook my head and bit my lip. Tears welled in my eyes, but I didn't blink for fear that they would fall. He stepped closer, but I stepped back. If he comforted me now, I would cry.

"Blaire?"

"Give me five minutes to get dressed, and I'll be right out."

I went toward my bedroom but stopped in the doorjamb and peered inside. The light was as bright as it usually was, as was the lamp. When I blinked, the tears came, but I wiped them away quickly and closed the door behind me.

The closet door was open, but I must have left it that way when I had packed the overnight bag.

I pulled on underwear, jeans, and a three-quarter white-and-blue striped top with black sneakers. I also added a scarf and a hooded black winter jacket made from down feathers.

When I realized my hair was still wet, I slipped the jacket off, blow-dried my hair until it resembled something close to being dry, and then pulled the jacket back on again.

Before I left the room, I grabbed the overnight bag, added toiletries, and joined Sebastian in the lounge.

"See, all done."

"What happened?"

"Nothing. Can we go now?"

The look on his face said he didn't believe me. But I didn't feel like explaining how I had freaked out because of the wind outside and the dim light in my bedroom. It was easier to just ignore it and move on.

He stepped closer to me and cupped my face in his hands; they felt so warm against my cheeks.

"You're freezing."

He leaned in closer and kissed me. His lips were hot against mine, and I kissed him back. I placed my hands over his hands, and the tips of my fingers hurt from being cold and touching something warm. When he pulled away, he left his hands on my face.

"What happened? Why are you so cold?"

"I don't know," I whispered, clenching my jaw to stop my teeth from chattering.

He lowered his hands from my face, and I entwined mine in his. They were so warm. I turned to look over my shoulder, but there was nothing in the hallway. He glanced over my head to see what I was looking at.

"What is it?" He asked with concern in his tone.

I shrugged again. He let go of my hands and went down the hallway into my bedroom, and I followed closely behind. The room was as I had left it; nothing out of place.

"Is there a window open somewhere?"

"There shouldn't be."

He went into each of the rooms and checked the windows, but they were all fastened in place.

"It's just your room that's freezing." He went back into my bedroom and checked the windows again, including the windows in the adjoining bathroom, but they were all closed.

He came back into the room, looked me up and down, and frowned. I followed his eyes downward and saw my feet were touching the border between the hallway and the bedroom. It was like my body didn't want to go inside the room again, as if it somehow knew that it was safer out there in the hallway.

"It's only cold near your bed." He looked at the rumpled covers where I had sat down after I showered. "Did you sit here?"

"Uh-huh." I crossed my arms over my chest and huddled myself.

He knelt down and touched the bed.

"It's freezing," — he felt the bed where it was still neat, — "but only in the spot where you sat." He reached for the mattress and pulled it up. "Shit."

"What? What is it?" I took a step back into the hallway.

"Don't come here," he said. He reached for something and dropped the mattress. He was holding a doll; a doll that looked identical to those the police had found sewn into all those victim's chests.

"Pack enough clothes to stay at mine for a while. You aren't coming back here until that priest is dead." His eyes darkened to a seaweed green color, and the muscles along his jaw tightened. I'd never seen him this angry before.

"Do you have any zip-lock bags I can put this thing in?"

"In the kitchen." I moved out of his way as he walked past me. "In the middle drawer," I called after him.

I kept my body pressed against the wall in the hallway, my hands flat against the wall. The coolness of the surface soothed my aching hands. I opened my jacket and aired it out; I was sweating again. At least that was a good sign.

Sebastian came back into the hallway with the doll in a bag. He held it up for me to see. The doll was made of brown material, and it had two buttons for eyes, a smile stitched with red cotton, and a little bell sewn to the middle of its body.

There was no mistaking it. It was exactly the same as the dolls found in the victims.

I kept my hands pressed against the wall. I would not touch it.

"Pack extra clothing, Blaire. Can you hear me?"

My eyes went from the doll in his hand to his eyes, and they were now summer green again. Not trusting my voice, I nodded and pushed myself away from the wall. I took a larger bag out of the closet and packed enough clothing and underwear for a week. When I was done, I found Sebastian in the lounge.

"Where are your weapons?"

My gun was downstairs in the basement. I didn't know how to get my weapon without letting Sebastian know I had a secret room. I didn't think it would be a disaster if he knew. We were sharing things about each other and this was part of me.

"Stay here," I said, entered the kitchen. I pulled the lever, and the fridge moved away from the wall to reveal an opening in the floor. It was dark below. I tentatively took the stairs one at a time until I reached the switch on the wall near the stairs and switched on the light.

My gun and shoulder holster were in the armor cage. I entered the combination on the lock, and it clicked open. I grabbed the holster and my gun and took a small bag and filled it with extra ammunition, two knives, and a wrist sheath. I locked the cage, switched off the light, and went back upstairs. The fridge moved back into place.

"Secret basement?" Sebastian asked with a smirk on his face. He was still standing in the lounge with the zip-lock bag in his hand, but he held it away from his body.

"Something like that." I removed my jacket, slipped on the holster, and fastened it onto my belt to keep it in place; that way, it wouldn't rub against my side. I slid the Glock 19 into place, added the wrist sheath to my left arm and secured one of the knives. I placed the other knife in the special sheath built onto my holster and pulled the jacket back on.

"Okay, now I'm ready." I picked up my overnight bag.

Sebastian held his left hand out for mine, and I gripped it tightly. The jolt of electricity his touch generated within me was comforting.

I locked the front door, and we walked hand-in-hand to the car. Rory, the guard I had met last night, was in the driver's seat. He jerked his chin in greeting when he saw me. He was a very quiet bodyguard. I wasn't quite sure which were-animal he was, but if I had to guess, I would've said werewolf. He just had that demeanor that screamed wolf. His olive-skinned frame was large and muscled, and he had brown hair and dark eyes.

Sebastian opened the door for me so I could climb in. He took the overnight bag and placed it in the back section of the Jeep and sat beside me. He dropped the zip-lock bag with the doll onto the front seat.

"We need to take this doll to Seraphine."

"No," I said. "Let me take it."

"I know this is connected to the target you and Ralph are watching, but Seraphine can handle it for you."

"We have someone who can take it."

Rory started the engine and pulled away.

"Who?"

"He's new. Started today."

"Fine, but it stays in the car. After what it did to you, I don't want you handling it."

"I need to find out whether the same thing happened to Ralph."

I dialed Ralph's number, and he answered on the sixth ring.

"Hello." He sounded distant, even more so than what using a cell phone would usually do.

"Ralph, are you okay?"

He didn't answer.

"RALPH," I yelled. I glanced at Sebastian. "We need to go to him. He isn't answering me."

"I am... h-e-e-e-r-e," he drawled. He sounded as though someone had drugged him.

"Are you on your bed?"

Silence.

"RALPH! Are you on your bed?"

"Uh-huh," he mumbled eventually.

"Get off your bed and try lifting your mattress. Ralph! Do it now!"

"Okaaay."

Something thumped onto the floor, and I heard a faint cry followed by swearing.

"What's the address?" Rory said, looking at me in the rearview mirror.

"Fuck, it's one of those dolls," Ralph said as I was about to answer.

"Ralph, get a bag, any bag, and scoop it in. Do it without touching it."

There was another thump followed by scuffling sounds, and then footsteps. Followed by drawers opening and plastic ruffling.

"Okay, I have it," he said a few seconds later. "Now what do I do with it?"

"We're coming to fetch it from you. I was thinking we could ask Devan to take them from us and break whatever the fuck spell is on it."

"Okay."

I gave Rory Ralph's address, and we arrived within twenty minutes. As we pulled onto his driveway, Ralph was sitting in his porch chair. Sebastian walked with me.

"How did you know?" Ralph asked. He lifted the doll in its plastic bag so we could see it.

"The same thing happened to me, but luckily Sebastian arrived just in time." I touched his arm when I said his name. His smile warmed me to my bones. It was a small gesture, but it meant more than that. The look in his eyes was a flurry of emotions; a combination of being afraid of losing me and grateful he had found me in time.

"Are you going to be okay?" Sebastian said, taking the doll from Ralph.

"I'll be fine, thanks." He ran his fingers through his wavy brown hair and rubbed the back of his neck.

"I thought you had a date?" I said.

"She cancelled on me."

"Is there someone else you can call? Marcus, maybe?"

"Don't worry about me; I'll be fine." He turned his dark blue eyes on me and frowned.

"Why are you angry with me?" I matched his frown with one of my own.

"I'm not angry with you. I'm angry that I got us into this mess."

"Do you want to come with us?" I asked, glancing at Sebastian, who widened his eyes at me. It was our date; he was taking me to his leap and opening up his world to me, and here I was trying to drag my colleague with us.

"Nah, I don't think so," Ralph said quickly. "But thanks anyway. Have you phoned Devan yet?"

"No, not yet."

"Okay, let me phone him. Give me the dolls and I'll drop them off at his place and text you when I'm done, okay?"

"Are you sure?"

"Yes, I'm sure."

Sebastian fetched the other doll from the front seat.

"Promise me you won't stay here alone, Ralph," I said. "Otherwise the next body Martin will find is yours."

Ralph pulled out his cell and dialed a number. "Hey, Marcus. Can you give me Devan's number?" He rose to his feet and entered his house as Sebastian walked toward me.

"Are you ready?"

"Give me a minute. I just want to make sure he goes to Devan."

Ralph came back outside and slipped his cell back into the pocket of his jeans.

"Okay, Devan is at home," Ralph said. "And he's fine with me coming over to drop off the dolls. Then I'm going to a hotel. You still staying with him?" Ralph pointed to Sebastian.

I nodded.

"She'll be staying with me until this case is over," Sebastian said matter-of-factly.

"Good, good," Ralph said, nodding quickly and added, "You can go now."

"Not until you grab your jacket, get in your car, and drive to Devan's."

"Still pushy, hey?" Ralph went back inside his house and disappeared from view. When he came out again, he wore his jacket with a bag over his shoulder. He locked the front door and picked up the two zip-lock bags containing the voodoo dolls. We walked down the driveway and climbed into our respective vehicles.

"Wait until he starts his car and drives away," I said to Rory.

"You know he can just drive around the block and come back here again."

"I know, but ignorance is bliss. At least I can say I saw him leave while I was still here. It'll make me feel better."

I waved at Ralph as he drove past us.

Chapter Nine

We drove with the radio playing softly in the background. The headlights from the car lit up the road in front of us and the tall trees alongside. As we came around a bend, two sets of eyes glowed in the dark, then they disappeared into the woods. My hand was in Sebastian's, and I squeezed it gently. He turned to look at me.

"Are you all right?" I whispered. Sebastian told me that Rory was in fact a were-wolf, and even though he could hear from a distance, I whispered anyway. It felt intimate, like it was just the two of us.

"Why wouldn't I be?" He squeezed my hand back.

I shrugged. In leopard form, he could see perfectly in the dark, but I wasn't sure whether he saw my shrug.

"Your hands feel sweaty," I said.

"It's not my hands," he chuckled.

He let go, and I wiped my hands on my jeans. He was right; it was my sweaty hands but I'd never admit I was nervous about meeting his leap. Most of the were-leopards and the alpha female—their leader—would all be present.

I turned to face Sebastian. He unbuckled his seat belt and scooted over to me. He put his arm around my shoulders and started bringing me closer to his body. I pushed away from him.

"What's wrong?" he whispered near my ear.

"Is it too late to turn around?"

"Don't you want to meet them?"

"I do," — I stared out of the window, and the trees blurred past us, — "just not right now."

"There really isn't anything to be nervous about."

I kept thinking about what Ralph had said; about how the old me didn't like shifters, any of them, but he hadn't known why.

Galina, one of Sebastian's exes, had shown a pretty distinct dislike for me when we had met. She had asked me if I would allow her to help me; to help mend what was broken inside my head. If it was possible she could help me, I wouldn't let her near me again. The last time we had seen each other, her jealousy over Sebastian had almost killed me.

Perhaps Devan could help, if I asked. I needed to know what the old me knew, but I didn't want the old me to come back. My head started to ache from thinking so hard.

The car slowed down then stopped. I glanced out of the window and saw a large house. Rory must have taken one of the side roads when I wasn't paying attention.

A knot formed in the pit of my stomach. Shit. I didn't want to do this anymore.

I turned to say something to that effect, but I was the only one in the car. I didn't notice everyone get out of the car.

I flinched when my door opened, and Sebastian held his hand out for me. It was too late to run away; he could catch me easily. I ran track at school, but I was nowhere near as fast as a leopard.

Sebastian's hand was still outstretched, waiting for me to take it. He bent down and put his face close to mine.

The lights from the house and the car shone on Sebastian's summer green eyes so perfectly that I could see, among the slivers of gold, that they were more than one shade of green. The expression in his eyes and on his face meant that he was trying to be gentle with me.

"It'll be okay. This, I can promise you. Anne and the leap are like family. As close to a real family as I've ever had."

If he had the guts to bring me here, then I could do this. It wouldn't be so bad. I could do this. I took his hand and climbed out of the car.

As we approached the house, three people—a man and two women—were standing near the doorway. The light was behind them, so I couldn't see their faces. We walked toward them with Rory close behind us. I wasn't sure why he was accompanying us, given that he was a were-wolf and this was a leopard-only leap. Sebastian said he was around for my protection, but surely I wouldn't need protection here.

"Sebastian, my dear! So glad you came." The woman who spoke was small and petite, and much shorter in height than I was. She moved toward Sebastian, he let go of my hand so they could embrace. When they let go of each other, she turned to me.

"Blaire, I've heard so much about you, dear," she said kindly.

My glance flicked from the woman to Sebastian as I wondered what he had been saying about me.

"All good, I can assure you," she said, coming closer to hug me.

I stood there with my arms at my sides as she embraced me. I put my head on her shoulder and moved my arms around her tiny waist. She smelled familiar, like warm grass on a hot day. Like leaves after a summer rain. Like leopard. Like Sebastian.

She let go, and I stood back from her and felt my forehead crinkle. I glanced at Sebastian and then back at the woman in front of me. Her smile reached her eyes, and her happiness swarmed around her, spreading through the two people beside her and through me, Sebastian, and Rory. The hair on the back of my neck stood on end, and I shivered as it ran down my spine like cold water.

"I'm glad you came." She touched my arm and started pulling me gently behind her as she walked toward the front door.

I glanced over my shoulder, and Sebastian was right behind me, the smile on his face sincere.

"My name is Anne," she said as we walked through the entrance and into the vast living room. She let go of my hand, pointed to a chair, and said, "Sit."

Anne looked like she could be close to sixty years old, with blonde hair styled short in a pixie cut—not gray like it usually would be for a woman of that age. Her eyes were a mixture of green and brown and looked like they could change with her mood.

She was short, with a naturally athletic build; you didn't have to see what she looked like naked to know, but you could tell by the muscles in her forearms and calves. She wore shorts and a t-shirt beneath a winter jacket, which she removed when we came inside the house. Her heart-shaped face, straight nose, and soft cheeks completed her pixie look; few women could pull off that look. I couldn't pinpoint which part of her was beautiful. She just was.

I sat in the loveseat across from her, and Sebastian sat beside me.

"This is Greg and Ivy," Anne said, pointing to the two other people in the room. They sat beside her on the larger sofa. "They are Sebastian's brother and sister."

Both were in their early twenties, with brown eyes and brown hair. But where Greg had copper streaks in his hair, his sister, Ivy, had blonde streaks.

With all three sitting alongside one another, you could tell they were related, courtesy of their similarly straight noses and heart-shaped faces. But the shape of their eyes differed, except for the kid's eyes, which were also a similar shade of brown. My guess was their father had brown eyes similar to theirs.

I knew they weren't Sebastian's real brother and sister, but the way in which she had introduced them was odd. My frown deepened, and the look on my face must have shown.

Anne immediately addressed it by blurting, "Not in the true sense, you understand, but family all the same."

"Nice to meet you all," I said in a pleasant voice.

"There is something I need to tell you before the meeting starts," Sebastian whispered near my ear, took my hand in his and squeezed gently.

But before Sebastian could say anything more, a gust of wind blew through the room, and men's voices grew louder as they entered. Everybody turned to see who had arrived.

"Sebastian, call off your dog," a man said as he entered the room. He must have been talking about Rory, who was still standing by the entrance; we shared eye contact for a few seconds before he went back to scanning the room.

The man who had spoken stood between the couches so we could see him and glared at Sebastian.

"And what is she doing here? This is leap business."

"That's quite enough, Phillip," Anne said, standing. She was at least a head and shoulders shorter than him, but her power oozed with rightful dominance. "Nobody needs to hear your whiney voice."

"I'll ask again, Anne. What the fuck is she doing here? And why is that dog standing at the door? This is leap business."

"Phillip," Sebastian growled, letting go of my hand and stood up. I could tell that one word was a stern warning. Sebastian was taller than Phillip, and his shoulders were broader. I knew he could beat Phillip with one hand tied behind his back.

Phillip's shoulder-length mousy blond hair was in desperate need of a brush or a trim and a wash. His haunting green eyes were a little too close together, and he had a long nose and a square jaw.

Another man entered the room to stand beside Phillip, but he didn't stand too close to Sebastian; almost as if he knew not to get in his way. This man had shaved brown hair and a black goatee, a small nose, and only one brown eye. He also had a vertical scar across his closed eyelid which ran from his forehead to his cheek. No amount of shapeshifting could heal a missing eye.

Phillip turned to face Sebastian and put a foot behind him to maintain balance if there was a fight. Which was not a good sign.

"Phillip?"

"What?"

"Are you sure this is what you want?"

"I've been waiting long enough, Sebastian."

"No!" Anne yelled, and stood between the two men. She placed a hand on each of their chests. "Not tonight," she said, staring at me. "We have a guest."

"Well, shit! We got here just in time to see Phillip's ass handed to him on a silver platter."

I turned to see who had spoken. Lee and Kai walked in and stood closer to me. The two were-leopards had helped us escape Roland's goons during his betrayal two months ago. They managed one of Léon's warehouses, where he kept all his priceless artifacts.

"Hi, Blaire," they said together, smiling at me.

"Hi, boys."

Both men had been in boxers the last time I saw them. Luckily, tonight, they were clothed: white sneakers, faded blue jeans, white t-shirts and jackets.

Lee's short blond-brown hair had curled over his ears, and his green eyes looked different from how I remembered them.

Kai still reminded me of a Roman soldier, with his aquiline nose and square jaw. His brown hair had grown out as well, and his brown eyes were bleeding to green and yellow.

"Boys," Sebastian said without looking at them.

Lee and Kai stood on either side of Sebastian; not exactly in a defensive stance, but they were there, waiting for further instructions.

"Three against one. Now that's not fair." One side of Phillip's lips curled upward, and then he hissed.

"They're going to make sure you fight fair," Sebastian said.

Phillip blinked. Sebastian was quick, hitting him in the jaw. His head rocked backward, and he crashed to the floor. I rose to see if he would get up, but he didn't; it had been a knock-out shot. Were-animals could take a panel beating and still walk around, but the force of that one blow had been powerful enough to make him fall down and not get back up.

"Not in my house," Anne said through gritted teeth. Her anger was directed at Sebastian and Phillip.

"Sorry, Anne," Sebastian said, turning to the other man who stood beside Phillip's unconscious body. "When he wakes up, Grant, tell him to stop pulling these stunts. Next time, I won't be gentle."

"Jesus! If that was you being gentle, then I don't want to see you in a real fight," Grant said.

"Exactly, now take him to Anne's infirmary."

Grant didn't argue; he did as instructed. He picked Phillip up like he weighed nothing, threw him over his shoulder, and proceeded down the hallway.

"Right, can we start now, please?" Anne said with a heavy sigh.

A few more people entered the living room, most of whom I had never seen before. Some stood while others sat on the floor.

Anne started the proceedings.

Through the Were-Animal Alliance, the WAA, all were-animal groups knew when something happened to any of the other groups. For centuries, they had each lived in isolation, and many had died because of this. But through the WAA, they worked together and grew in strength and numbers. They blocked outsiders from taking over territories, and when were-animals went missing and the police couldn't assist, the WAA sent out distress calls and everybody pitched in to help.

From the sounds of it, in recent months, something had happened every month: a missing teenage were-wolf who was later found with his were-lion girlfriend; a rogue vampire group who had attacked a were-rat and had been sentenced by the Vampire Council. Everybody worked together for the sake of all, and to keep humans safe and everybody within the law.

It was reassuring to know that the WAA was working so well.

A woman commented that although there had been no attempts from outsiders to encroach on anyone's territory during the last two months, they had heard that someone, a scientist, was busy developing a serum that had the potential to make a were-animal's inner beast dormant.

I glanced at Sebastian. He took my hand but didn't look at me; he didn't want anyone to know that we knew who this woman was.

The scientist in question, Melinda Cromwell, was a were-lion like Marcus. She had been dating Marcus until she almost killed him and left him for dead, which was when we had found him in an alley with his two fingers missing.

It was dangerous for any were-animal to try to kill off their inner beast. Their animal was part of who they were; if that side of them went dormant, nobody knew what happened to the human side. It was too risky; nobody knew what the side effects were; death or deformities.

Someone had to stop Melinda before she hurt somebody else. Perhaps Sebastian wanted to handle her, or perhaps it was something Ulysses Assassins would have to take care of. I needed to raise the issue with Ralph; perhaps we could handle it.

After an hour of discussion, the same woman who had mentioned the serum stood up and pointed to me.

"We've been quiet this whole time, Anne, but we think it's only fair that you enlighten us. Who is she, and what is she doing here? She isn't even a leopard." Her top lip curled over her emerging fangs, clearly unimpressed with me.

I leered at her. My free hand went to my side, reaching for where my gun was nestled. I felt safer knowing that it was there. Luckily, I had listened to Sebastian and Ralph and had chosen to carry it tonight. I was only human, and I guessed that she could throw a small car at me and not break a nail, so I needed all the help I could get.

"Greg..." Anne said, looking to her son to control the situation.

"Lauren," Greg sighed. "Now isn't the time."

Lauren crossed her arms over her chest and pouted.

"We might be together, Greg, but I'm still allowed to ask relevant questions. And she," — she pointed at me again, — "isn't one of us."

Greg didn't flinch. The look he gave her said she needed to be careful.

"Yeah, why is she here?" someone near the front added.

"That is enough. All of you! Her name is Blaire, and she is with Sebastian," Anne said, her voice loud enough to quieten all the murmurs.

"So what? I don't bring my buddy to our meetings," said someone at the back.

"She doesn't smell like a human," a man said, standing and approached us. He sniffed the surrounding air near my head. "What is she?"

"I can't be sure, but she does smell a little like us..." Another person sniffed.

I wasn't sure what that meant but I leaned forward to prevent them from sniffing me again and glanced at Sebastian, raising my eyebrows. Sebastian mouthed the words *'I'm sorry'* and rose from the couch.

I didn't know what he was sorry for. He didn't know how they would react to me.

"I brought her here so she could see who we are and how we do things in our leap."

I didn't understand why he said it like that. He could've said he wanted to introduce me to Anne. I frowned up at him.

"By now, I'm sure you have all heard about Blaire," — he jerked his chin in my direction, — "who was attacked two months ago by a were-wolf and a were-lion. Mel used my blood to replace the blood she had lost, in effect cancelling out the other two strains. Or so we thought at the time."

I bunched my hands into fists. My tongue stuck to my palate. And my frown deepened.

He glanced down at me with tenderness and continued talking loud enough for the others to hear. "When Mel took more blood, she had it tested, and it seems the strains didn't cancel each other out as we'd hoped."

"What are you saying, Sebastian? And why didn't you tell me this in private?" I sounded angry. Instead of informing me in private, he raised it now, in front of people I didn't know.

"Okay, everybody, that's enough," Anne said, standing. "I think it's time to leave. Everybody get out." She moved around the couch toward the hallway. "Come, you two," she called to us.

Sebastian reached for my hand. I ignored him and walked toward Anne. Sebastian and I followed her to a private room just off the main hall.

"What is wrong with you, Sebastian? Why did you do that in front of everybody without talking to her first?"

Anne said, chastising Sebastian, as she closed the door behind him.

He leaned against the wall with one foot against it and crossed his arms over his chest.

"You left before Mel could give you the results," he said, staring angrily at me. "I called you every week for two months, and you didn't bother to return any of them. It amazed me you even bothered to show up to the concert last night. I wanted to tell you after the concert; I tried to tell you last night, but you didn't want to hear it—" He didn't finish his sentence. His voice was strained like he was controlling his emotions.

"You should have tried harder, Sebastian. Telling people I don't know my life story, and that I may be infected with not one, but three, different lycanthropy strains, is not right." My neck heated, which happened sometimes when I was mad.

"You're right. I should have tried harder. I should have told you last night, but the look on your face..." His shoulders dropped, and his expression softened. Power trickled in the air like falling pins and then receded as quickly as it had appeared.

"I know it's a lot to take in right now and you're scared, but I was thinking that maybe you could visit the various animal groups and try to understand what all this might mean for you. I've arranged with Marcus for you to go to the Lion's Den on Saturday night, and then you're going with Mel to the Wolf Pack on Sunday."

"You didn't have to do it in front of everyone." I rubbed my arms and blinked back tears.

"You were ready to bolt when we first arrived. If I had told you this earlier, you wouldn't have come at all."

I opened my mouth to say something but closed it

again. I looked around the room: two of the walls were covered from floor to ceiling in bookshelves, and there was a desk with a laptop and two chairs. I sat in one chair, crossed my arms over my chest, and slouched. The look I was giving him wasn't a friendly one.

I exhaled a frustrated breath. Sebastian was right: if he'd told me beforehand, I wouldn't have come. I would've freaked out knowing I had three strains of lycanthropy inside of me. I would have gone home.

In the last two months, I had made plans to meet with Mel so she could help me manage my anger, and both times I had called to cancel. If I had kept those appointments, she could have told me about the strains. I now understood why she had specifically asked to see me face-to-face. This wasn't something you could tell someone over the phone, but I didn't want to see her. I didn't want to be reminded of that night and how everything in my life had changed. I also didn't want her telling Sebastian or Léon how I was doing.

Sebastian pushed away from the wall and kneeled in front of me, placing a hand on each armrest. The look in his eyes was intense. I glared at him.

"I'm sorry it came out the way it did. I didn't mean for it to be this way." Then his expression changed, and sadness spread to the rest of his face as he glanced at Anne then back to me. "I told Anne, and she suggested that I bring you here to tell you, but in private. But when everyone started asking those questions…" He swallowed hard. "I had to tell them. They would have found out eventually."

I tightened my fists until the knuckles whitened and clenched my jaw. I exhaled slowly, relaxing.

"You could have told me in the car ride here, Sebastian. If we are to have any kind of relationship, you need to be honest with me." I leaned forward. "You need to talk to me first. Always. You can't go around doing stuff like this and making decisions that affect me on your own."

"I'm sorry. Would you have stayed if I had told you beforehand?"

"Probably not. To find out I'm carrying three strains of monster isn't exactly great news, no offense. I don't even know what it all means." I sat back against the chair.

"I'm sorry," Sebastian said, smiling. He closed the distance between us, his kitty-cat green eyes leering mischievously at me, and I couldn't be angry at him for long. He leaned in and kissed me gently.

It was unfair how he could look at me like that and I would just melt in his embrace.

"Do you know what this means, having three strains?" A loud sigh escaped my lips. "Will I shift into one of them?"

"Honestly, we don't know. Best guess is that if you could, it would have happened already. We think it has something to do with how you can absorb power and then use it when you need it. This may be an extension of that power." He stood and sat in the chair across from me.

"How do I use this now?"

"I have no idea. How has your training with Seraphine been going?"

"How do you know about that?" I narrowed my eyes.

"We keep in contact."

"Does she know about the strains?"

"No. Only Léon, Mel and I know the truth. I wanted to tell you in person, but not like this." His words were filled with regret.

"It's okay, Sebastian." I went to him and straddled his lap. "Is that why you want me to go to the other animal groups? To meet them in case I shift into one of them?"

"Yes."

I put my arm around his neck and rested my head against his shoulder, but the holster dug into my ribs, so I sat up again.

Suddenly, we heard the sound of glass shattering, and something heavy crashed into the wall. Footsteps ran toward the room we were in, and then there was frantic knocking on the door.

"Anne, Sebastian, you have to come quickly."

Anne opened the door to find Kai and Lee standing there.

"It's Phillip," Lee said. "He's awake, and livid."

We ran to the living room, and everyone was scattered against the walls as Phillip and Greg fought in the middle of the room. Lauren was lying on her side on the floor, bleeding, with Ivy beside her. The loveseat I sat on earlier was in pieces against the fireplace, and the glass table was shattered on the floor.

Greg had bloody scratch marks down his arms and blood coming from his nose.

Phillip had partially shifted, and his hands ended in sharp black claws. He looked up at me, and his eyes glowed yellow.

Something moved to the side, and I turned toward it. It was someone in their leopard form; a very fluffy snow leopard the size of a small pony. He stalked me. With each step he took, he moved like he had liquid muscles; he made it look effortless yet careful. It reminded me of how leopards stalked their prey before they pounced.

I stepped backward, and the wall stopped me. Anne stood beside me, and suddenly Rory was here as well. I hadn't seen him move from where he had originally been standing near the front door. He stepped in front of me and lifted his right arm to keep me back, protecting me like Sebastian had asked him to.

"Phillip," Sebastian said, loud enough to make the other man look at him and not at me. "Are you challenging Greg?"

"He isn't strong enough to change his claws. How can he be third?" Phillip said, before leaping onto Greg with one claw in the air and swiping down across Greg's face.

Greg crashed to the floor, and blood splattered around him. He cried out in pain and then a low deep growl escaped his mouth. Phillip jumped on top of him and tried to go for his face again, but Greg held onto Phillip's claws to stop him.

"It's not that I can't, Phillip. It's because I choose not to," Greg said through gritted teeth.

Two things happened at once; Greg partially shifted, and his hands changed into orange-yellow-brown claws with black spots. He drove his sharp claws into Phillip's sides, splitting flesh. And the leopard on my left jumped in the air toward me, but Rory was there to take the full impact. The snow leopard collided with Rory, both crashing into me, toppling the three of us into the wall behind me. We hit the floor hard, and as the two men fought, they pinned me between the wall, the floor, and their bodies.

Rory half-shifted; his face and claws were that of a gray wolf, and he used those large teeth to bite into the leopard's neck. The leopard kept pushing forward in an attempt to get to me, and that's when I saw that it was missing a left eye. Grant was trying to hurt me.

That one eye fixed on me no matter how Rory tried to move him away, but leopard claws were held back by those of a gray wolf.

Grant moved quickly, knocking Rory into me and slamming my head against the wall. Stars swam before my eyes for a second. Then someone grabbed my hands and dragged me away.

When I came to, I was sitting against the wall in the hallway with Anne beside me.

Rory, in half-wolf, half-man form, was still fighting Grant and trying to keep him in the living room.

"I'm okay," I said to Anne. "Help me stand."

Anne pulled me to my feet. I opened my winter jacket and pulled my Glock from its holster. I gripped it tightly in my hand until it hurt, and walked toward Rory and Grant.

Greg was on the floor with his claws in Phillip, whose claws were now in Greg's sides; a standoff.

"Stop," Greg said through gritted teeth.

"You first," Phillip growled.

Sebastian moved closer to the fight, wrapping his arm around Phillip's neck, and putting him in a chokehold.

"Remove your claws," Sebastian said gravely. He now stood in his t-shirt, having removed his jacket while I was in the hallway; the muscles in his arm flexed around Phillip's neck as it cut off his air supply.

Phillip's head lulled to one side, and his arms went limp. Lauren pulled Phillip's claws out of Greg's sides, while Greg removed his own from Phillip and slid out from under him.

Rory had his back to me, trading punches with my would-be attacker. Both he and Grant fought well, even though Grant was bigger in his leopard form than Rory was in his partially-shifted wolf form.

Grant saw me walk toward them, and his one yellow eye glared at me.

"Let him go, Grant," I said, lifting my gun, aiming for that one yellow orb. "I have silver in the chamber, and I will fire."

Grant knocked Rory's head against the wall and lunged at me. I raised my hand in the general direction of his body as he was in midair and fired the gun. Grant fell to the floor and stayed there.

The room went quiet and people moved away from me. My ears were ringing from firing the gun indoors.

Rory pulled himself up from the floor and stood beside me.

"Are you okay?" he asked, placing one hand on the gun and lowering it to the floor.

I nodded too quickly and it hurt, the knock to my head starting to show signs of life. Something dripped down my back. I touched my head, and my hand came back with blood on my fingertips.

I didn't want to put the Glock back in my holster until I knew we were out of danger and there were no more leopards trying to kill me.

Sebastian laid Phillip on the floor and said something to the woman who sat next to his unconscious body before approaching me.

Someone caught my eye as they went to Grant, now back in his human form. I couldn't see his chest moving. Shit.

I went down on my haunches to feel for a pulse in his neck and moved him onto his back. The bullet had left a hole where his heart was meant to be. There were gasps coming from people all around me, but I didn't look at any of them. The bullet had shredded his heart exactly as it had been designed to, which was why Ulysses paid so much for these bullets.

There was nothing we could do for Grant.

"Why did you have to kill him?" the woman asked as she sat beside Grant's body.

"She had no choice, Vivian," Sebastian said from behind me.

He touched my arm, and I flinched.

"It's okay. You can put the gun away."

He touched my arm again, but I didn't jerk away this time. I put the gun back in my holster, shivered, and then zipped up my jacket.

Anne stood in front of me, her green-brown eyes filled with sadness and unshed tears. With her so close, I realized it was her eyes that made her beautiful, in the way that the green and brown interlaced with each other. And there was a yellow ring around the iris. One would think the yellow would only show when she was in her leopard form, but it remained with her in human form, too. Her lips were moving, but they were too fast for me to read. My ears were ringing louder now.

I caught some words: 'trouble', 'shock', then 'danger'.

I stared beyond Anne at the woman sitting near Grant's body and she was crying. She pulled something from Grant's wrist and made as if to throw it to one side.

"No," I yelled. "Don't throw it away." I went onto my haunches beside her.

The woman froze with the armband still in her hand. I reached out for it and she handed it to me. The armband was woven from rough brown material and had a small pouch containing tiny bones, pieces of leather, a feather, and a number of herbs inside.

I brought the pouch near my nose and regretted smelling it; it was pungent.

"What is it?" the woman asked.

Finally, I could hear again.

"It's a medicine bag," Sebastian said from behind me. He reached out for it, and I handed it to him.

"Why would any of your people need this, Sebastian?" I asked.

Sebastian turned away from me and approached Phillip, who was still unconscious on the floor.

"Show me his wrists," Sebastian asked the man watching over Phillip.

The man pulled Phillip's sleeves to his elbows to reveal his wrists. First, the left, where there was nothing, but then, on the right, there was an armband similar to the one retrieved from Grant's body.

"Does anyone know where these two went before they came here?" Sebastian asked as he glanced around the room.

"Grant told me they stopped off at a shop to buy special candles," a man in the corner of the room said, stepping out of the darkness.

"Do you know which shop?"

"No. Just some hoodoo shop."

"Do you know the street name?" I blurted. My heart sped up, and my hands were clammy.

"I think he said Jackson."

"What is it?" Sebastian said, turning to face me.

"That's the priest's shop," I whispered, even though I knew everyone present could hear, thanks to their wereleopard ears.

His eyes widened.

"How did he even know I would be here?"

"Anne, did you tell anyone else I was bringing Blaire here tonight?"

"Greg and Ivy were with me," — Anne said, scanning the room, — "and Lauren."

Ivy was still sitting beside Lauren, who was lying on the

floor. She was conscious now, watching the exchanges taking place in the room.

Greg sat on the floor with his back against the couch, pressing against his sides to stop the bleeding from Phillip's claw marks. He needed to shift in order to heal.

"Did any of you disclose to an outsider that Blaire was coming here tonight?" Sebastian said, first looking at the siblings, then at Lauren.

"No," Greg and Ivy said at the same time.

Lauren scowled at Sebastian.

"Lauren?" That one word questioned everything she may or may not have done.

She didn't blink as she sat up and hissed at Sebastian.

"Lauren, what did you do?" Greg said as he crawled to her, but she ignored him.

"Lauren." Anne sat on the couch in front of her, took her right wrist, and pulled up her sleeve to reveal the armband beneath. "Explain."

Lauren yanked her wrist from Anne's grasp and pulled her sleeve down. Sebastian stepped closer to her, and I followed him. Others moved away from us, most likely decided it was better to be away from the fight than near it.

"Take it off, then talk," Sebastian said with a hint of anger.

Her face was etched with pain, like it would hurt to remove it. Anne grabbed her arm and pulled the armband off. Like a light switch could brighten or darken a room, the look on Lauren's face changed from anger and pain to comfort and delight once the armband had been removed. She let out her breath in a long exhalation of relief. It sent shivers down my spine, like a cold hand trailing over my warm skin.

"What's going on?" Lauren asked, blinking sparkly eyes. She had confusion stamped all over her face.

"We were hoping you could tell us. Where did you get this from?" Anne asked, lifting the armband near her face.

"I bought it at the voodoo shop on Jackson Street. I think the owner, Ross or something, gave one to each of the four of us."

"Who else, Lauren?" Sebastian asked as he sat on his haunches in front of her.

"Me, Phillip, Grant, and…" She frowned. "Dammit, I can't remember who the fourth was." She brought her hand to her forehead and rubbed her temples.

"Think, Lauren, please." Greg sat beside her and wrapped his arm around her shoulders. "Who took the fourth armband?"

"Jeremiah," she said, glancing at Greg then up at Sebastian. She seemed as surprised as she sounded when she said his name. "It was Jeremiah, but he isn't here." Her brows furrowed, and she started rubbing her temples again. "I didn't know he was going out. Did he tell anyone where he was going?"

My cell phone rang, and I jumped in response. Everybody turned to stare at me.

"Sorry," I said, fishing the phone out of my pocket. "Hello," I whispered.

"It's Ralph. Can you ask Sebastian if he knows someone named Jeremiah?"

"Yeah, he does. Do you know where he is?"

"Sure do. He followed me, then attacked us when I arrived at Devan's apartment."

"Did you kill him?"

"No," he yelled so loudly I had to move the phone away from my ear.

"What did you do with him?"

"We tied him up."

"Tell Devan to look on his right arm. There should be an armband." When I said that, everyone stared at me again. Sebastian turned to me. I placed my hand over the mouthpiece. "My partner has Jeremiah. He attacked them, but he's fine; they detained him."

"Yeah, he has one," Ralph said after a moment of silence.

"Before you remove it, ask him who gave him the armband and why."

There were muffled sounds, and men's voices.

"The priest has our names and addresses," Ralph said. "He gave four armbands to the were-leopards who came into his shop this afternoon and instructed them to hurt us."

"He is one conniving bastard, I'll give him that. He won't stop until we're dead."

"What should I do with this one?"

"Don't hurt him. Can you bring him here?"

Anne gave me her address, and I repeated it to Ralph. He told me they'd be here within the hour.

Chapter Ten

I explained the evening's events to Ralph over the phone, and then gave the leap a short version of the case we were working on. I didn't include a lot of information, but it was enough for everyone to know not to buy anything from that shop ever again, and to stay clear of McNielty.

When I asked if anyone had previously bought anything from the shop, almost everyone put up their hands. So, any of them could have been there today and given the armband.

We waited for Jeremiah to arrive before speaking with Lauren and Phillip. Everyone else was welcome to leave.

Staring down at Grant's body, at the large hole in his chest, I thought he didn't deserve to die like a monster, like some contract target I had been assigned to. I had killed him with one of the special silver bullets that was custom-made for Ulysses Assassins. We used them to stop the monsters from hurting us, but this were-leopard was a friend.

I wanted to make this better, but I didn't know how. I hoped he didn't have a wife and kids.

I blinked back tears.

"What are you going to do with his body?" I asked no one in particular.

Anne, Greg, and Sebastian were standing nearby. I glanced at each of them. When I looked at Greg, something flashed through his eyes. For a second, I would have said it was pain or sadness, but it also looked like fear. The muscles in his jaw moved as he fought not to speak.

"What is it, Greg? If you have something to say to me, say it."

"I don't know you well enough, Blaire. I'd rather reserve my opinion."

"Say what's on your mind," Anne pushed.

"Fine." His anger flared through the room, and he no longer seemed afraid. "She knew her gun was loaded with silver bullets, yet she fired it directly at his heart anyway. If she'd aimed anywhere else, he would still be alive." He was pointing a long finger at me.

"I didn't mean to kill him. I warned him before pulling the trigger, but he still came for me. Before you say anything, I know he wasn't himself. I know that now, but at the time, none of us knew they weren't acting of their own volition. And perhaps a part of me didn't feel like getting mauled by another were-animal. If anything charges at me, I'll shoot it." As soon as the words flew out of my mouth, I regretted them.

Greg's mouth opened slightly, like I had punched him in the face, and his eyes glistened with tears.

I wanted to take the pain away.

"I'm sorry." My voice sounded strained as I choked back tears.

Rory came to stand behind me, and the air smelt like disinfectant and soap. He had washed his face and hands, and Mel had already patched him up.

Mel, the were-wolf doctor who worked with the were-leopards, had arrived earlier and was tending to each of the injured leopards. Now that Rory had returned, it meant that Lauren was now with her.

Phillip lay on the sofa, looking worse for wear, even though Mel had already seen him. All the leopards could heal if they shifted, but they were waiting for Jeremiah to arrive so we could hear his side of the story.

Anne and Sebastian spoke at the same time.

"She was only protecting herself," Anne said.

"It could have been any of us," Sebastian said.

Greg looked from his mother to his 'brother' and screamed as loudly as he could. He screamed until his face turned the color of the liquid lying beneath Grant's body.

I didn't stick my fingers in my ears to block his screams; I heard them all. I felt them vibrate off the walls. I needed to hurt, even though I knew it wasn't my fault. Greg's power explode into the air, and it took my breath away.

When he stopped screaming, his eyes glowed yellow and his hands had changed into claws.

"Sorry," he said in a hoarse voice and skulked toward the back door in the kitchen and left, leaving the door open.

Sebastian wanted to put his arm around me, but I stepped back.

"If you console me, I'll lose it."

"There's no shame in breaking down," he whispered. "You just shot and killed someone. If you didn't break down, I'd worry."

"What do you mean?" I frowned.

"If you killed him and didn't feel something, whether it

was sadness, pain, or guilt, then I'd worry about your morals. It would tell me that you would kill anything without thinking twice."

Like a cold-blooded killer.

I was cold. Empty. Numb. Was that the same as not feeling? Was the old Blaire returning? Apparently, she could kill without feeling much of anything, whereas I regretted for feeling this way. Maybe that was the difference between us.

I felt regret.

"What are we going to do with his body?" I asked again, changing the subject.

"The blue moon will be full in five days' time. We will feast on his body then," Anne whispered.

I blinked very slowly as I processed this information. I turned to Sebastian, but he avoided eye contact.

Was he ashamed that this was what his leap did; they consumed the dead? My mouth opened, but no words came out.

"Not all were-animals do this, but it's a ritual we perform if we want one of our own to join the others and stay with us metaphysically. I would like for you to join us when it takes place. We need you to be there," Anne explained.

"But," — I cleared my throat, — "I'm not one of you."

"Yes, you are," Anne whispered for my ears only and glanced at Sebastian. "You are one of us. No one else knows Sebastian's secret except for me, but I know how you are tied to him, the were-leopard strain excluded. I can also feel the attraction between you, and I feel that there is something else buried deep inside of you. Your mind became clouded after your attack, but when your light shines clearer, you will know what to do with many of the things you have consumed."

I was about to object when banging started on the front door.

Ralph, Devan, and Jeremiah arrived before midnight. Ralph had deep scratches on his forearm, and because he was human, Mel treated him first. Devan stood off to one side with Rory, as far away from any were-leopard as he could get.

Jeremiah was young. He looked younger than his nineteen years and was exactly my height; five foot five. He had soft brown curly hair, the lightest blue eyes I had ever seen and chubby cheeks. He looked innocent, like someone's younger brother or son, or a next door neighbor. But the exterior was deceiving; his eyes whispered hints of a hard life, and when he shook my hand, power jolted through my arm like lightning and I had to jerk my hand free of his.

"What was that?" he said with wide eyes.

"That was you, Jeremiah," Sebastian said, rubbing his arms. "Tone it down, dude."

Jeremiah flinched when I moved away from him. He had a stab wound to his gut, but it appeared superficial. He walked around the room giving the other were-leopards hugs and chest-bumps.

Mel called him next, and Ralph came out.

"Are you okay?" I asked, staring at his forearm.

"Jeremiah used his claws on me. Mel took some blood. She'll let me know the results."

"Shit, I'm sorry, Ralph." I hugged him.

"Can all leopards shift their hands into claws without shifting completely, or is it only certain people who can?" Ralph asked.

"Only those powerful enough can shift a body part at a time," Sebastian said.

"Jeremiah is only nineteen. Is he really that powerful?"

"Yes, he is."

"What happened to him? He seems so young and innocent, but that's not the case, is it?" I asked Sebastian.

"No, it isn't, but he hasn't elaborated on all that has happened to him. All we know is that his family was attacked and he was the only survivor. He came to us through a mutual friend and has stayed here with Anne ever since. She's helping him to control his powers, because, at the moment, they are all over the place. As you saw when you shook his hand."

"Yeah, I can still feel it." I rubbed my hands together.

Jeremiah came out with Mel trailing behind him and stood near the fireplace.

Phillip was still lying on the couch with Lauren tending to him.

Greg came through the back door, looking much calmer than when he left.

"Right, everyone; come closer. Let's hear from Jeremiah exactly what happened," Anne said, nodding at the young leopard.

Jeremiah's account matched exactly with what Lauren had said, and Phillip nodded in agreement. The four of them had often shopped for candles or incense and had never spoken more than five words to the owner, but they knew his name was Ross.

They described McNielty as pale, so pale that his skin seemed translucent, with white hair and eyebrows. They didn't think he had any eyelashes, and if he did, they were white and couldn't be seen from across the counter.

I began making notes in a little booklet I kept in my pocket.

One thing the three of them couldn't agree on was the color of his eyes. Jeremiah said they were blue; Phillip said they were lilac; and Lauren said they were green. I wrote all three colors down with question marks next to them. The police report had varying descriptions of his eye color as well, with one even stating they were red.

"And..." Jeremiah started, then stopped, thought about it, and continued. "His accent. I can't place it, but it's different."

"Do you remember him saying anything specific?" I asked.

"No, I only remember him saying he had armbands for us to wear and that they would guide us spiritually." Jeremiah frowned like he still wasn't sure that that was what McNielty had said.

"I remember now that you mention it, Jeremiah," Phillip said, wincing as he sat up and glanced at Sebastian. "I'm sorry I acted like such a dick, Sebastian. I know I can be a pain in the ass," — he shook his head gently, — "poor Grant. I still can't believe he's gone."

An ache burned in my stomach. I focused at a spot on the floor as I felt the stares of the others boring holes into me.

"It wasn't her fault, Phillip," Jeremiah said. "I almost killed someone tonight, and you know I am the last person to do anything remotely violent. I attacked Ralph. That has never happened to me before. Ever. I felt possessed." He shuddered. "If Blaire hadn't shot Grant, he would have torn his way through her, and then what would have happened? Cops would be here, and who would we blame? They would have the right to kill us all on the spot, because human law protects humans first."

Jeremiah seemed very practical and wise for his age. I wanted to jump up and give him a hug and a kiss on the cheek for standing up for me. An edge of a smile played across my lips, but I stopped it there. I didn't want to look pleased about what I had done.

Jeremiah glanced at me and winked. I stiffened, then scanned the room, but no one else had seen it; they were busy talking amongst themselves.

"Okay, I think that's it; we have all the information we need. Or does anyone have anything to add?" I asked. Taking their silence as proof that there was nothing more to be learned here, I pocketed my notebook.

"We have lost enough tonight," Anne said sadly as she rose from her chair. "There will be no further punishment. And you three, shift so you can heal."

"Yes, ma'am," Phillip said, and started to undress.

When were-animals shifted, they tended to shred their clothing because their bodies became so large. Most wore the bare minimum or old clothing and were usually happy to shred it during their transformation.

Lauren removed her clothes but kept her underwear on. Nobody seemed to mind, but after all, there was nothing sexual about the process. It wasn't something to lust after: it was part of who they were.

Lauren shifted first. Her turning furry was smooth and graceful; her muscles moved like flowing water beneath her skin until she was covered in orange-brown fur with black spots, or rosettes. I thought with her jet-black hair and blue eyes, she would be a black leopard, but she wasn't. And her eyes were grass-green in leopard form.

A growl escaped from her large jaw and she opened wide to reveal sharp teeth. Lauren stretched her massive body, and dug her claws into the carpet. She approached Greg to rub her face on his body, marking him with her scent. He scratched her head and led her away down a corridor.

Phillip was next, and I fought not to look, but I wanted to see his change. His shift wasn't as graceful as Lauren's, but he shifted just as quickly and was much larger than her: he was bigger than a pony. He made a husky coughing sound, and a woman led him down the same corridor that Greg had taken Lauren through.

"Where are they taking them?" I whispered, my mouth near Sebastian's ear.

"Shifting can take a lot out of us, so when we change, we are usually hungry. It's only new leopards that have to be secured for the first few moons. Us older ones can control our animal and don't always have to feed soon after, but if we can eat, we will. There is a feeding den downstairs where we keep live animals."

"Ah, I see." The thought of seeing an animal mauled to death didn't sit well with me but it was something they had to do.

Jeremiah stripped down to his birthday suit. Although I had avoided looking at Phillip's entire body, I couldn't avoid staring at Jeremiah. He stood tall and removed pieces of clothing almost provocatively, teasing all the eyes watching him. The baby fat in his face was a youthful look that would fade as he got older. When he removed his shirt, the muscles beneath his skin rippled and moved flawlessly. Once he had slipped off his underwear, it became obvious why he moved the way he did: he was well endowed and relished in people staring at him.

My face heated because he watched me the entire strip show and smiled mischievously.

"Jeremiah loves to flirt," Sebastian whispered near the shell of my ear; his hot breath against my neck, causing all the little hairs to stand on end.

I turned to meet his gaze. His expression hinted at

something I couldn't put my finger on. I didn't know him well enough to discern all of them yet. Was he somehow suggesting that no matter how well-endowed Jeremiah was, Sebastian could compete?

My body heated and I turned away from him, but as I did so, I stared straight at Jeremiah and felt a little dizzy with embarrassment.

Too much movement, too quickly.

Luckily, the strip tease didn't last long because Jeremiah suddenly shifted. Like snapping your fingers, there he was: large with thick black fur and brown-green eyes with a yellow hue.

He roared loudly, then a purr trickled from his mouth as he started pacing. He walked past everyone, brushing his big furry body against them, and they rubbed either his head or along his body, like one would pet a dog.

When Jeremiah reached me, he scent-marked me and licked my hand, sending shivers down my spine. I tickled behind his ear where his fur was smooth and silky.

One woman rubbed his head and started pulling him away from me. At first, he didn't want to go with her, but after some gentle persuasion, he went reluctantly with her down the hallway.

"He has a crush on you," Sebastian said, with a laugh that didn't sound entirely happy.

When in doubt, say nothing. I couldn't get into trouble for keeping quiet. If Jeremiah had a crush, I'd ignore it. And besides, I was way too old for him, anyway.

"I'm heading out," Ralph said as he walked toward us. "I'm going to crash at Devan's place. We'll fetch you from Sebastian's place around five tomorrow afternoon."

"Okay. I think we're going as well?" I said, glancing at

Sebastian. I was tired; it had to be close to one in the morning.

"Sure," Sebastian said, then he went over to speak with Anne.

Ralph was a friend, but we weren't the type of friends who hugged each other each time we said goodbye. We only engaged in the mushy stuff if either of us was hurt or there was something going down where we might not live to see each other the next day. But with Jeremiah having attacked him with his claws, there was a chance that Ralph could now be carrying the were-leopard strain.

I approached Ralph and hugged him. I held onto him and felt a tiny white spark as I wished away his pain and the strain that might have infected him. I didn't want him to become a were-leopard. I needed my friend to stay as he was, and I could only assume he didn't want to turn into a were-leopard, either. Everything would change, and as selfish as it sounded, I didn't want that to happen. I was also having my own thoughts about the strains I carried, but the difference was I hadn't yet changed into any of the were-animals.

"When will Mel call you?"

"She said the results would be quick. Two days, if she pushes it."

"Does your forearm hurt a lot?"

"It hurts, but Devan said he will make me a special herbal tea when we get to his place. Apparently, it'll sort me out." He glanced back at Devan, who was still standing against the wall, eyes wide.

"Devan, are you all right?" I asked, walking over to him. He was paler than before, and his eyes flitted around the room.

"I'll be fine," Devan said, clearing his throat. He

squinted at me, but the lights in the living room were soft, gentle dinner lights.

Some clairvoyants knew what one did through skin-to-skin contact, while others only had to touch clothing or objects. Then there were those clairvoyants who were powerful enough that being in the same room was good enough. I wondered whether Devan had the ability to sense things by only needing to be in the vicinity, and when he touched the person or object it was that much clearer.

"Are you always this sensitive to light?" I asked, not wanting to bombard him with all the questions inside my head.

He bit his lip and stared down at me as though he was trying to read my thoughts.

"I don't have to touch anyone to feel."

"Did you read my thoughts?" I asked, frowning.

"No, but I saw the question on your face," he grinned.

At least I took his mind off everyone else. His shoulders visibly relaxed, and color came back into his face.

"Is it difficult for you to switch off like that? To tune people out?"

"It was hard at first. I was ten when my parents sent me to live with my aunt. She was a priestess. She taught me how to control my power and how to focus. But, yes, if there are too many people in a room, it becomes harder tuning them out."

"Were your parents gifted like you?"

"No," he chuckled lightheartedly. "My parents were plain human. But the priestess I stayed with helped them to understand my gift. Which is why, when I was old enough, I went to live with her. She taught me everything I know." He smiled, but behind that smile was sadness.

I wanted to take his sadness away, and not ask whether

his parents were still alive or not. I changed the subject instead of asking more questions about his childhood.

"What do you think of the dolls Ralph and I found under our mattresses?"

Until now, with everything that had happened that night, I had completely forgotten about the dolls the voodoo priest had left Ralph and I in each of our rooms. The voodoo priest knew who we were, where we lived, and he had been able to manipulate the were-leopards into attacking us by supplying them with those charmed armbands. Yet we were still no closer to pinning any of the murders on him. My hands balled into fists, and my head started to ache from being thrown against the wall earlier.

"I think it's best if we discuss it tomorrow when we fetch you. You're tired, and your anger just spiked a few notches."

"How did you know?" I frowned again.

"I can taste your anger, and it's hot. If I had to lick the air, it would burn my tongue like a chili."

"Jeez," I said, pressing my hands flat against my jeans. "And now?" I tried to relax.

"Pepper. It's like pepper now."

I started to say something else when Ralph headed for the front door and opened it. Ralph wanted to leave, and he gestured for Devan to follow him. The boy smiled at me briefly and then darted out the door after him.

Sebastian drove, I rode shotgun, and Rory was laying in the back. Grant had clawed Rory so badly that he had missing pieces of flesh on both sides of his hips and a deep scratch over his chest.

He needed to shift but would do so when we got back to

the Labyrinth; we didn't want anyone seeing a large gray wolf in the back of the Jeep and start shooting at us. Although there were laws protecting were-animals, there were still some gun slingers who shot at anything bigger than a dog. That kind of hunting was illegal, yet they still killed were-wolves, were-tigers, were-hyenas, and were-bears. Apparently were-leopards were too fast for them to kill. Go leopards.

It was after one on Friday morning by the time we arrived at the Labyrinth. Since there were no other cars on the road, the journey didn't take us long.

Sebastian took my bag and carried it to his room. The walls were different and the way to his room was a mystery once again.

Rory left us and went to his room, which I assumed was to enable him to shift and heal.

I thought of the voodoo priest and how easy it was for him to enter our houses and put a doll under our mattresses. I hoped this fortress prevented him from getting inside.

"How tight is the security here?"

"Why'd you ask?" Sebastian said as he set my bag beside his closet and sat on a chair.

"I want to make sure the priest can't get in here and leave another present for me." I sat on the chair across from him and started undressing.

"It would be difficult for him to get in, we have great security. And even if he did, how would he know which room you were staying in?" He made a good point.

"I had to check." I shrugged.

My shoes were off, and I slipped out of my shirt, opened my bag, and pulled out my pajama top. Just as I was about to remove my bra, I realized he was watching me, and froze; I was getting too comfortable around him. I grabbed my pajama bottoms from the bag and headed for the bathroom. He chuckled as I walked past him.

I dressed in my sleepwear and entered the bedroom. Sebastian was in his boxers and pulled the covers back without noticing me. As I watched him, I tripped over my feet but corrected my balance before I crashed to the floor.

I giggled like a sixteen-year-old with a school crush. Apparently, I was utterly clumsy as well; which was terrible for a thirty-year-old to admit to.

I threw my clothing on the floor near my bag and went to the side of the bed I had slept on last night. I wasn't sure whether Sebastian had seen my 'almost fall,' but I was glad he didn't mention it.

Sebastian switched off the bathroom light but left his lamp on and climbed under the covers. He was very much on his side of the bed, avoiding the middle. I didn't like the distance he had created.

Being this close to him, I wanted to touch him, to hold him, and to be held by him. I crawled to his side of the bed and forced my hand between his arm and his waist, and held him.

I snuggled my head onto his pillow with my face against his back and breathed in his scent: the ocean, a hint of cologne, but beneath all that was his leopard. The warm sun, tall grass, and wet leaves. I breathed it all in and exhaled. I held him tightly, and he moved my hand up to his chest until I felt the rhythm of his heartbeat beneath my fingers.

The feel of him against my face and under my hand felt so right, and I took it all in. I pressed as much of my body against him as I could, and my lips curled upward.

Being away from him for two months had felt right at the time; not being near him had helped me to think and to fight whatever connection there was between us. I fought to push us apart and kept it that way, thinking I was meant to be on my own.

But, being so close to him now, this was where I was supposed to be. This was what I had been missing all those months. Perhaps it hadn't been the broken pieces of my mind or it was pieces of him I was missing.

My memory fully returning would take time, but until that happened, I would try to be happy. And perhaps I could be happy with him.

The bed moved, and I jolted awake. Sebastian turned around to face me and pressed his body against mine. Moving my hand holding him, he placed it around his waist and pulled me closer to his body. He was taller than me, and his hardness pressed against my body.

He stared at me, like he was studying my face; like he was counting every pore of my skin. I fought not to look away; not to squirm. I gazed back at him, staring into his eyes, then those soft lips that always kissed me gently, tenderly.

It brought back a memory of a kiss we had shared when we were running away from danger in the sewers beneath Léon's warehouse. We had both stunk of sewage, but he had kissed me like it was the last day on earth, and it was a kiss I would never forget.

"What are you thinking?" he asked, bringing me out of my daydream.

"I was just thinking of that one time you—"

Before I could finish my sentence, his mouth was on mine with a growing need. His hands were everywhere on my body. I touched his back, arms, waist, and the soft mound of his ass. He moved his right leg between mine, forcing my legs apart. I lifted my leg over his hips, and he pushed me closer into his body. Somewhere low in my body tightened, and my own need for him grew.

A soft purr escaped his lips as we kissed. I pulled away to look at him. His face held an expression all men had when they were intimately close to a woman. It was a look that said, 'mine'.

I kissed him and smiled in that kiss. His hands went under my top, and I tensed. He brought his hand back out, but he still held me.

"We don't have to do anything else." He traced his thumb across my swollen lips, then kissed my cheek, temple, forehead, and neck.

He pulled me closer into the circle of his arms. My eyes closing from the calming feel of his body against mine.

"You are like a magnet. And I can't get enough of you. It's good to have you back," he said, his words sounding dreamlike. "You're the only one to capture a piece of me..." he whispered

I didn't hear anything else as I drifted off to sleep.

Chapter Eleven

Heavy concrete ground against concrete, and the earth moved. I sat upright and felt the room shift sideways. I wasn't sure if I could get used to the place with its walls moving every twelve hours. The clock on Sebastian's bedside table read 10:47am. I must have been exhausted to have slept for so many hours.

Sebastian was still asleep. He was lying on his stomach with his left hand under his head, his right arm over his pillow, and the covers falling over his hips. I lay against his back and felt his body rise and fall with every breath; he was so warm and comforting.

Then I remembered the words he had said last night, and it felt like butterflies were loose inside my body. I smiled and kissed him lightly on his shoulder blade. My index finger caressing his skin and my heart contracting with exhilaration. The thought that only I had managed to capture a piece of Sebastian was a treasure, something I needed to explore.

And, if he was exhausted, then he should sleep. Ralph

was fetching me after five that afternoon, so I could take my time.

Sebastian didn't stir when I moved off him.

I climbed out of bed, grabbed clothing and toiletries, and went to the bathroom to shower. There was nothing like a hot shower to wake me up in the morning.

I took my time in the bathroom. When I was finished, I dressed in black cargo pants, a white vest, and my shoulder holster, with a loose-fitting navy top over it so I didn't scare civilians by having my gun on show. The loose navy top had buttons going halfway which I could leave undone, allowing me to grab the gun easily.

When I entered the room, Sebastian was still asleep. As he was half-were-leopard, half-vampire, he could walk in daylight without the risk of death, which other vampires could not. He was one of a kind. Amazingly, no one had tried to kidnap or kill him. He could potentially be perceived as either a threat or a miracle, depending on the group of people and their level of crazy.

Here I was, metaphysically tied to him, and he wanted us to be something more. As I stood there, soaking up his presence, it would be so easy to fall for him, and hard.

With light fingertips, I touched his face, but he didn't stir. He was in a deep sleep. I'd never seen him sleep so much in all the time I had known him.

Gurgling sounds echoed from my stomach. Over the last couple of days, I had eaten little, but this morning I needed a good breakfast with eggs and bacon. Finding my way to the kitchen would be a challenge since the walls kept changing, and I could never remember where anything was. Wandering around the Labyrinth, however, would alert the bodyguards, and I could ask one of them to take me to the kitchen.

When I opened the bedroom door, there was someone standing in my way.

"Morning, ma'am," the guard said with a British accent. He loomed over me and gave me a boy scout smile; it was all innocent, yet scary at the same time.

"Please don't call me 'ma'am'. Blaire will do just fine. Who are you and why are you standing here?"

"Sawyer, ma—I mean, Blaire."

Sawyer was over six feet tall, with broad shoulders and enough muscles to scare any human away. He had a number of tattoos peeking out of his clothing which ran down both arms. He had an all-year-round tan and curly black hair, a black beard, dark eyes, and a smile so big and genuine that it would easily make most ladies melt in his arms. When he smiled, he revealed perfect teeth, the tips of his canines subtly showing.

"Where are you from Sawyer?"

"Britain, but my parents are Egyptian." That explained the dark features and perma-tan.

"Why are you so far away from home?"

"I used to be in the British Armed Forces, but when I was attacked, I received an honorable discharge and moved here for work."

From what I understood, England was a little slow with their laws in protecting vampires, witches, and were-animals. The monsters were allowed to work, but only if no one found out what they really were. It was unfair, but it still happened in some parts of the world.

"I'm sorry. Which animal attacked you?"

"Were-jackal," he said, and the boy scout smile was back.

"I didn't know there was a jackal pack in the city?" I asked, frowning.

"There isn't. I'm the only were-jackal in Sterling Meadow. The wolf pack took me in as their own."

"It's rare for an animal group to accept a different species. It was generous of Shawn. I hear he is a tough nut to crack."

"That's putting it mildly," Sawyer chuckled. "But yeah, it was kind of him to offer me a place in his pack."

"You didn't mind the change?"

"Nah, not at all. I've never been this strong, and it takes a hell of a lot to kill us. Plus, we are in demand by master vampires, so we get to travel."

There was movement behind us. I excused myself and closed the door again.

"Morning," Sebastian said groggily. He sat up slowly and leaned against the headboard. "Where'd you go?"

"Nowhere. I was up before you and in need of food. When I opened the door, Sawyer was standing there, so I was just chatting to him."

He smiled lazily at me.

If I didn't know Sebastian was with me last night, I would have said he had been out drinking and was nursing a hangover.

"Are you all right? You look kinda sleepy still." I sat on the bed near his feet.

His eyes rolled back into his head.

"I just feel sleepy, otherwise I'm fine," he said when he focused again.

"Has this ever happened to you before?" I asked, my frown deepening.

"Never," he said, shaking his head slowly. "But I feel utterly relaxed. It's usually what I do to others; not the other way around. I could never do this to myself."

"I wonder," I said, thinking out loud. "When I woke up,

you were still sleeping. All I did was lie against your back and think that you should carry on sleeping if you were tired."

He frowned.

"Sebastian, I've never asked you about the full extent of your abilities. I know you can melt metal, but can you help someone sleep?" I didn't wait for him to answer and continued speaking. "Usually it takes me a short while before I sleep. But the last two evenings when you pulled me into your arms, I fell asleep immediately."

Something I'd said was like a shot of adrenaline that brought Sebastian out of his dreamy haze.

"The last two evenings," — he cleared his throat, — "I pushed some power into you, but it was just enough to help you sleep. With everything going on with that voodoo priest, I wanted you to get a good night's rest." His last words trailed off softly.

"These last two months Seraphine and Désiré have been trying to teach me how to use my abilities. To help me absorb power, and to use it against its source. I finally got it right two days ago when I was with Seraphine."

"Which means when I held you last night and helped you to sleep, you stored some of that power and used it against me this morning."

"Not on purpose, I swear." I shrugged. "But you looked so peaceful this morning, I just wanted you to sleep. I wanted you to rest."

"We need to speak to Léon about this," Sebastian said, climbing out of bed.

"What do you mean?"

"In all the years I've lived, I've never come across anyone who could do what you did. And you aren't a witch, or a necromancer, or a vampire. You are human. When Seraphine mentioned she wanted to teach you, I didn't fully comprehend what that would mean." He grabbed some clothing out of his closet. "Léon might know more or know of someone we could talk to. He has more connections than I do."

"Why do you think it is that important?" I asked nervously.

"Who knows what it means? But if any powerful monster or being hears about this and knows what you can do, there's no telling what they might do to you." He stared wide-eyed with a flash of panic behind his gaze. I stared back at him as I tried to process this bit of information. "Let me get ready," he finally said, and entered the bathroom.

My mouth was dry, and my clothing clung to my body. I replayed the conversation with Sebastian, trying to come to terms with the fact that I had been able to put him to sleep using the little bit of power he had pushed into me the night before, whether it had been accidental or not.

Shit. I needed to be careful what I said around others, and what I did going forward.

I wasn't hungry anymore.

Once Sebastian was dressed, we maneuvered through the different hallways and grabbed lunch. I moved food around my plate, ate a piece of chicken, and drank a cup of coffee.

Sawyer, the bodyguard, walked with us, but he sat at a nearby table to give us our privacy.

Sebastian looked up. It seemed as though he was staring at something I couldn't see.

"Léon's awake," he said.

"How do you know?" I asked as we rose from the table.

"He's my brother. How could I not know?" He winked wickedly.

That didn't answer my question, but I guessed they shared a metaphysical connection with one another, perhaps something similar to what Sebastian and I shared.

We left our dirty dishes on the counter, with Sawyer trailing behind us.

It was late afternoon, and the three of us were sitting in Léon's office and Sawyer stood by the door like a dark angel.

We gave Léon the short version of what had happened earlier and what had happened a few days ago with Seraphine.

Léon sat in a chair across from us behind a glass table, pressing his index fingers together in the shape of a steeple and holding them against his forehead.

He went still like all vampires could, like they were sculptured out of stone: beautiful, flawless, and cold. I focused on his chest to see if he was breathing and immediately kicked myself. Vampires didn't need to breathe, but they had to inhale to speak.

"Is this something you can do with little thought?"

"Like I said," I shrugged. "It's new to me, so I don't know."

"Stand up," Léon said, rising to his feet. He moved like liquid; quick and fluid. He took a step toward us and held out his hand.

"Why?" I asked as I stood, but I didn't go to him. He took another step, placing his hands on my shoulders.

"I want to try something, and then you try it on Sebastian," Léon said.

"What are you going to do? It better not hurt," I said, narrowing my eyes.

He laughed softly; the sound was smooth and velvety, and it swirled around the room, caressing the back of my neck and tickling down my spine. It tightened things down below, and I shivered with pleasure.

A surprised 'O' sound escaped from my lips, and I stared up into Léon's eyes. Normally, I wouldn't look any vampire in the eyes; they had the ability to control your mind with just a stare, but, somehow, it either wasn't working now or Léon wasn't trying to use his wiles on me.

Léon's dark blue eyes had bled into the white, and I wanted to drown in their deepest ocean color. His hands were still on my shoulders, his fingers massaging them ever so gently. The heat from his fingertips vibrated through to my bones.

The silky sensation of his laugh still swirled around me: as lightly as a feather, it moved up and down my back, then switched to my front and moved below, to my hips and between my legs. I pushed him away from me.

He didn't hold on, even though he could've, and fell to the ground. I fell onto the couch beside Sebastian.

Léon laughed again, but it wasn't like before. It wasn't soft or smooth; it was loud and diabolical.

"Now use it on Sebastian," he said, still sitting on the floor.

I moved away from Sebastian as far as I could whilst still staying on the couch. I didn't trust my legs to stand and keep me steady.

"No," I said, crossing my arms over my chest and scowled at him. "What was that, Léon? What were you trying to prove?"

"Léon's power seeks your undisclosed desires, Blaire,

and offers them to you," Sebastian said kindly. "He can pleasure you without touching." He grimaced at his brother. "Usually, although I see that, today, he made an exception."

"I'm sorry, brother." Léon stood, but he didn't hide the fact that the front of his black pants was damp. "What a fucking ride. Hold on to this one," he said, pointing at me.

"Did you just—" I pointed at his crotch.

"Oh yes, my dear." He winked darkly. "I wouldn't mind doing it for real sometime. Should you ever get bored of my little brother, you know where to find me." He started undoing his belt buckle as he walked toward his desk.

Heat crept up my neck, and my cheeks flushed. I moved on the chair to straighten my shirt, and the orgasm caught me again; I whimpered in pleasure, writhed on the seat and fought not to squirm. I dug my fingernails into the armrest to keep still.

"Why aren't you touching Sebastian? It won't stop until you give it to him."

The look on Sebastian's face must have shown Léon something.

"You mean the two of you haven't done it yet?"

"No," Sebastian said, with either a hint of frustration or regret; I couldn't tell which.

I wasn't looking at either of them; I was too busy concentrating on a book on the shelf. It was bound in leather and covered in dust. I couldn't read the title on the spine, no matter how hard I squinted at it.

"Oh, I'm sorry, brother." Léon chuckled. I heard a door open. "Touch him, Blaire, otherwise it won't stop."

Shit, mother... asshole.

My fingertips pulsed with his power. I reached out for Sebastian, but before I touched his shoulder, he grabbed my hand. I pushed the orgasmic power Léon had given me into him as fast as I could.

Sebastian writhed with pleasure in the chair beside me and let go of my hand. I forgot about the old book I was staring at and watched Sebastian. As he hardened against his pants, I noticed the length and girth of him and how he was pressed against his right hip.

"You're an asshole, Léon," he said to his brother before glancing at me. He reached for himself and rubbed over his pants until he orgasmed.

We kept staring at each other: I watched him enjoy himself, and he watched me take pleasure in the view. It was very erotic, and I struggled to avert my eyes.

Where Seraphine's power had hurt as it had made its way up my arm and neck, Léon's power was most pleasurable. I prefer pleasure over pain any time of the day, but a warning would have been nice.

My mouth was dry, and I had to swallow a few times before I could eventually speak. "What the fuck was that, Léon? You can't do that to people without consent."

Léon walked out of the bathroom in clean underwear, but still wore the same shirt.

"I had to see what your power could do; whether it was something real and worthwhile testing. I couldn't warn you. I needed your response to be raw and genuine." His smile split his face in two, enough to show the points of his fangs. "Didn't you enjoy it?" he asked, oozing with confidence.

"I'm not a guinea pig for you to test on, Léon." My anger was back, and it made me feel better.

"My apologies, Blaire, but I had to see for myself what you were capable of." He gave a slow bow of his head.

Sebastian stood and went to the bathroom.

Léon opened a closet door, removed a pair of pants, and started pulling them on.

"Do you like what you see?" he whispered seductively.

My glance swept up to his face, and he watched me carefully. His dark gaze caused things down below to contract in fearful pleasure.

He stood straight, slowly pulled up his pants, and fastened them. His long fingers ran down the front of his pants, and my eyes followed as he cupped himself, then touched his stomach, and moved up to his chest.

I dug my fingernails into my skin until it hurt. Heat crept up my neck and cheeks, and the lines between my eyes deepen as I shook my head.

He must've done something to me.

"No," I said, turning my head to face the bookshelf.

"No?" he asked with sarcasm in his tone. "'*No*' because you dislike what you see, or is it that you do like what you see?"

Vampires smelled lies, so I didn't bother.

"That I do," I said, squeezing my eyes shut.

"Open your eyes," he purred.

When I did, Léon was in front of me. I hadn't heard him move. One of his hands was on the armrest and the other on the back of the couch, which left his face and body uncomfortably close to mine. I leaned back into the couch so that our faces didn't touch and closed my eyes again. I didn't want to look into his eyes; the drowning blue of the sea. I didn't want to be under his power again.

"Do you want to touch me?" His smooth whisper caressed my cheek.

I didn't trust my voice, so I nodded. He took my right hand and placed it on his bare chest, which made me look at him. A minute ago, he had been wearing a shirt; now, he was naked from the waist up. I could feel his heart beating in his chest. Vampire hearts would only ordinarily beat if they'd recently consumed blood.

"You make my heart beat," he whispered. "Can you feel it?" His tone sounded desperate. His mouth was close enough that I could feel his warm breath on my face.

The bathroom door opened, and a blur came past, swiping Léon away. Sebastian and Léon hit the bookshelf hard enough to dislodge all the books and break half the shelves. They were too fast for my eyes to follow; there were cries, the snapping of teeth, and punches. They stood, then Sebastian flew into Léon again, and they went crashing into the opposite wall.

I jumped off the couch. Sawyer came behind me, lifting me over the couch, and pulled me into him. We stood safely against the far wall.

"We should leave," Sawyer said near my ear. "They won't stop until first blood."

Sawyer opened the door and we left. He closed the door softly behind us. We stood in the hallway listening to the sounds of yelling and things breaking. They crashed into the wall and the door shook, causing a crack to form at the bottom of it.

"Shouldn't we try to stop them? They'll kill each other."

"They can't kill each other."

"Have they done this before?"

"They disagree often enough."

"I'll take that as a yes, then?"

"They get into it at least once a month."

After ten minutes of things being smashed and both of them yelling at each other, the door finally opened.

Sawyer and I backed up against the far wall. Léon and Sebastian had their arms over each other, like one was trying to keep the other upright. Sebastian's shirt was torn, each had a bloody nose, and Léon's left eye was swollen.

"Who won?" I asked with a hint of sarcasm.

"Sebastian," Léon said, slapping Sebastian's chest. "He always wins." He grinned, then pulled his brother in for a hug and gave him a light pat on his back.

"As I mentioned to him," Léon said, fixing his shirt. "We need to be careful now that we know of your talent." He warned. "There are others out there who would kill to get their talons on you. And, I do, however, have to apologize to you, my dear. It would seem you enthralled me to such an extent that I forgot my manners. Besides, my brother doesn't share well," Léon said the last part playfully and smiled mischievously.

Sebastian punched Léon in the ribs, who cried out.

"There. Now we're equal."

Chapter Twelve

It was early evening, and I had enough time to freshen up before Ralph fetched me.

Sebastian had healed by the time we got to his room, so he didn't need any medical attention, but he showered again.

By the time Sebastian was done, Ralph was already outside, waiting for me.

"Before you leave, I want to talk to you about what happened in Léon's office."

"Which part?" I snapped.

"All of it."

Heat crept up my neck and onto my face. In hindsight, I would have preferred avoiding any conversation that related to what Léon's 'touch' did to me, and how he did all those things without really touching me at all. The feel of his hands on my shoulders, his heat moving through my bones, under my skin and…

"Firstly," Sebastian said, pulling me out of my

daydream. "I need to apologize for how my brother behaved."

"Why are you apologizing?" I said, trying desperately to sound normal, and failing. The tone of my voice was slightly high-pitched and I couldn't look Sebastian in the eye.

"I should have spoken with him in private before taking you to him," he said with regret. "I should have known he would try something like that. He is a vampire."

"You don't say," I replied sarcastically.

More to the point, Léon was male, and being a vampire wouldn't change that part of him; men had insatiable desires to satisfy. Even though I had an immense attraction to Sebastian, there was something burning for Léon, too. But I suspected it was just his vampiric wiles at play. It had to be.

And, following their fight afterward, I didn't want to be in the middle of, or the cause of, a feud between the two brothers.

"Anyway, can we move forward?" I said, needing to drop the subject and wanting to go. "I need to bring my A-game if I'm going to catch this voodoo fucker with Ralph. I can't have this," — I waved my hands in the air, — "at the back of my mind while I deal with the real monster."

"Are we good?"

"We're good, but whatever you and your brother keep fighting about, please don't drag me into the middle of it."

He smiled, took my hand in his, and led me down the various hallways until we met up with Sawyer, who stood near an open door. Dusk sunlight greeted us. Both men trailed behind me as I approached Ralph's parked car.

"What are you doing?" I said with one hand on the door handle.

"Coming with you," Sebastian said.

"Nah-huh. This is my work, Sebastian. This is what I do. I can't have you with me while I work."

"Then take Sawyer with you." Sebastian glanced at the tall dark man behind him.

"I don't need a babysitter," I grumbled, opening the car door. Sawyer advanced closer. I lifted my hand to stop him. "No," I commanded. "If you want to know if I'm fine, call me on my cell," I said, lifting my phone.

"Please humor me. That priest has tried to harm you twice already. I want to keep you safe. Please let me. If you don't want me with you, allow Sawyer to tag along. What's wrong with the extra firepower? He's one of our best."

I opened my mouth to argue, but I didn't see the point. It was true; we might need him. And it didn't look like Sebastian would stop until he got his way.

"Okay, fine, but don't interfere, Sawyer. Unless we need backup."

"Yes, ma'am."

"What did I tell you about calling me 'ma'am'?"

Sebastian came to my side, cupped my face, and kissed me chastely. I melted in his arms and forgot about everything except his soft lips on mine, his tender touch on my face and how hot his hands were. All I could think of was how I wanted to touch more of him.

He smiled in our kiss. He pulled away and gazed lovingly at me. I stared into his kitty-cat green eyes and was lost.

I flinched at the sound of Ralphs horn, breaking my concentration. When I blinked, I could think again. I smiled shyly and climbed into the backseat, with Sawyer joining me.

I introduced Ralph and Devan to my bodyguard, and we set off.

We were a block away when I remembered I didn't say goodbye to Sebastian. I touched my lips; his kisses seemed to pull me in deeper, to the point where I forgot things. I wanted to say bye.

I pictured his arms around me as we embraced, and thought of his kissable lips. I closed my eyes and pictured him.

"See ya later," I said in my head.

"You're sweet," I heard someone say in my mind.

"What?" I said out loud.

"What?" Ralph said back to me.

"Nothing. I wasn't talking to you."

Ralph frowned.

"It's the mark, Blaire," Sebastian whispered inside my head again. *"It's one of the perks of being tied together. We can communicate metaphysically. But only if you want to."*

"Holy shit! We don't even need a cellphone?" I responded.

His chuckle echoed inside my head like a ghost and then he was gone.

I smiled as I buckled in.

Ralph turned his vehicle right and headed for the highway.

"Okay, Devan, talk to us," I said. "Tell us what you think about those dolls and how we can get this priest without dying in the process?" I stared at Devan in the mirror on the sun visor in the passenger seat.

"The dolls you found under your mattress was cursed, but they were only directed at each of you," Devan said, swallowing hard. "I think someone told him who you were; he had to have had help. There was no way for him to know where you lived. Voodoo doesn't work that way. Someone told him." His eyes darkened slightly. "Who would benefit if neither of you survived this? What would the priest gain, or what would anyone gain from your disappearance?"

"The only people who know about this case is Martin and Désiré. And we only told her about it yesterday," I said, looking at Ralph as he drove.

"What about Marcus?" Ralph said. There was something in the way he said it that left me on edge.

Two months ago when I was attacked, and our colleague, Shane, was murdered, Marcus had disappeared on us when we needed him the most.

Shane's torso had been dumped in the trunk of my car, and his limbs had been left in Marcus's bathtub; which he didn't dispose of until we discovered it. Only then did Marcus explain everything to us; but we believe Marcus only gave us part of the truth.

"See where Marcus is, and then let's go over to the priest's shop."

Ralph pulled into a parking lot and dialed Marcus's number, but he didn't answer. He pulled a device out of a bag from the glove compartment, plugged it into his phone, and started tapping into it. A map showed on the screen of his phone, and he asked Devan to hold it. He pulled back onto the road and followed where the map said he needed to go. The end of the map's red line brought us to a warehouse, where Marcus's car was parked out front. Ralph parked around the block.

We walked past open windows and found a door on the side near where Marcus's car was parked. As we walked in, Sawyer stopped Ralph and mouthed that he would go in first. Ralph stepped back and allowed Sawyer to go ahead of him. Sawyer took his Beretta 92 out of his pants holster and pointed it at the ground.

I was not a fan of that gun; my hands were too small to handle it, and the safety wasn't in the best spot either. You needed big hands with long fingers to switch the safety off and aim at the same time. The other thing I didn't like about it was the recoil. If you didn't know how to take care of your gun and clean it properly, the recoil could be a bitch.

We heard echoes of a woman talking. We entered a hallway and followed the sounds until we came to a large room. In the far corner, Marcus was sitting on a chair next to a bed, with an occupant lying motionless under the covers. The woman was tinkering with the drip and talking about various drugs she had tried on her patient.

All four of us walked into the room and didn't hide the sounds of our footsteps as we approached them.

Marcus spun around and pointed a gun at us, but Sawyer's gun was already pointed at his head.

"What are you guys doing here? How did you even find me?" Marcus commanded, a soft growl trickling from his lips. When he saw the large, dark man with a gun pointed at him, he lowered his own.

Sawyer kept his gun aimed at him regardless. I was starting to like Sawyer even more.

"You weren't answering your phone, douchebag. We had to trace you," Ralph said with an edge of hostility.

"Who are these people, Marcus?" the woman behind Marcus said.

"They work for me, Melinda."

"Is this the same Melinda who dumped your ass and left you for dead?" I asked as I walked closer to them. The person on the bed still wasn't moving. I wanted to make sure they were alive. Pointing at the bed, I added, "What's going on here?"

"This is Tommy. Melinda used to work with him at the Med Tech Lab before her attack. A were-wolf bit him last night, and he called her for help. He knows what she's been working on, and that's why he reached out to her."

"Is Tommy still alive?"

"Yes," Melinda said defensively. "And what happened to Marcus was a mistake. He wasn't breathing, and I panicked."

"It doesn't look like Tommy is breathing either." I walked right up to the bed and touched Tommy's hand. His pulse was strong. "Are you still trying to cure Marcus of his were-animal?" The look I gave her was not a friendly one.

She glanced from me to Marcus, then back to me, trying to figure out what to say.

"Well?"

"Yes," she yelled. The veins on the side of her forehead bulged.

"Marcus?"

"What?" He turned to look at me and shrugged.

"You can't be serious? You've already lost two fingers to her incompetence. Do you want to lose your life?" I said to Marcus, before turning to Melinda. "And you, Melinda, is your animal still with you?"

"Yes," she yelled again.

"Sweet Mother, Marcus, this is wrong. What the two of you are doing to poor Tommy is wrong. He needs medical treatment, not a scientist poking and prodding him."

Melinda edged around the bed and started walking toward me. I reached for my Glock 19, pulled it from the holster, and aimed it at her.

"Don't fucking try it, Melinda, or I'll shoot you in the face." I glanced at Sawyer; he still had his gun pointing at Marcus.

Ralph had his Glock 43 out and pointed it at Marcus and then Melinda. We covered them from all sides. Devan was the only one without a gun, but a firearm was superfluous in the hands of a nineteen-year-old born with metaphysical weapons.

Melinda's stare was icy; full of rage and anger.

I went to that dark place I knew was mine. It's the place I went to to switch everything off and focused on the gun and the person I wanted to shoot.

Something must've shown on my face because Melinda's face thawed. Her icy stare now replaced with fear. She lifted her arms in the air and stepped back.

My lips curled upward, but it wasn't a happy smile: it was a smile that showed, 'I'll shoot anyone who tried to get in the way'.

"If I hear you are still doing this shit, I will turn you in myself, Melinda. And if you hurt Marcus or anyone in the process, I will kill you." The look I gave Marcus was the same one I gave Melinda, and he put his gun away and lifted his hands in surrender. "You really need to stop seeing her, Marcus. She's bad news."

In all the commotion, I had almost forgotten why we were looking for Marcus in the first place. "Who have you been speaking to about the voodoo priest, Marcus?"

"No-one." He swallowed hard.

"Liar!" I yelled, lifting my gun with both hands and aimed it at his face. "Who have you been speaking with? Who did you give our addresses to?"

"No-one," — he closed his eyes for a second then opened them, "I swear." The corner of his left eye twitched.

"You're lying," I said in a calm voice. "What have you done?"

"I've done nothing. I swear, I'm not lying." The twitching stopped.

Ralph waved to get my attention. I lowered my gun just a little, taking the strain off my shoulders.

"Yeah?"

"It's time," Ralph said. "We need to get to the shop so we can follow the priest."

Shit.

"This isn't over, Marcus." I placed my gun back in its holster and walked around the bed and equipment, out of Melinda's reach, to stand beside Marcus. "Think hard, Marcus. This is the second time your name's come up where there has been a disaster while Ralph and I are in the thick of it. We've already lost Shane. Do you want to lose two more?"

"No, I don't want to lose any more people," Marcus said, shaking his head and squeezing his eyes shut.

"Then stop fucking around."

Marcus nodded fiercely.

"And one more thing." I remembered another reason why I wanted to speak with Marcus. "I understand I'm coming with you to your Lion Den tomorrow evening?"

"Yeah," — he swallowed hard, — "Sebastian called me last night to arrange. He thought if you visited the various animal groups you were infected with ahead of the next full moon, if you shifted, you would be comfortable enough with that animal group."

"What about you, Melinda? You seem to be the expert on all things furry. What do you think about all this? Do you think I'll shift?" I said, leering at Melinda.

"From what I've heard, it's rare to be infected with more than a single lycanthropy strain," Melinda said matter-of-factly. "But through my research, I came across four cases.

They didn't change into any were-animal, and one of them died when their inner animals fought; metaphysically, of course."

"I guess I'll see you tomorrow?"

Melinda nodded and averted her eyes. She was about five foot eight, which made her taller than me. She had curly black hair that swept her shoulders and brown eyes, a small nose, pursed lips, and olive skin. She was voluptuous and wore a dress that would attract any man: no wonder Marcus couldn't stay away. She wore glasses, which was for show; as a were-lion, she had perfect eyesight, along with super-strength, faster agility, and impressively sharp teeth.

"And get Tommy home," I said, pointing to the now-stirring figure on the bed.

"I will," Melinda said nervously, and she set about pulling the needles from his arms.

"Let's go," I said to Ralph.

Chapter Thirteen

We parked across the street near the shopping center. No one had said a word after we left Marcus and Melinda at the warehouse.

In the silence, I kept thinking about the three lycanthropy strains I now carried within me and about going to the Lion's Den tomorrow night with Marcus.

The clock on the dashboard read 7:08pm, and the center was busy and noisy. Inside the car, the silence was suffocating.

"Will you come with me tomorrow night?" I said to Ralph. "To the Lion's Den?"

"Sure, but we should go in my car. That way, we can leave when we want."

"Thanks."

I was now in the front passenger seat, having swapped places when we left the warehouse. I turned in the chair so that I could see both Devan and Sawyer in the back seat.

"Is there anything else about McNielty you can tell us,

Devan?" I asked. "You saw him up close when you were in his shop."

"No, like I said yesterday, he has the standard stuff. It's what he has out the back that interests me."

Devan squinted at something behind me, and I turned around. The voodoo priest was closing his shop for the day.

"Let's go," I said, and Ralph started the engine.

We kept a short distance away from McNielty's red Chevy truck. The drive around Sterling Meadow lasted for over an hour. McNielty stopped at various houses, knocking on doors with something under his arm and leaving empty-handed. It seemed that he offered a personalized home delivery service of sorts. Probably one of the ways he supplemented his income.

Another hour had passed by the time we stopped outside his house. Ralph parked around the block like the first time we'd been here, but we stayed in the car. We could see his car in the driveway from where we were and would know if he left the house. We agreed to take turns watching it.

It was close to midnight, and McNielty still hadn't left his home.

"Are we sure he's going anywhere tonight?" I asked Devan.

"Who knows?" Ralph interjected and faced me. "But at least we're here if he does."

"It doesn't help us catch him." I frowned.

"I know, but it's all we can do for now."

Dammit.

Ralph faced the window for a better view of the house.

"Has anyone searched his car?" Sawyer said from the dark corner of the backseat behind me.

He was so quiet I'd forgotten he was there.

"I like the way you think," I said, glancing over the headrest. "Who's going?"

"We can't. He knows what we look like," Ralph said.

"I'll go," Sawyer said, opening his door.

"You sure?"

"Yeah," he said, then added, "Anything specific I should look for?"

"Anything you think a voodoo priest really shouldn't have in his car, like the appendages of other men," I said. "Good luck, and don't get caught."

Sawyer held two fingers to his forehead in a salute and exited the car. Like a tall, dark shadow, he blended with the night and was gone.

Twenty minutes had passed.

"Shouldn't he be back by now?" I said to no one in particular. "Can you still see the front door, Ralph?"

"Yeah, no one has opened the door or gone out the back."

Someone knocked on the car's bonnet, and I jumped in my seat. Sawyer came around the car, opened the door, and climbed inside.

"It's clean; been vacuumed recently. There's even that new car smell. So, whatever you were hoping to find, it's not there anymore. Sorry."

"Thanks, anyway."

Ralph switched the radio on to break the cold silence,

and we waited quietly in the shadows of our own consciousness.

"We should have brought coffee," I said, yawning and rubbing my eyes. Stakeouts were the boring part of the job, waiting in anticipation for anything to happen.

By the time it was one in the morning, I honestly didn't think McNielty was going anywhere.

"Devan, you sure McNielty was up to something tonight?"

"Yeah. When I was in his shop, I saw it clearly. He was planning to kill again tonight. A man with gray eyes. Appearance or hair color doesn't matter, just as long as he has gray eyes, is six foot two, and weighs between two hundred and two-hundred-and-twenty pounds."

We hadn't shared any of the details from the police reports with Devan; he'd said he didn't need to see it to know the details.

"You sure you didn't take a peek at those police reports?" I asked as I turned in my seat to see his face.

"No, like I said, all I had to do was focus on him while I was in his shop, and that was the feedback he projected."

"Jesus, I'm too afraid to ask you what you see when you look at us," Ralph said, a hint of distress in his voice.

Devan glanced at me and held his gaze. "I learned from a young age not to talk about everything I see. It affects people too much. Then they sit around waiting for it to happen instead of just living their lives. So, if I can, I prefer not to say." He glanced down at his hands and started rubbing the pressure points on his palms with his thumbs; first, the right hand, then the left.

"Why are you working with us, Devan? You could make plenty of money on your own," I asked.

"I'm interested in what you do. It's a better cause than

telling someone they will die from cancer in twenty years' time. Or telling a mom that her son will not make it out of hospital. Or feeling what someone did to their own child when I shake their hand. I'd rather be part of a team who put the monsters away, then help them."

I couldn't argue with that; they were all valid points.

"You're still so young," I continued. "Isn't there something you wanted to study or somewhere you wanted to go before you settled down with a job?"

"No, I prefer to limit my contact."

"Gotta take a piss," Ralph blurted, and climbed out of the car.

It's so easy for men; they can go wherever they want. Women needed toilet paper and a seat. Just thinking about it made me need the bathroom.

"Do you think they'd mind if I knocked on their door to use the bathroom?" I thumbed toward the house parallel to the car.

"At this time? Rather not," Sawyer said. "It's safer to go in that bush over there. It's big enough to hide you."

I stared at the hedge Sawyer pointed at, and it was a huge japonica near where Ralph had disappeared. I didn't want to tinkle out in the open; we weren't camping.

I found some tissues in my bag, and went to the hedge. The air was icy, with the smell of rain edging near.

The hedge was large and trimmed into half a circle, with the opening facing another hedge. It hid me well enough to do what I needed, and buried the tissue in some loose soil beneath the hedge.

As I walked out of the hedge, I saw McNielty's porch light switch off, followed by those in the kitchen, and then his house was swarmed with darkness. The time on my cellphone read 1:18am.

I walked between the houses toward his residence and stopped alongside a dark tree. In my black cargo pants and black winter jacket, I blended easily into the darkness.

McNielty's house was quiet, dark, and eerie.

I thought of the woman with the white dress and blood stains. Her short hair, mutilated ears, and missing tongue. I didn't know how we could get her out from McNielty's basement without involving the police.

I glanced back at Ralph's car. I saw all its occupants clearly from where I stood. If McNielty had come out of his house, he would have seen us. This was not good. Perhaps he'd seen us already and wasn't prepared to go out tonight to complete his four pairs: two of each eye color and enough organs to feed the black market. I walked back to the car among the shadows.

"It looks like he's turning in for the evening," I said to Ralph through his open window. "Plus, I could see you from where I stood. There's a possibility he saw us and canceled his nocturnal plans."

"Should we call it a night?" he asked.

"Perhaps we should." I walked around to get into the passenger seat, and buckled in. "Let's go home and get some sleep. There's nothing else happening tonight."

Devan squeezed his eyes shut, exhaled loudly and frowned. He seemed to be concentrating on something; or someone.

"The victim with gray eyes is already dead," he drawled.

We stared at him.

"He dumped the victim near a warehouse on the far side of town," Devan said, opening his eyes. "I don't know how he did it, but he did." He sighed exhaustingly. "Now we just need someone to find the body."

"Fuck! How did we not see him leave?" It was almost a

yell, but I was angry. We'd been out here watching his house all evening, and we didn't see him leave. His car didn't move since he pulled into his driveway.

"I don't know. It's impossible, but we did miss him." Devan frowned. He sounded like he couldn't believe it either.

"Have you ever been mistaken, Devan? Has anything like this ever happened to you before? Not getting it right, I mean?" I asked carefully, not wanting to insult him.

"No, I've never been wrong before. Ever." He shook his head gently, then leaned into the seat and put his head back. "I felt him inside the house the entire time. He didn't leave."

"Can he feel you?"

"I doubt it; I shield pretty well," he said, lifting his head. "But," — he stared at me, — "I can feel and see you."

"What does that mean?" My frown matched his.

"Why didn't I think of it before? If I can, so can he. You need to shield yourself better, Blaire."

"How the fuck do I do that? I only recently learned how to absorb someone's power and return it, and I haven't even grasped that concept properly. What do I have to do to shield myself?" My anger boiled to the surface and I didn't bother hiding it.

Sawyer shivered and rubbed his arms.

Devan blinked wide eyes.

"What's going on?" Ralph said. The lines between his eyes deepening.

"It's your anger, Blaire. You mustn't let it out like that. You need to learn how to control it."

"If I knew how to do that, Devan, I would." I crossed my arms over my chest.

"Give me your hand." Devan reached out for me with his hand, palm-side up.

"No, tell me what you're going to do first." My arms were still crossed and I shook my head. After being violated by Léon earlier I trust no one.

"Don't you trust anyone?"

"No. She never has, and I don't think she ever will," Ralph said.

"Gee, thanks, Ralph."

"Please, I rarely want to touch anyone like this," Devan pleaded. He looked wounded.

My frown deepened, but I placed my hand in his.

The moment our hands connected, an electric shock ran through my fingertips. It was different to what I'd felt before; it wasn't a power like Seraphine's, which was intended to hurt me. This was a soft tingle that sprinted through me, searching. His power was looking for something within me.

Devan held onto my hand while he metaphysically navigated through me: up my arm, around my shoulder, through my rib cage, and close to my heart. It hovered for a second before moving up to my neck and my head.

While he searched, it sounded like a bee inside my skull. I shook my head out of reflex and not fear; I trusted this kind of power not to hurt me.

His power traveled down my spine and into my legs, then came back up along my spine, through my hand, and back to where it started.

Once Devan let go of my hand, I opened my eyes. He was paler than before, and fell limply against the back seat.

"Holy crap, that felt weird," I said, surprised by my experience.

"It didn't hurt, did it?"

"No, you didn't hurt me. What were you looking for?" I asked.

"I can either tell you in front of these two," — Devan swallowed hard, — "or we can speak privately. It's your choice," he said in a hoarse voice.

"I don't like the sound of that, Devan. Is it bad, or is it just private?" I frowned again.

"Just private. There's nothing bad, I promise." He closed his eyes and looked asleep.

"Ok, in private then," I said, nodding at Ralph that we should go. There was nothing more we could do until we found the body anyway.

Ralph started the engine and pulled away from the curb. He would drop Sawyer and I off first and then go to Devan's apartment. He would be spending another night on the sofa there. Which was a relief, as I didn't want any of us to be alone with the voodoo priest walking around a free man.

We arrived at the Labyrinth, and Ralph parked near the same door he had fetched us from earlier.

"Come on, Sawyer; let's give them some privacy." Ralph climbed out and Sawyer followed him; they stood near the door of the Labyrinth, waiting for us to join them.

"Okay, Devan, talk to me. What did you see, or rather, what did you feel?"

"You knew about your ability before you were attacked." Devan sat up, still deathly pale.

"Yeah, I had to have known. But Ralph was unaware."

"You must've shielded yourself well enough from everyone then. Otherwise me and every other witch or clairvoyant would have known about you a long time ago. Before yesterday, I hadn't known about your gift, and it was only recently that I started to see a glow shining at night. Now I know that glow was you. Your white aura shines brightly on a clear evening sky. You have it in you to shield again."

I did my slow blink as I thought about what he said. I must have previously had training to hide myself from everyone. Someone must have taught me.

"Can I suggest something?" Devan continued, bringing me out of my thoughts.

I nodded.

"All I can tell you is what I was taught. Close your eyes and picture what you think your aura and your ability looks like, even if it's a token of some sort. Place them behind walls: make them metal or brick—anything—just as long as your aura and ability are behind that wall," he said.

"Then, when you need to use them, imagine the wall coming down one brick or one slate at a time. You need to figure it out for yourself before someone powerful tries to challenge you. Your recent discovery—absorbing someone's power and using it at will—is dangerous. There are people out there who would seek to use you for it." His pale eyes darkened; his sky-blue eye looked like a storm before thunder, and his light green eye looked like an emerald that had been left in the shadows. He looked haunted and scared.

"I don't—"

"You have to try."

"Okay." My frown was back, and I wiped beads of sweat from my forehead. I unzipped my jacket. "Fine, I'll try."

I rounded my shoulders and closed my eyes. I pictured my ability and wrapped it in the white of what I thought my aura should look like. Walls came out of the ground, made from brick at first, but they slowed changed to metal. That way, there wouldn't be any holes for the white light to seep through. The metal wall was so high that when I looked up,

I couldn't see where it ended. And the metal wall was wide, and the white was... gone.

"Good! That's excellent! There's still a small spark, but it's nowhere near as bright as that beacon you were omitting. One would need to be near you to see that spark."

Muscle memory working at its best, I supposed. I had to do it to protect my own ass. My smile reached my eyes, but Devan's attempt faltered at the sides.

"Did it take a lot out of you to search through me like that?"

"Just to take a peek? Yes, but I didn't want to do any more than that. And there's one more thing," he said gravely. "There is something stopping you from moving forward. You need to figure out what's causing it and undo it."

"Yeah, I know, but I'm struggling."

Devan gave me serious eyes, like my life depended on me finding out who I truly was. I shifted uncomfortably in my seat. His solemn look softened as his shoulders sagged, and he leaned against the seat again, utterly exhausted.

"I guess I'll see you tomorrow, then," I said when he didn't answer. I opened the door and climbed out.

I approached the two men chatting near the door. Ralph and Sawyer were discussing football when I reached them. I had no interest in the sport, so I waited for them to finish.

Before Ralph left we arranged that he would phone me if he heard from Martin about the discovery of the victim; the latest one with the gray eyes.

Once Sawyer and I were inside the Labyrinth, the walls had already shifted, and the hallways were different again.

Sawyer guided me to Sebastian's door, which stood open but the room was empty. Sawyer used his radio to find out who would take over from him so he could get some sleep. Apparently, Rory was on his way.

I closed the door with Sawyer on the other side of it and went to the bathroom.

When I was back in the bedroom, there was a soft knock on the door.

"Yes?" I said while removing my shoes.

"It's Rory. Can I come in?"

"Sure."

Rory entered as good as new. The injuries he'd sustained the previous night were gone, like nothing had happened.

"Sebastian wanted me to tell you personally that he is busy assisting Léon with vampire business, and that you should get some rest," Rory said in a serious tone. He sounded well-rehearsed.

"What's really going on?" I stood and approached him.

"It's vampire business."

I narrowed my eyes. He stepped backward. He was a were-wolf and, from what I could tell, was dominant in the pack, so him stepping away from me said something. Either he was afraid of me, or he didn't want me to know what was really going on.

I closed the gap until I was close enough to almost touch him and stared daggers into his face.

"Tell me, Rory. Now!" I commanded.

He stared down at me with such intensity, but I didn't blink. The look I was giving him was the same one I gave when I held my gun, courtesy of where I went to in my mind. My dark, quiet place.

"There are vamps visiting Léon," he said, blinking first and sighed. "It's the group Envision and two others."

"See, that wasn't so difficult, was it?" I patted his left shoulder. "And don't worry. I won't go looking for trouble."

His shoulders dropped, and he exhaled.

Normally, I would've asked what they were doing here, but it wasn't my business and I was tired. I would rather sleep then discuss vampire business with a were-wolf.

"I'm going to sleep. Will you be standing outside all evening?"

"Yes, until Sawyer wakes up."

Rory left and closed the door behind him. I climbed under the covers and tried to sleep.

"When are you coming to bed?" I thought inside my mind.

"Sleep," Sebastian responded. *"I will be beside you soon."*

The sheets were cold, and I kept turning from one side to the other. I couldn't get comfortable. I eventually fell asleep from sheer exhaustion.

Chapter Fourteen

It was before noon when we stopped outside an abandoned warehouse with an open lot. Police personnel were hovering around something on the ground covered in brown rags.

Some personnel were taking photographs, while others were busy cordoning off the area with yellow police tape.

Detective Martin Everett was on his haunches, looking over the rags on the ground.

Somehow, despite our surveillance of his property, McNielty, our voodoo priest, had left his house undetected, driven across town to kill a gray-eyed father of two, and made it back in time to switch off his house lights. We needed to check whether his house lights were on a timer or if he could operate them using his cellphone.

Red, the clairvoyant the police used, and Devan were both positive that Ross McNielty was our killer.

Martin lifted his head and scowled when he saw us. He stood over six feet tall and walked over to us; towering over me like a stormy cloud.

"I thought you were watching our voodoo boy?" Martin grumbled, like dark thunder.

"We were," Ralph said, sounding angry. "But, as you know, he's a slippery fucker." Ralph stood straighter and stared Martin in the eyes. "Otherwise you'd have caught him yourself by now."

Martin opened his mouth to say something but closed it, pursing his lips tightly. It looked like he might be counting to ten. A vein along his neck pulsed. He closed his eyes and exhaled; and slowly calmed down.

"Fair enough," he said when he opened his eyes. Then he pointed to the brown rags on the ground. "Our victim: six foot two, male, weighs between two hundred and two-hundred-and-twenty pounds. It's the same M.O. as the others, but this one has gray eyes like the last victim. Killer stitched his abdomen together, like the others, so we can assume his organs are missing and we will no doubt find a little voodoo doll inside. But we can only confirm this once the autopsy has been done." He sighed. The rings under his eyes were visible, even though he had a dark complexion, and his eyes were red.

"Do you think he's finished now that he has killed two of every eye color?" I asked from the side, lifting my hand in front of my face to keep the sun out of my eyes. It was unusually bright for so early in the day. I could have stood in Martin's shadow, but I didn't feel like staring directly up at him.

"We hope so," Martin said.

"Can I have a look?" Devan asked.

"Who are you?" Martin grimaced.

"He works with us," Ralph said. "Let him have a look. Maybe he can pick up something we can't."

"Hell, why not," Martin said, sighing again, and it

sounded like it hurt. He raised his arm to point the way. "Be my guest. I'll be over there if anyone needs me." He joined uniformed colleagues from his unit where they spoke in hushed tones.

We walked over to the body in rags. The victim's eyes were open, and his mouth was slack. The dark soil smeared on his face was different to the tan-colored soil beneath him. The dark soil looked like potting soil, or that which was typically found in gardens; much like the soil beneath the hedge I had my bathroom break in last night.

Unlike the other victims, who had looked as though they had been pushed out of the car and rolled in the dirt, this one was neatly positioned on the ground.

If I had to guess, McNielty planted the potting soil on the vic's face to throw us off his trail or to confuse us; either way, we knew it was him.

The victim's hands were missing; they had been cleanly removed. There were no jagged edges to show that the monster who did this had struggled to take the hands off. All it had taken was one quick swoop of something sharp and they'd come clean off.

The killer had wrapped the victim in the rags, which were either an old sheet or a curtain: it was paper thin and shredded in some parts. The victim was naked, with a long cut from neck to pelvis that had been sewn back together with fishing line.

Martin hadn't mentioned this, but our gray-eyed victim was missing his private parts, similarly to the other gray-eyed victim, the homeless man.

Devan stood beside me, went down on his haunches, and bent over the body as though he was about to touch it, but his hands hovered just above it. A warm wind blew in from the side and then it was cold again.

Devan stood, dusted his hands on his clothing—except there was no dust on them—and faced us.

"It's our boy," Devan said. "I saw him do this." He rubbed his chin. "I don't know how he did it, though. How he was able to be in his house and kill this man at the same time, but he did this." His cell phone pinged, interrupting his sentence.

"My aunt had a vision about you," he said to me after reading the message. "She says you're in danger."

"We know that already, but tell her I said thanks, anyway."

"She also says you mustn't get caught."

"Okay." I shrugged. "Was that it?"

Devan nodded.

"Very cryptic, but I should be fine. I have a bodyguard," I said, smiling at Sawyer.

The Lion's Den looked like a large barbecue and picnic area. There were eight barbecue stands positioned in a semi-circle around a fire pit in the middle. Behind it all was their clubhouse. There were four other cars in the parking area when we arrived.

"He can't be here," Marcus said, walked along the footpath toward us, and pointed at Sawyer.

"I can stay in the car," Sawyer said, with the car door open and his right leg still in the car. "I'm not here to mess with another were-animal's territory."

"Put her on if you want music." Ralph gave him the car key.

"Thanks," Sawyer said, closing his car door and went to the driver's side. "Blaire," he said to me. "Yell if you need me; I'll hear you. If you get hurt, Sebastian won't be pleased." His eyes flitted to Marcus as a warning.

"Thanks, Sawyer, but I should be safe here." I glanced at Marcus as I said, 'safe', but he wasn't paying attention.

We left Sawyer at the car and followed Marcus to the clubhouse entrance. We entered through double doors and into a room with a round table where there were people already sitting around it.

There was one chair which reminded me of a throne: it was large and painted gold with a red cushion. The man who sat on it, the king, rose when we entered.

"Blaire, how wonderful to finally meet you," the man said.

I walked up to him and shook his hand. It was a good, strong shake.

"I'm Troy, and you know Marcus, obviously. And Melinda," — he pointed in the direction where she sat at the table, and then to the person next to her, Léon's private investigator, — "Kit, and this is Keegan, my second." Troy placed his hand on Keegan's shoulder. Keegan was a large bald man with the fattest black mustache I'd ever seen. "Please sit."

Marcus sat beside Melinda; Devan, Ralph and I sat on the other side of the were-lions, with several empty chairs separating them from us.

"As you know, we are all part of the Were-Animal Alliance, and there has been talk of your attack," Troy continued. "More specifically, it has come to light that you now carry three different lycanthrope strains. You haven't shifted into any of them yet, have you?"

"No," I said, shaking my head.

"Sebastian suggested it would be a good idea for you to meet with us, the leopards, and the wolves."

"Yes, that's why I'm here today."

"And what do you think about what's happening to you?"

"Everything is still very new and strange to me. And I won't lie, 'cause I know you guys can smell it, but I'm relieved I haven't shifted yet." I glanced at Melinda. "I do have one thing to ask, though. Why is she here? From what I understand, she wants to eradicate her animal."

I shouldn't have ratted her out, but her king needed to know what she had been up to with the serums she had concocted.

Melinda shifted uncomfortably in her seat, and averted her eyes for a second before staring up at Troy.

"Because she asked to be here. We know what she's been trying to do, and what she did to Marcus," Troy said. His eyes flitted to Marcus but instead of compassion in his expression I detected something else; possibly contempt. "But don't worry; we're keeping an eye on them."

Melinda blushed and looked down, but there was no smile.

Marcus moved in his chair, and turned his body away from Melinda.

Troy glowered at both of them.

"What do you think of me being here, meeting you?" I asked, wanting to change the angry atmosphere now suffocating me.

"Not sure yet," Troy said, rubbing his chin with his hand.

"Why are we meeting with only a handful of your were-lions?"

"We heard what happened at the leap, and we thought it would be safer keeping it small."

I couldn't argue with that; things didn't go according to plan.

Marcus shifted in his chair again, which made everyone turn in his direction.

"Marcus, what is bothering you so much?" Troy asked.

"Nothing." His eyes flicked from Troy to Keegan, and then to me. His face had that sweaty glaze I had seen before. When Melinda had injected him with her serum, he had shown signs of flu. For a were-animal to show any signs of a cold was odd because lycanthropes didn't get sick, and Marcus had lied to us by telling us it was a byproduct of him taking strong medicine.

"Are you medicated again, Marcus?" I asked, leaning forward so that I could see his face.

Heat crept up his neck in maroon blotches. Melinda was still staring down at her hands. She wouldn't meet my eyes.

"Marcus?" Troy commanded.

Marcus rose from the table, lifting it slightly and letting it drop with a loud thud. He moved closer to where I was sitting, dark shadows danced across his face. His small blue eyes were dark. He stood in a fighting stance with his feet pointed in my direction.

Ralph and I rose from the table at the same time. I touched his shoulder and shook my head. I could handle this. I approached Marcus in anticipation.

"What's up, Marcus? Why do you want to fight me?"

Marcus frowned, anger flashing through his eyes, then his facial features softened.

"It's not me," he said through gritted teeth. He doubled over, holding his stomach and moaned in pain. When he stood straight again, his small blue eyes bled into a glittered sky; a vast darkness void of the human that should be there.

"I have been waiting for you, Blaire." The voice coming

out of his mouth wasn't Marcus's. "You must visit me soon."

"Who are you?"

"Don't you recognize me?" the voice asked.

"Can't say we've met before."

"But you have been the one following me. You are the one invading my life. I thought I would return the courtesy." The man using Marcus's body stood using Marcus's feet and shifted them apart, both hands in fists protecting Marcus's face.

At over six feet tall, a were-lion like Marcus could throw a small car around without breaking a sweat. The man using his body was both powerful and dangerous.

There was no way this would be a fair fight.

I touched the gun in my holster and felt the tension ease. I could draw my gun and shoot him. But there was one problem with that; Marcus was our boss. The only choice I had was to knock the voodoo man right out of Marcus.

Without thinking, I ran and grabbed Marcus's back while lifting both my legs and came up toward his face. He grabbed my lower body and held on. I swiveled my body and legs so that his head was between my legs, and I grabbed his back from the other side. I squeezed my legs around his head and brought his body down while I held onto his back; the head-scissor-takedown was a great Brazilian Jiu Jitsu technique I'd learned.

As my legs dropped to the floor with his head still between them, and before he could hit me, I kneed him in the face, knocking his head backward. A sharp, snapping sound vibrated around the room, and Marcus fell to the floor.

My gun was out and pointed at him before he even hit the floor.

It took a while before Marcus opened his eyes, and when he did, they were small and light blue once again.

"Are you okay?" I asked, the gun still pointing at his face.

"Yeah," he whispered as he exhaled. He flinched in pain as he tried to move his head.

I stood back and observed the room. Everything had happened so fast I didn't see Ralph grab Melinda.

And as if from nowhere, Danny—the were-lion who had attacked me, infected me, and left me for dead—had arrived. He stood back and raised his hands into the air when I pointed my gun in his direction.

"What are you doing here, Danny?" My voice wasn't friendly.

"The pride asked me to be here. I didn't want to, I promise, but I came for them." His hands dropped to his sides, and he lowered his head. "And," — he glanced at Troy, — "I need to beg for your forgiveness."

I looked at Troy, who was now closer to the action. He nodded once.

"He will pay for what he did to you for years to come," Troy said. "I promise you. No member of my pack can do what he did and think he can get away with it."

"What are you making him do?" I said, keeping my attention on Marcus.

"He lost his rank within the pride, and he has become our errand boy. We also forbid him to associate with vampires."

"You don't know me. Why do you care what he did?"

"My pride only hunt animals, never humans." The tone of his voice now icy, and when I glanced at his face, he showed no emotion when looking at Danny. "And we don't do the dirty work of vampires, no matter who they are." To me, he said, "And, as you might become one of us, it's the least we could do." He smiled.

I didn't know what to say. The punishment was more than I could have asked for; apart from death.

"Thanks, Troy."

Melinda helped Marcus to sit up, and he had already healed his neck without shifting.

"How did the priest get to you, Marcus?" I asked as I went down onto my haunches near him and tapped the side of his head with my gun.

Melinda sat on the floor with Marcus between her legs, leaning him against the front of her chest. She wrapped her arms around him, an armband dangling from her wrist. Marcus and I stared at each other; I wanted to make sure his eyes stayed blue, and he wanted to make sure I didn't pull the trigger. My gun was still pointed at him.

"I don't know," he said, in between short and shallow breaths.

"Where did you buy the armbands, Melinda?" I pointed my gun at her left wrist. They were similar to the ones Grant, Lauren, and Jeremiah had been wearing a few nights ago.

Marcus strained to look at her wrist, lifted his arm, and pulled his sleeve up. He was wearing one, too.

"I bought it for him. The two came together in a love packet."

"From a voodoo shop?"

"What did I do wrong?"

A long sigh escaped my lips.

"How did McNielty know you were coming here tonight, Melinda? It's rather convenient, don't you think? Do you know him personally?"

"N-no," Melinda stuttered. "I buy from his shop every

month. He said I seemed different; that I was glowing. He suggested that love had brought out a sparkle in me, and that these were new." She raised her wrist, revealing the armband.

"You love me?" Marcus finally said, the shock of her confession evident.

Her cheeks flushed, and she nodded, averting her eyes.

"He offered these love bracelets for free when I purchased the candles," she said sadly, looking at me. "I didn't know what they were capable of doing. You have to believe me." She glanced at Marcus with pain in her expression. "I didn't know."

It was all perfectly timed. I couldn't understand how McNielty managed to stay one step ahead of me. Of us.

"I want to go to the priest now," I said, standing. "I've had enough of this fucking case. It ends tonight—"

"My aunt advised you need to stay away from him. Don't go," Devan said.

"I don't care!" I yelled. "For all we know, your aunt saw wrong. Did she see that this would happen?" I pointed to Marcus.

"No."

"Exactly. The bodies keep piling up, and he keeps coming after me. And I'm expected to just stand around and wait for him to hurt me? Fuck that." I touched Ralph's shoulder. "Either you drive me there, or I'm taking your keys from Sawyer and going alone."

"No, I'll drive," Ralph said, jumping to his feet. "Are you coming, Devan?"

"Yeah… I'll come," Devan said, hesitating.

"Thanks for the welcome, Troy. I'm sorry for what happened here." I waved my hand in the direction of Marcus and Melinda, who were still on the floor.

"No need to apologize; it wasn't your fault. We'll keep an eye on them," Troy said, then turned to Keegan and whispered in his ear. Keagan nodded and turned toward the back of the room, from where Danny had appeared.

I holstered my weapon headed for the exit.

Ralph parked right in front of the priest's voodoo shop. The doors were closed, as were a number of other shops.

"I thought the voodoo shop stayed open till 8pm?" I said. It wasn't six, and the shop was dark inside. The little 'Closed' sign hanging loosely behind the glass door.

"Not tonight, Blaire."

"Thanks, Ralph, I can see that." I climbed out of the car, approached the closed doors, and pulled on them. When I touched the metal handle, a surge of electricity passed through it and zapped my hand.

"I felt that, and I didn't have to touch it," Devan said from behind me.

I flinched, not hearing him behind me. I was too focused on the case, instead of paying attention to my surroundings.

"Magic?"

"Oh, definitely! That's one of the first spells you learn as a witch, a priest, or a warlock."

"Really?" I asked, turning to stare at him.

"Yep," he said with a quick nod. "It's a fun spell and super easy to do. A lot of owners ask witches to enchant their businesses to keep burglars at bay. It's a good income."

"Do you do it?"

His smile reached his eyes. He didn't say, 'yes' but he didn't have to. That smile said it all. I smiled back at him.

"It's not the right time to meet our priest," he said, sounding wiser than his age.

"He keeps fucking with us, Devan. I've had enough."

"You need to get to the Labyrinth," Sawyer said. His tone urgent.

"Why?"

"I don't know, just that you need to go."

What a disappointment: I had been reluctant to use my gun the last two months unless in self-defense... until tonight. Tonight, I wanted to use it on McNielty. The old Blaire might finally be peeking out from her hiding spot.

We all piled into the car again, and after a scenic road trip, we were back at the same door Ralph always parked near; the one near the garage door.

As he parked, Elena, another of Léon's bodyguards, stood by my door. I hadn't noticed her until she opened my door.

"Where did you come from?" I asked as I climbed out.

She gave me a half-smile, one that was full of mischief. "I knew you were on your way." She glanced at Sawyer. I turned to look at him, but the were-jackal was already out of the car and heading toward us.

"What's going on, Elena?" Sawyer said, deep lines showing between his eyes. "I thought she had to stay away."

"Apparently not."

"Who's here?"

"The two big ones."

They were talking to each other like I wasn't there.

"Can one of you please tell me what's going on?"

Sawyer glanced at me, those dark Egyptian eyes swimming in mystery. There was something else there, too. Concern?

"The Vampire Council has sent emissaries to hand down Roland's sentencing."

"What does that have to do with me being here?"

"That's what I want to know." His dark eyes flicked to Elena then me, then back to Elena.

"I honestly don't know. Just that the emissary wants to meet you and you should be present for the judgment," Elena said.

"Jesus, when you say it like that, it makes me not want to meet them."

"Is everything all right?" Ralph asked, standing beside me.

Devan was also out of the car, hovering near us.

"This doesn't concern you. You may go," Elena said with a flare of hostility.

A tiny spark of her power touched my torso. When I rubbed my arms, she stopped whatever she was doing.

"Do you want us to stay?" Ralph said, ignoring Elena's jab.

"No, it's okay. Thanks, Ralph. I should be fine." I patted his chest. I wasn't sure everything would be fine. If things went wrong, it was no use getting us both killed by vamps. One of us needed to be around to kill the priest.

We agreed that Ralph would fetch me in two days' time. Tomorrow, Sunday, we would rest, and if I made it through the evening with the Vampire Council and Roland, then tomorrow Rory and Sawyer would take me to meet their alpha, their Wolf King, just in case my body shifted for real and I picked a were-wolf.

Chapter Fifteen

I followed Sawyer and Elena into the large hall where everybody had gathered. The walls of the banquet hall were high and dark, like a drowning sea so blue and so dark that it looked black.

Sebastian caught my eye first, his tall body standing out among the vampires. He wore dark jeans, a gray t-shirt, and a black jacket. He looked very casual yet businesslike, with his blond hair styled like an executive.

There was a man I had never seen before, shorter than Sebastian, talking to him and Léon.

When Sebastian saw me, he smiled and called me over. Elena stopped and stood against the wall, like the security guard she was, while Sawyer continued to walk with me toward the men.

Salvador, Sebastian and Léon's father, was sitting on a two-seater couch with Charlotte. Salvador was a tall man; even while he sat, you could see those long legs stretched out in front of him. His straight hair was more salt than pepper and was kept neatly off his face. His skin was pale and smooth, with high cheekbones. He, too, was in smart-casual attire, wearing jeans and a black collar dress shirt.

Charlotte wore a green blouse that made her flaming red hair look like it could burn when touched, and her crystal-colored green eyes were vivid; I could see the bright color of her eyes from across the room. She completed her look with a tight black skirt and heels so high I wouldn't be able to walk in them.

From what Sebastian had told me, Charlotte was Léon's lover. I wondered what she would think of Léon's display of power toward me. And if she was the jealous type like Galina, then I should watch my back.

"Blaire, this is Alex and Genevieve. They are from the Vampire Council and are here to sentence Roland," Sebastian said when I reached them.

Alex was dressed in dark jeans with black boots, a dark green shirt, and a black jacket. His blond hair was cut short with light brown streaks, and the color of his eyes were a mix of both green and yellow; because he wore a dark green shirt, his eyes seemed greener. His features were soft and delicate, but you knew he was a man by the way he carried himself, and because his clothing was tailored, you could see it fit his athletic build perfectly.

Alex had been staring at me from the moment I arrived. I crossed the floor toward them, and felt the weight of his glare. Alex was slightly taller than me, and I noticed a sly smile across his face.

The woman Sebastian introduced as Genevieve came into my view. She was standing between the two men and, because she was short, I didn't see her until I reached them.

Genevieve was a redhead, but the color was not a flaming red like Charlotte: it was a shade closer to auburn. Her blue eyes held dark secrets, and there was a scar across her right cheek, which she must have sustained before she turned into a vampire.

She was petite and dainty, with small sharp features. Her smile seemed genuine when I greeted them, but the look in her eyes was not. Tension crawled along my spine, telling me to be careful. She wore a purple blouse and a skirt that stopped above her knee, with low heels.

I felt underdressed in my sneakers, jeans, and t-shirt.

"You are probably wondering why we called you here," Alex said.

"Yes, this looks like vampire business?"

Shattered glass got everyone's attention. We all turned toward the commotion near the doorway on the far side of the hall. Envision, the three superstar vampires Sebastian had introduced me to, were having an altercation with one of the guards. Elena and a few others ran to them.

"Why do they always have to make a grand entrance?" Salvador asked loudly from his seat.

"Because without us, your life would be fucking boring, old man," Heath said, walking into the hall with his hands on his hips. His leather pants looked like they were painted on, and he was naked from the waist up.

"I made you who you are today. Best you remember that," Salvador scolded the younger vampire.

"Oooh, I'm so scared." Heath flashed fangs as he smiled. "Besides, you love this body too much." He touched his chest seductively and slowly. When he reached Salvador, he stopped in front of the other vampire and kept his legs spread apart. He was still touching his chest, running his fingers over his nipples, giving Salvador a private show.

"Is that all you have, little vampire?" Salvador said, watching Heath's performance, and licked his thin lips.

Heath moved closer to Salvador so quickly, I didn't see

it. One moment he was standing, the next he was sitting on top of the other man, grinding his hips into Salvador's front, and they started kissing.

Sebastian glanced at Léon, who shook his head.

"Okay, Heath, Father," Léon eventually said. "Would the two of you like to take that somewhere else?"

Salvador laughed and tapped Heath's ass, then pushed him off.

"Are you jealous that I didn't come to you first, Léon?" Heath said, approaching Léon with a sway of his hips.

I was missing something here, but before I could think to ask, someone's power flared through the room. It was hot against my skin, and it stopped the other vampires from their bickering.

"Show some respect, Heath. I don't care how famous you are. At the moment, you are acting like the little shit we all know you to be, and we still have business to attend to. Let's get that out of the way, and then you can do as you please," Alex said, his voice deep and authoritative.

Heath gave a small bow and waved his hand in front of him, like he was holding a hat. Kris and Steven came in behind Heath, then the three of them sat on a sofa near Salvador. Heath blew Salvador a kiss.

Three more vampires entered. From earlier interactions with Léon, I knew one was Zachary; he managed the apartment blocks for him. With him was Jean-René, Léon's oldest and dearest friend.

Jean-René had the coolest blue eyes I had ever seen; an icy contrast to his warm personality. He was one of the more pleasant vampires to be around. He had naturally curly brown hair that I assumed would touch his shoulders if you straightened out. He was also one of the few vampires who had stubble, which suggested he had died before he had started shaving regularly. It suited him, framing his square jaw. He wore black slacks, a tailored white dress shirt, and black boots. His eyes stayed on Léon when he walked in.

I had only seen Zachary once before. Not only was he tall, but he was wide in the shoulders. His clothing was tight against his body, and you could see his muscles moving underneath. He did some heavy weight-lifting, which was odd for a vampire. Sebastian had mentioned that he worked out with some of the guards, and fought well.

I incorrectly assumed all those muscles would make him stiff, but apparently, he was surprising limber. I doubted the guards would let him win, yet he always did; the guards eventually tapped out. Which meant he was much stronger than most of the guards, who were mainly were-rats, were-hyenas or were-wolves. They weren't just muscle: they were ex-cops, ex-military, or ex-special forces. They knew how to fight.

I knew Zachary was one of the few vampires who carried a gun. He scared me, and there weren't many vampires who did that. He tied his long brown hair in a ponytail which opened up his face and showed his big brown eyes, and square jaw.

As Zachary walked across the floor, the dim lights and shadows played along his features. His face went from its usual pale marble to a dark spine-tingling glare. The last time I had seen him, he had had a woman on each arm, but today he was dragging Roland behind him.

Roland was the vampire who had tried to usurp Léon and take his place as Master Vampire of Sterling Meadow. He had ordered Miles and Danny to hire an assassin to kill Léon. That assassin was me. But Miles had had a crisis of conscience and changed his mind. He and his brother

Danny had attacked me in that shady alley, to prevent Léon's assassination. Since then, Roland had been in vampire lockup—a coffin wrapped in crosses—rendered powerless. The treacherous vampire was no longer in a position to reattempt his coup.

The Vampire Council was here to see to that justice and Roland's final judgement.

Roland was bound from hand-to-foot. His eyes were sunken, and his skin was leathery and gray; reminding me of a mummy. I guess being in a coffin locked with a cross and deprived of blood would do that to a vampire. The rope Zachary used to pull Roland was tied around his waist.

"Just the vampires we've been waiting for," Alex said, grinning.

Zachary let go of Roland's rope and came to stand beside Léon and Sebastian. He didn't even bat an eye in my direction. Sebastian had said I shouldn't take whatever he did personally. Apparently, it was Zachary's belief that women were around for only two things: fornication and blood donations.

I shuddered at the thought, and would stay far away from him as possible.

Genevieve glanced at Alex, who gave a small nod, and she glided toward Roland. She stood above him, with one foot on either side of his waist, went onto her knees, and sat down, straddling him.

"No, please, anything but her," Roland whimpered, his eyes pleading desperately with Alex.

"Because of your hate for Genevieve, this is only part of your punishment, Roland." Alex said.

"Do you remember the first time we met?" she asked, leaning forward so that she was near Roland's face.

Roland shook his head from side to side. I think if he could melt into the ground, he would've.

Roland had been a gray color when Zachary had dragged him in. But when he saw Genevieve, his body stiffened more than any vampire should and paled. He looked gravely ill.

Genevieve moved up until she was sitting on his chest, loosened the rope enough so that his hands weren't tied to his feet, and lifted his bound hands above his head. She started kissing him like she was patiently waiting for him to kiss her back and open his mouth to hers. But when that didn't happen, her kissing became forceful, and he whimpered.

Everyone stood closer to watch the scene unfold; to ensure Roland was punished. But I didn't understand how her kissing Roland could be a punishment or why Roland cried out; it made no sense. Genevieve was beautiful, and she was kissing him.

Roland tried to move his arms in front of his body again to block her, but she pinned his hands to the floor with one hand.

She made moaning sounds as she kissed him; she was enjoying the taste of him. He tried to move away from her, away from her grasp, but she held him firmly in place.

She kissed his cheek, then his mouth again, and then her skin started to pull away from her muscles, dripping over him. His cries grew louder. The more he struggled beneath her, the more her skin and muscles started to sag away from her bones and rot.

Pieces of green and brown flesh fell onto Roland, and he cried out again. Her arms were nothing but bones, and her face had sunken to little more than rotting meat. She looked like a zombie, freshly raised from the grave.

I gasped.

"Are you all right?" Sebastian said in my head.

"Yeah, just grossed out," I thought back. *"Is that why Roland cried out?"*

"They have history, and none of it was pleasant. His main power is rot, albeit not as bad as Genevieve's, but he is ashamed of it all the same. That's why he asked Léon to share his power with him when he worked at Kiss nightclub."

"No wonder he didn't want her near him."

"It should be over soon."

Relieved that this wouldn't last long, but it was disgusting. I stepped backward. My movement caught Genevieve's attention. She stopped kissing Roland, stared at me, and laughed. That gave Roland a breather and he cried for help again.

Genevieve's muscles started forming on her bony arms and her face puffed out until she was beautiful once more. When she was whole again, she sat up and tapped his chest.

"Now, now, Roland, that wasn't so bad, was it?" Her smile reached her eyes. "You should be used to this. You and I share some of these qualities."

Genevieve had enjoyed herself; I mean, she really enjoyed kissing him.

Then her right arm reached behind her and she grabbed his crotch, and arched backward.

"You cry for help," — she purred, — "but your body loves me touching."

"I'm nothing like you, Genevieve," Roland cried. "Please get off me." He moved his hips around but couldn't throw her off balance. "Please get her off me," he yelled.

Her hand was still behind her and she squeezed, which stopped him from moving. He was very still. Genevieve pushed herself lower over his body, lifted herself up, positioned him, and sat down.

Roland closed his eyes and his mouth parted as she started to ride him, gently at first, then harder and harder. She was having sex with him, in front of everyone.

With each thrust of her hips, Roland emitted a guttural, grunting sound. Genevieve moved her hips faster and harder with him inside of her, then, with each thrust, she started changing again. The skin and muscles on her abdomen started rotting, forming holes until we saw her ribs. Some areas on her arms and neck turned green with a putrid smell.

Roland moved his arms to try to dislodge her, but Genevieve held his arms in place, and her fingers rotted around him.

He continued crying, but no one helped him. This was his punishment; at its cruelest.

She lifted his arms above his head again, and with one final thrust, they both screamed at the same time. She licked his cheek and left rotting meat in her slimy wake, and kissed him again like she wanted to eat him from the inside.

I held my hand over my mouth and swallowed hard. *I would not throw up*. I turned around so I didn't have to see any more. There were noises coming from them, and then they were done, but I didn't turn around. I'd seen enough.

I flinched when someone touched my shoulder. It was Zachary.

"Don't turn away. All this is for you. It is justice for you and Léon."

"Torture doesn't do it for me," I grumbled.

"Let her be, Zachary," Alex said, then turned to me. "What would you rather we do?"

"You can do whatever is necessary; I just don't want to

witness any more of it. And, if you need to kill him, get it over and done with already."

"Fine. No more torture. Get off him, Genevieve. Any last words, Roland?" Alex said.

"Please don't, Alex; I beg of you!" Roland cried. I turned around to look at him. He was tucked back in his pants and on his knees, begging. "Please, please. I have been in my coffin long enough. I will do whatever you wish to make this right."

"You were warned before, Roland. The Council has decided." Alex lifted his arms, palms facing the ceiling.

Roland was airborne, screaming. Alex clapped his hands, and a fire started in the fireplace behind us. He clapped twice, and Roland's body smashed into the wall on the far right. Bones broke, the snapping and cracking echoing in the hall. Then his body split in half. His screams pierced my ears. He was still alive. For vampires to perish, you needed to remove their hearts and head and burn them.

I covered my ears as best I could to drown out his cries.

Every joint of his body pulled apart, then each limb split, and blood sprayed down over us like rain. Blood hit me in the face, in my eyes, in my mouth, and I gagged.

Alex dropped his hands and the pieces of Roland's body was flung into the fire, which sparked into tall blue flames.

I screamed, staring at my blood soaked hands.

Sebastian came to comfort me, but I didn't want anyone touching me. I ran for an exit but slipped in a puddle of blood near the door. Sebastian was there to pull me to my feet, and I cried into his chest.

"Are they always this brutal?" I whispered through sobs.

"It was necessary," he whispered near my ear. "I'm sorry you had to witness it, but Roland needed to suffer, and we needed to teach the others a lesson. Just in case someone wanted to do the same."

I was crying, almost hyperventilating. There was blood all the way down my side, and my clothing clung to my body. The blood on my skin was hardening.

"I need to get this off of me. I need to shower. Please, Sebastian, help me."

"It's okay," Sebastian said, wiping blood from my eyes with a white handkerchief. "Let me take care of you."

I washed my body and hair twice to make sure I was free from Roland's blood. Sebastian left me in his room while he used Léon's bathroom to clean up.

Sawyer was drenched in blood, but remained outside the bedroom door, guarding me. There was a soft knock on the bathroom door.

"Who is it?" I said, switching off the water so I could hear the answer. I grabbed a towel and wrapped it around my body.

When no one answered, I opened the bathroom door, but the room was empty. I frowned, closed the door, and dressed into sleepwear.

I was in desperate need of sleep, and I'd had enough of vampires and the voodoo man to last a lifetime.

My shoulder holster was on the table. I grabbed the gun and held it in my hand. I picked up my blood-soaked clothing, threw it in the laundry basket, and entered the bedroom.

Sebastian had said that after he showered he needed to return to his brother in the hall. I, on the other hand, was going to sleep.

There was another knock on the bedroom door, but before I answered, someone opened it slowly.

"Salvador is outside," Sawyer said, sticking his head in. "He would like to speak with you."

"Salvador? Why does he want to speak with me?"

Sawyer shrugged those large shoulders.

"Fine, let him in."

The tall man came in smoothly that it looked like he floated above the tiles, rather than walking. The motion was both graceful and eerie. Despite being Léon and Sebastian's father, Salvador still looked twenty-eight, as he had for over a thousand years. He was old and, from what Sebastian had told me, powerful.

He was so powerful that he had fathered two sons after becoming a vampire. Fathering one child showed strength enough, but two; that was unheard of.

Salvador was as tall as Sebastian, but with hair that was cut short and more the color of salt than pepper. His skin was the smoothest I'd seen on any vampire, like he had been carved from marble and brought back to life with a kiss. The resemblance between him and his two sons was unmistakable; they all shared a similar bone structure, but where Sebastian had green eyes with golden slivers, Léon's were an ocean blue, and Salvador's were a shade lighter.

He stood before me, and I'd never felt as uncomfortable with any of the vampires as I did then. He stared at me, deeply into my eyes, like he could see inside my soul. I wanted to put my gown on, but I remembered I hadn't packed it. I saw my jacket on the floor and pulled it on.

"It's not cold. Why wear the jacket?" he chuckled.

"I don't know. Just that I needed to," — I didn't want to look into his eyes, so I looked at his nose, — "put something on."

The corners of his mouth curved upward, but the rest of his face didn't match the smile.

"I'm sure you were wondering why I am here." He stepped closer and leered down at me. "I wanted to hear it directly from you." He paused. It wasn't so much a pause for breath as a pause to see my reaction, as vampires only really took in air as they spoke.

"What?"

He removed stray hair out of my face, but there was something in the way he hesitated that told me he was being careful not to touch me.

"Your light is so bright. I want to touch you, but I'm afraid I might burn."

Dammit.

Since I was by myself, I had relaxed, and may have dropped my metaphysical shields ever so slightly. I thought of metal, tall and wide.

"You've been practicing."

I nodded. I thought only witches and clairvoyants saw the white of my aura, and frowned.

"You can see my aura?"

"Yes, Blaire, I can. And before you ask, I am that powerful," he said, nodding and lifted his hand and shushed me with his index finger.

I closed my mouth.

"Have the nightmares stopped?"

"How did you know I was having nightmares?" I asked. My frown deepened, showing my confusion. It was a peculiar question, especially since he and I didn't converse, and I hadn't mentioned to Sebastian that I kept having them.

"You are metaphysically tied to my son. I needed to know if you are all right," — he arched an eyebrow, — "if anything happened to you, it could affect Sebastian."

"I'm fine," I said quickly, hugging my body. The tension in my back and shoulders eased a little, and I tried to relax without dropping my shields.

"Good. Has he been treating you well?"

I opened my mouth and closed it again. My frown was back.

"You don't trust easily, do you?" He laughed. It was deep and throaty.

"No, I don't. Sorry, it's just I don't know you." I was quiet for a moment, then added, "You might be Sebastian's father, but I still don't understand why you're here talking with me. You could've asked Sebastian these questions."

The bedroom door opened.

"Father, what are you doing here?" Sebastian said, entering.

"Having a little chat with Blaire." He winked at me.

"And what was the topic of your little chat?" Sebastian drew closer to me.

"So suspicious, Sebastian."

"When it comes to you, Father, always."

The same deep, throaty laugh echoed off the walls. Salvador bowed.

"Her light brought me here, son. Like an insect to a candle."

"You must forgive him," Sebastian said. "My father has always been this way."

Salvador placed a hand on each of our shoulders and squeezed.

"I only wanted the chance to hear how she was doing."

"As you can see, she's fine."

"Indeed." He squeezed my shoulder again. "Right, I'll leave you to it." Salvador turned and exited.

"Are you okay? Did he do anything to you?" Sebastian asked with concern in his tone.

"No." I shook my head. "He was just asking questions."

He pulled me into the circle of his arms, and I held him tightly around his waist, my face against his chest.

"I need to leave again. Léon has asked that I return, but I shouldn't be too long. Why don't you sleep, and I'll see you a little later?"

"Okay." I stared up at him and gave him a sleepy smile. "When you hold me like that, you make me so tired," I said, yawning.

He kissed the top of my head, cupped my face, and kissed me chastely.

"I'll be back soon."

He let go of me, and as I walked to the bed, he smacked my ass lightly. I gave a playful yelping sound and climbed onto the bed. When I set my head on the pillow, I fell asleep immediately.

Chapter Sixteen

Sebastian drove while I rode shotgun, with Sawyer and Rory in the back. Despite Sebastian being a were-leopard, the Wolf King, Shawn, had agreed for him to join us for our little meet-and-greet.

As he drove, Sebastian informed me that Miles, one of the were-wolves who had attacked me, would be there, too. I wasn't sure how to feel about it.

I hadn't seen Miles since Roland's capture, where it had been revealed that Miles had been in league with the rogue vampire. He had hired me to take out the Master Vampire, but at the pivotal moment, as I had been preparing to assassinate Léon, Miles had realized that Léon was the lesser of the two evils and that Roland would never accept him as his second-in-command. He had attacked me in order to stop me from fulfilling the contract.

Miles had been punished for his role in my assault, for what Roland had asked him to do, but as a result of his actions, I had been left close to death and infected with three strains of lycanthropy; I wanted none of them.

We arrived at the Wolf Pack and found a parking spot not too far away from the building. A throng of people flowed in that direction, like a dark wave reaching shore. We joined the wave and headed toward the entrance.

The Wolf Pack congregated near to the forest, just like the other were-animal groups. This was done on purpose; each were-animal group had easy access to the forest so that they could hunt during the full moon. By being part of the Were-Animal Alliance, each animal group agreed to hunt in certain areas, and not hunt in each other's territories. It was a gentleman's agreement that everyone adhered to.

"Is it always this packed?" I asked no one in particular.

"Always," Sawyer replied. "Plus, everyone wants to meet you."

"Why?" I glanced at Sawyer with raised eyebrows.

"Well," — he shrugged, — "we lashed Miles in front of the whole pack for what he did to you, so everyone knows who you are. You're something of a myth at the moment; the human who hasn't shifted. So, naturally, they want to meet you."

A knot formed in the pit of my stomach, and I flinched as someone touched my back; it was Mel, the resident doctor and were-wolf. She had an uncanny ability to calm me down, much like Sebastian.

I'd been avoiding her the last two months, much like I had done with Sebastian; much like I had done with everything else that had happened to me. I had been afraid that if I saw her, she might tell Sebastian how I was really doing. I'd also avoided her when she had helped the leopards a few days ago.

Mel had chocolate brown eyes and a beautiful smile. She was in her mid-forties but didn't look it: apart from her platinum bob hair, everything else about her seemed younger.

"I've missed you," Mel said, wrapping her arm around my shoulder and giving me a sideways hug. "Every time we made plans, you canceled on me. And I really needed to speak to you about your blood, but I understand Sebastian has informed you already."

"I'm sorry I kept canceling." A sigh escaped my lips. "Yeah, I know about my blood." I didn't know what else to say without sounding lame or lying, and I couldn't lie; were-animals could smell a lie much like vampires could.

"It's okay." She squeezed my shoulder and whispered, "If you'd kept the appointments, I wouldn't have said anything to anybody. I'm here to help you, to try to answer any questions you may have about your situation. Just remember that."

"Thanks, Mel." I hugged her back. When I looked ahead, the three men were already at the entrance to the building.

"We still need to talk about them." She jerked her chin in their direction. She meant Sebastian and Léon.

"We will." I smiled, but it didn't reach my eyes. I wasn't sure how that conversation would go, but I would meet with her and listen to what she had to say.

We followed the men through the hallway of the clubhouse until we were outside again. There was a man sitting in a chair on top of a large step, which had to be Shawn, the Wolf King.

There were at least a hundred were-wolves sitting or standing around the large step. The talking died down as we started walking through the crowd.

My hands started sweating and my clothing clung to my body, even though it was cool outside.

Shawn rose from his chair and held his hand out. From where I stood, Shawn seemed tall, but he was only around six foot. It was his build that made him seem larger, though; it was pure muscle. His dark hair shone black in the sunlight and framed his blue eyes and square jaw. Few people had pure black hair—it was usually dyed—but Shawn's hair was naturally black. It was cut short but still outlined his face, somehow making his sky-blue eyes seem brighter.

"Blaire. Welcome!"

Sawyer and Rory stopped by the step and stood to the side to allow me through, like a gauntlet.

Mel squeezed my elbow, let go, and stood next to Rory.

Sebastian went up the stairs and shook the man's hand.

"Blaire, this is Shawn, the Wolf King."

My hand reached his, and the moment I touched his skin, a jolt of power shot through my hand. I would have collapsed if Shawn hadn't reached for my elbow and Sebastian hadn't grabbed my other hand. For a moment, I was held up by them.

"I'm sorry," Shawn said.

When I was standing on my own, both men let go of my arms.

"I'm sorry, I usually shield better than this. Plus, I'm used to humans not being able to feel it at all."

"It's all right," I said, rubbing my palms on my jeans. The power he had pushed into me was still lingering, and I shuddered as it dripped slowly down my spine like an ice cube.

The sun was instantly gone. When I glanced up, there was a large, dark man hovering over me.

"Are you all right?" the man asked, holding a chair in one hand.

"Yeah, I'm good."

"Thanks, Djimon," Shawn said, sitting down.

Djimon was big and wide, not fat but strong. He was all dark muscle on that large frame. He had a tattoo on the right side of his face, but you could hardly see it against his dark skin. He set a chair down beside Shawn's throne and stood behind his king.

"I'm here if you need me," Sebastian said, stepping onto the grass.

"You want me to sit beside you?" I asked, looking from Sebastian to Shawn.

"Yes," — Shawn tapped the arm of the chair beside him, — "I want to introduce you to everyone."

I realized I was holding my breath and exhaled slowly. I climbed up the step and sat down beside the Wolf King. All eyes were on him and I.

"Welcome, everyone. I'm glad to see so many of you could make it at such short notice. As everyone is well aware, this is Blaire, the woman Miles attacked two months ago." As Shawn said Miles's name, I saw him standing to one side of the crowd. He was pale for a were-wolf and thinner than the last time I'd seen him.

"Because she holds our lycanthrope strain," Shawn continued. "And could turn at the next full moon in two days' time, she is here to meet us, to see what we do and how we do it. Please make her feel welcome, and no attacking." Only a few snickered at the joke.

The rest of the introduction was pleasant and cordial. There were a few questions from the others about whether I would join their pack even though I hadn't changed yet. I didn't know and left it at that. I answered the questions I could, even though I didn't fully know the answers.

Someone asked why Sebastian was there. He was a were-leopard at a were-wolf meeting. Shawn answered that they were friends and that they both belonged to the Were-Animal Alliance, which was one way they shared information. It was a good way to keep out those who wanted to infiltrate one of the were-animal groups and for everyone to keep Sterling Meadow safe.

"Is she trying out to be your mate?" Asked a woman near the front. She scowled at me with hate written all over her face.

My mouth gaped open. The look of shock on my face must have been enough because her face softened, and her cheeks glowed; she wouldn't meet Shawn's eyes.

"No, Michelle," Shawn said, then threw his head back and laughed. "She is only a guest for today," he added once he composed himself.

"What did she mean by that?" I asked under my breath. I could feel my frown lines deepen when I glanced at Shawn.

"I've been their Wolf King for over two years, and it's time that I settle down and have a family of my own. So, at the moment, I'm looking for a mate."

"Do women have to try out? What exactly are you making them do?"

Shawn laughed again; it was deep and throaty, with an edge of a growl to it. "Humans call it dating. And I don't make anyone do anything they don't want to do. It's dating, only quicker. Speed dating, if you like."

"How many speed dates have you been on?"

"I only started this week, so two or three per night."

"Are you only looking for were-wolves?"

"Yes, only were-wolves. Why, are you looking to try out?" he teased.

Heat crept up my neck, and I fought not to touch my

cheeks. "No, I don't think I qualify. Plus, I'm already taken." My eyes flicked in Sebastian's direction.

"I heard. You can't go wrong with him. He's a good guy." He grinned at me.

Shawn continued with pack business for another hour before everybody started to leave. They would reconvene in a couple of days to hunt during the full moon.

I'd learned that Shawn had fought the previous king two years ago and won. As with most wolf packs, to fight for this title was to fight to the death. Nobody had challenged Shawn in the two years since he had become king, not out of fear but because he was a good king. I could tell by the way in which he interacted with the pack. He answered their questions like he had all the time in the day for them. Putting people at ease came second nature to him.

When it was just our little group left by the steps, Shawn rose and approached Sebastian, grabbing him by the shoulder in that sideways hug men do, and they walked a short distance away from us.

I stood near Sawyer and Rory while Djimon remained like a tall, dark building behind us, his eyes scanning the trees behind us as he watched over his king.

Sebastian and Shawn walked back in our direction, their private conversation over, and the three of us walked to meet them.

"Do you want to take a walk through the forest?" Sebastian asked, pointing to the trees behind him. "Shawn was telling me he thinks there might be real leopards on this side of the forest, and I'd like to check them out."

"Sure. If we're allowed?" I said, glancing at the two guards, then at Shawn.

"Absolutely, we'll be coming with you." Shawn motioned for Djimon to follow.

We all headed for the path that started at the edge of the forest. At first, the path was neat, then it branched off in different directions. We followed Shawn, with Djimon bringing up the rear.

The farther we traversed into the forest, the more shadows played along the trees and ground. With the icy air of the night surrounding us, there was a smell of wet sand, leaves, and shrubs everywhere, and it reminded me of something.

A tightness formed in my gut.

We walked deeper into the darkness, the sounds of broken branches creaking underfoot, our feet shuffling through leaves on the uneven ground.

As I pushed a hanging moss out of the way, a spider's web came back on my hand and I had to shake it off and wipe it down on the rough bark of a tree. It relieved me there was no spider.

A light fog started moving in through the trees and headed toward us. It reminded me of all those horror movies I'd seen, but I was grateful knowing that the werewolves in this area were the good guys.

There were hooting sounds coming in on my right. Wings flapped to my left, as something large flew over us.

My chest tightened as I felt a gaze so heavy I feared I would sink into the soft, wet earth below me.

I glanced over my shoulder, but Djimon didn't look away. He kept the full weight of his stare on me. Rory and Sawyer turned around to look at the man.

"Djimon, what's up, dude?" Sawyer said lightheartedly.

Djimon ignored Sawyer, even when he slowed down to walk alongside him. Djimon kept his eyes locked on me. It wasn't until that second that I began to feel unsafe.

I touched Sebastian's back. He turned around, and followed my gaze to focus on Djimon.

"Shawn?" Sebastian tapped Shawn's shoulder.

"Yeah?" Shawn stopped to see what Sebastian wanted.

Sebastian jerked his chin toward Djimon.

Shawn's eyes settled on his sentry.

"Djimon?" Shawn asked. "Why are you looking at Blaire like that, big fella?"

Shawn walked past Sebastian and I and stood in front of Djimon.

The dark shadows played over Djimon's face, and his threatening eyes stared past Shawn at me. Shawn touched the big man's arm.

"She's white," Djimon finally said, lowering his eyes. "She white witch."

Sebastian took my hand in his, a warm contrast to my freezing fingers. I let go of his hand to stand closer to him, my back against his chest.

"No, Djimon, she isn't a witch."

"White witch, Shawn. Look her." He pointed at me with both hands as he outlined my body from head to toe.

Shit. I thought of a metal wall and shielded as best as I could.

"What do you mean, Djimon?" Shawn turned to look at me and shrugged.

"White gone," Djimon said.

I didn't understand how he could see my aura. He was a shapeshifter. I thought only witches, voodoo priests, clairvoyants, warlocks, and Salvador could see it.

"Djimon, lift your hands," I said, walking toward the big man.

"Don't," Sebastian said, trying to hold me back.

"It's all right, Sebastian." I gave him one of my most reassuring smiles.

Djimon lifted his arms and pulled up his sleeves.

"Shit." I whispered under my breath. "Can I take this off?" I asked.

He nodded. I hesitated at first, then, with my index fingers and thumbs, I reached for the armband.

When I touched the armband, Djimon jumped high in the air. In those few seconds, time stood still. Sebastian pushed me out of the way as Djimon came crashing down. He would've landed on top of Sebastian and Shawn if they were human, but they weren't, and they were quick enough to see what he was doing and got out of the way.

When Sebastian pushed me, it was so hard that I flew into a nearby tree, the trunk connecting with my right shoulder.

I struggled to my feet. When I looked up, Djimon approached with determination. Sebastian crashed into him with the entire weight of his body behind his shoulder, but it was too late: Djimon was too close to me. They both collided with me, and I slammed into the tree once again.

Darkness surrounded me.

When I came to, I couldn't hear Rory and Sawyer shouting, but I saw their mouths move. Shawn tried to grab Djimon, to pull him off and away, but the big man was tough.

Djimon fought Sebastian and pushed Shawn away at the same time. I understood why he was Shawn's bodyguard; he was a tough fucker.

Something trickled down my head and neck. I touched the wound and found that it was the size of a large coin. Every time I tried to sit up, I fell over; realizing my right arm wasn't functioning properly after I had hit my shoulder on the tree.

Sebastian got Djimon off my legs, and they fought a few steps away from me.

Rory and Sawyer were beside me, talking to me, but I still couldn't hear them. I shook my head and pointed to my ear with my left hand. They nodded, spoke to each other, and nodded again.

Sawyer bent down and scooped me in his arms. The moment my shoulder touched his chest, I cried out in pain.

The last thing I remembered seeing was Sebastian kicking Djimon in the head and the big man crashing to the ground.

Chapter Seventeen

Léon held my hair between his long fingers as he brushed the ends. I was sitting on a chair in front of a large mirror, wearing a navy lace bodice dress from centuries ago. He took his time brushing my long hair, from the top of my head all the way to the ends. My hair was much longer than I remembered and darker in color. He set the brush on the side table and placed his hands on my bare shoulders.

"There, all perfect again," Léon said, smiling.

"What's going on?"

"How do you feel?"

"Fine. Where are we?"

"Safe."

Léon pulled me to my feet. He lifted my hands to his mouth, his soft lips caressing my knuckles. The look behind his sea blue eyes held concern, his face a graven image. It was only the flash of sensitivity behind those eyes that gave any kind of emotion away.

"What is it, Léon? You're hiding something. What is it?" I tried to see myself in his eyes, but they were too dark.

"You were hurt. I wanted to make sure you were okay."
"Where is Sebastian?"
"He will be fine. He is healing as we speak."
"How can you be here? You don't have a mark on me."
"No."

Léon let go of my left hand and caressed my cheek. His hand was warm against my skin. I closed my eyes with his touch and leaned into his hand. He cupped my face and pulled me in for a gentle kiss. My eyes were closed when he pulled away. As I opened my eyes to see where he was, his mouth found mine again.

The kiss was no longer gentle; it was desperate and wanting. I remembered what he could do with his touch, how he could find my deepest, undisclosed desires and give them to me. I wanted to pull free of his embrace, but he held onto me tightly. He drew me in closer, the line of my body touching his.

I didn't know what to do with my hands. It felt silly to leave them by my side, so I slid them around his waist. I ran my fingers up his back and felt the strength beneath his shirt.

Léon pushed against me until my back touched a wall behind us. His tongue explored my mouth, and I explored his. My tongue found his fangs, and I nicked myself, flinching from the pain. A moan escaped his mouth and it echoed inside mine. His kiss intensified with my blood inside our mouths. And I swallowed the metallic liquid.

It was all distracting; his mouth on mine, his tongue inside my mouth, his hands exploring my body as I explored his. When he pushed against me, I felt the hardness of his body.

A moan of frustration came out of my mouth. I wanted to feel his skin directly on mine, to see whether he was as cold as the dead or if there was some warmth to him. I wanted to feel all of him.

But this didn't feel right. Léon kissing me, felt wrong. It was all wrong. I was with Sebastian, his brother. I had the metaphysical connection to Sebastian, not to Léon; so why was he here kissing me?

I dug my nails into my skin until there was pain, and I could think clearly.

I remembered the way in which Djimon had looked at me. How I had hit the tree and hurt my right shoulder. And how Sebastian had kicked Djimon to the ground. And then Sebastian had appeared hurt.

When I could think of things besides Léon's passionate kiss; his body against mine. I thought that this was only a dream, that Léon had somehow invaded my mind while I was unconscious.

My hands moved to his chest; his heart beating beneath my fingertips. The rhythmic duh-dum of his heart was strong; he almost felt alive.

Léon had the same look in his eyes that a junkie would for a fix. And it told me he wanted more.

"No, Léon!" I said, pushing him away.

"Forgive me," he said with regret in his tone. His eyes glittered like stars. He was using a lot of power to do this, to invade my unconscious mind in this way.

"What's going on, Léon? Why are you behaving like this?"

"I couldn't help myself," he said desperately. "Don't you feel it, Blaire? I know you don't carry my mark, but I wish it hadn't failed. I am completely drawn to you like an insect to a flame. To your flame." He looked me over.

I thought of metal, large slabs of metal pulled high and all around me, and suddenly Léon was gone.

When I opened my eyes, I was gasping for air. The room I found myself in was dimly lit and in a place I didn't recognize. As I tried to sit, pain shot through my shoulder and into my head, forcing me to lie back down.

"Don't sit up just yet," said a voice I recognized; Mel.

"You always seem to be around to stitch me back together," I said and smiled, but it didn't reach my eyes.

She laughed, and it was a good wholesome laugh like she hadn't laughed in a while.

"Yeah, you seem to get into a lot of trouble."

"It's not my fault. Help me sit up."

She walked away and came back with two pillows. She wrapped her left arm around me and pulled me up by my back; I held onto her arm while her right hand placed the pillows behind me.

I saw the room properly; it was painted an off-white hospital color, with a metal side table and a visitor's chair. We were the only ones in the room.

"Is everyone else okay?"

"Sebastian heals quickly. He was fine within minutes."

"How long have I been out?"

"It's been about four hours," she said, avoiding eye contact with me.

"What about Djimon?"

"Sebastian had to knock him out to pull the armband from his wrist. When Djimon woke up, he was back to his normal self."

"How did that priest get to him?"

"In his spare time, Djimon plays cards. He attended a game before he came here. He remembers nothing after arriving at the venue. He remembers the vampire he usually plays cards with, but today there was a tall white guy with white eyebrows and white hair. Then he woke up here. He doesn't remember anything in-between."

"Shit." I bit my fingernails. "White eyebrows and white hair! I need to speak to Djimon. I need to talk to him now."

"I know. We all know it sounds like the voodoo priest you've been after. Although it seems more like he's been after you these last couple of days."

"We need to know who this vampire is, Mel. What if it's someone in Léon's clutch or brood or whatever they call themselves? What if this vampire has been leading the priest straight to us?"

"Dammit." She turned and headed for the door. "I'll be right back." And she was gone.

The knot forming in the pit of my stomach started to ease, but only a little. I would relax completely once I found out who was helping the voodoo priest do all this. Someone was giving inside information to the priest; that was the only way for him to know where we were each time, and who would be there. It couldn't be coincidence that every time we tried to do something, someone would try to attack me.

I needed to know if Ralph had been attacked, and reached for the side table but it was empty. I would ask for my phone once Mel returned.

There was a soft knock on the door.

"You can come in." I should have asked who it was first, but it showed how hurt I was; I wasn't thinking clearly.

I saw his short, dark hair first, then his hard marble body that had been kissed by death. Léon entered the room, and my heart started to thunder in my ears. When I thought of the sensual dream we'd shared, things tightened down below, and my cheeks heated.

He smiled knowingly. His dark brown hair always stayed

off his face and showed his smooth, pale skin. His high cheekbones and strong jaw finished off his beautiful face. He wore dark jeans over black boots, a navy dress shirt, and a jacket.

When he wrapped his long fingers around my hand, I closed my eyes. The flashback of our kiss from earlier, the smell of his cologne, the ocean and the smell of him just beneath that was sensory overload, and my body reacted to it; reacted to him. I managed not to writhe on the bed and opened my eyes when I spoke.

"Is it still Sunday evening?"

"Yes." His smooth voice held promise, like velvet fingers caressing my skin. All the hair on my body stood on end with that one word.

I pulled my hand out of his. Without physical contact, perhaps I could think better.

"What are you doing?" I asked, holding my gaze. To stare into a vampire's eyes only spelled trouble, but I needed to see his eyes. I needed to see if there was any change in them. I needed to see if he flinched, or if he remained as hard as the marble they had carved him out of.

"What anyone else would do," he said. His voice a velvety caress against my skin. "Don't you feel it?" There was a hint of desperation in his smooth voice.

I shook my head a little too quickly, and couldn't trust what I wanted to say; what I felt.

He placed his hand over mine as it rested on my stomach. That one touch sent pleasurable heat burning along my hand, and lower on my body.

"Please don't touch me, Léon."

He removed his hand and placed both hands in his jacket pockets.

"You feel it, too, don't you? I will know if you lie."

"Yes, I feel it," I said, confessing to something that could cause trouble. "But is it real, or is it just your power that you are wielding over me?"

"The only power I have used was that which allowed me to see you in your dream. What is drawing me to you is not my power; it's you who is drawing me in, Blaire?"

"I can't," I whispered. "Sebastian…"

"You are drawn to him, too, I know. As he is attracted to you." He sighed. "It was never this strong before, but since your return—"

I opened my mouth to say something, but the door opened, and Sebastian came in with Mel behind him.

"What are you doing here?" Sebastian said, glowering at Léon. He moved to stand on the other side of the bed; the brothers scrutinized each other.

"I came to see how Blaire was doing."

"Were you not given the messages?"

"I received them."

"Then you didn't have to come all the way here."

They did that mind-to-mind thing they shared, and the air in the room became hot and stuffy. It felt like tiny flicks of hot ash falling on my skin.

"Sebastian! Léon! Enough!" I yelled. I had to stop what they were doing; I'd been hurt enough for one day.

Both men glared at me.

"Who did Djimon say the vampire was?"

We had a bad guy to catch. My head throbbed from the increase in blood to my head from screaming at them. I exhaled slowly and sank back into the pillow.

"He doesn't know; apparently no real names are given at the card game. As long as you show up with money, you can play. The only thing Djimon could tell us was that he had long brown hair and was big, like he lifted weights. Oh, and his eyes glowed red sometimes."

"That sounds like Zachary," Léon said.

"I thought the same thing," Sebastian said.

"What were you going to do, Sebastian? Go after him without informing me? We may be brothers, but I am still Master of this City."

"Yeah, so you keep reminding me, Léon. I needed to make sure it was him before doing anything."

"Mel, help me out." I lifted the hand with the drip in. "I need to go with them."

"You're in no shape to leave, Blaire."

"I can call Ralph. We'll handle it," Sebastian said.

"No!" I sounded angry, "I'm coming with you. Take this thing out or I'm pulling it out."

"You are one of the most stubborn people I know," Mel said.

"I've heard that before."

Mel started removing the tape from my hand and the needle from my vein.

"We'll be outside," Sebastian said, and they left.

"You know, I've never seen Léon so smitten," Mel said when it was just the two of us.

The comment caught me off guard. I swallowed air, and an 'ah' sound escaped my lips.

"Don't know what you're talking about."

"The brothers are fighting over you. It all started the night they found you."

"How do you know?"

"I was there that night, remember? It's the look in their eyes. When Léon couldn't tie you to him, he was furious."

"Why, though?"

"Why anything when it comes to them?" She shrugged nonchalantly. When I said nothing, she continued. "Those two boys have always had a lover here and there, but no-one they've wanted to keep around for longer than a week. Then their father comes to town, and a month later you're there, and this weird feud starts between them. And neither of them have had a lover since then. That is why I kept pushing you to meet with me. I wanted you to be aware of the entire situation. The only reason I'm saying this now is in case I don't get the chance again."

My head started to hurt, and I didn't think it was from the fight.

"I don't understand. Why? Why me?"

"I don't know, but there is something. It may have started when Sebastian tied himself to you, and Léon flipped."

That would explain all the power flares and stares between them. It would explain so much, but it raised yet more questions. I pinched the bridge of my nose with my fingers and pain pulsed between my eyes.

"Even Salvador is acting strangely around me."

"Curious indeed," Mel said, touching my hand; she was hot against my skin, just like all the other were-animals. That one touch took away my headache and the tension I was holding onto and, like magic, released it from my shoulders and neck.

"How do you do that?"

"It's my gift to you." She smiled.

"Thanks, Mel."

"You have my number. Use it this time. I'm here for you if you want to talk some more. And about anything."

"I will." I climbed off the bed and pulled on my shoes. My shoulder was sore, but it wasn't as bad as it had been. I wouldn't be able to throw a ball any time soon, but I could pull my gun out and shoot. If I had to, I would use my left hand; I'd been training to shoot with both hands, just in case.

I felt the wound at the back of my head. It had been stitched and taped.

"Is it my imagination, or am I healing quicker than humanly possible?"

"Definitely. I think it's because of all those strains inside of you. Were-animals heal faster. It might be worth seeing if you can tap into any of the other lycanthrope characteristics, too."

"Hmm, maybe."

But I could only focus on one problem at a time. I would do all the other stuff when I wasn't chasing the bad guy.

I combed my fingers through my hair and slipped on my shoulder holster and gun.

The priest who had been trying to kill me these last couple of days had to die. If I died trying, then so be it, but he couldn't be allowed to carry on with his murder spree.

And this vampire knew something.

Chapter Eighteen

The apartments Zachary managed were specific accommodation for vampires only. They were in a section of town the mayor had reserved for them when the laws allowing mystical monsters to join society had been passed. It was these same laws that allowed the vampires to own businesses and to employ vampires or humans; and not forgetting that they ensured they had to pay taxes, too.

To protect humans, laws had also been passed to allow assassins like Ulysses to attain contracts to kill any of these monsters: vampire; were-animal; faerie; witch; warlock; voodoo priest; dragon; the list went on. But each contract was only legal if it was sanctioned with the appropriate documentation; it had to be properly researched with enough evidence to confirm that the monster was the correct bad guy they were after.

They installed modern surveillance systems all around the city to monitor the interactions between humans and the monsters, just in case a human killed one of them and it wasn't in self-defense.

Also in these apartments were vending machines on each floor which supplied blood to those vamps who needed a light snack, and there was a cafeteria on the ground floor where willing humans offered themselves to those vampires who could afford it. Some humans offered themselves for free to the more powerful vampires, while others made a living out of it, especially those with the rarest blood type. Apparently, their blood was the most sort after by vamps.

Sebastian was sullen during the car ride. I had other things on my mind; a priest who had been trying to kill Ralph and I for four days. If we survived this, only then could we tend to our personal lives. Yes, it was awful of me to allow Léon to kiss me in the dream he had invaded, and I felt guilty about it, but it was out of my control, wasn't it?

Ralph had been attacked at the same time as when Djimon tried to assault me. Ralph and Devan had been sitting in the garden when a delivery man had jumped on his back and tried to strangle him. Ralph had shot him, but his intention was only to wound him. When they had removed the armband, the delivery guy had told them he had been playing cards with a vampire, a heavyset man, and a man with white hair.

All these attempts on our lives were too coincidental. Hopefully Zachary could shed some light on it for us.

It was already past midnight when we parked outside the apartment block, met with Ralph, and followed Sebastian to Zachary's apartment.

There was a chill in the hallway as we entered; it was warmer outside under the autumn moon. The farther inside the apartment hallways we traversed, the cooler it became; even the floor was a little slippery, as if we were ice-skating.

Ralph pulled his gun out, and so did I. I zipped my jacket all the way to my neck and pulled my hoody over my head. When we exhaled, we saw our breath in front of our faces.

"This isn't normal, Sebastian," I said as we arrived on the third floor.

Sawyer had his gun out, but it was pointed at the floor. He walked ahead of us while Ralph brought up the rear. Ralph had left Devan at his apartment where it would be safer. Sebastian walked beside me.

"No, it's not normal. That's his apartment over there," Sebastian said, pointing, then knocked on the door.

Sawyer came in behind Ralph and stood by the wall near the door. I stayed behind Sebastian. If anyone tried to shoot through the door, they would miss us and give us an opportunity to fire back at them.

Zachary opened the door without asking who had knocked. He wore low cut jeans with the button undone, and naked from the waist up. His brown hair fell loosely around his shoulders.

"Jeez, did you guys bring the snow indoors with you?"

"Can we come in?" Sebastian said, entering the apartment before Zachary could answer. We all followed him.

Zachary's apartment was warm; a stark contrast to the cold hallway. There were two women sitting on the couch in their underwear. When they saw us, they didn't budge from their seat. The four of us stood around while Zachary sat between the two ladies.

"So, what's this all about, Sebastian? Does Léon know you're banging on my door?"

"Where were you earlier, Zachary?"

"Here. Why?"

"Where is the guy with the white hair and white eyebrows?"

Zachary flinched, then went deadly still. He leaned back

against the couch and put his arms around the ladies' shoulders. His face adopted that blank look that told me he was thinking carefully about what to say next.

"I don't know what you're talking about."

"He's lying," I said, stepping closer. I held the gun tightly in my hand until it hurt.

"I know," Sebastian said. "Get out." He motioned for the women to move away so he could sit next to Zachary. They complied and went into one of the bedrooms. Sebastian sat down with one knee on the couch and faced Zachary.

What happened next was too quick for my slow human eyes to see. Sebastian pulled out a knife and held it against Zachary's neck. There was a spine-chilling darkness behind Sebastian's alluring green eyes, and I was glad not to be in Zachary's shoes.

"Have you been playing cards, vampire?" Sebastian said with an edge of a growl.

Zachary pressed his head farther into the couch as Sebastian dug the knife deeper into his throat and drew blood. His muscular arm held the knife in place.

"Vampires are not allowed to play, Zachary. Gambling is illegal for your kind."

"Okay, okay." Zachary lifted his hands, palms facing us.

"Talk, or I'll call Alex and Genevieve to make a ruling over your behavior," Sebastian said, lowering the knife.

"Please don't," he said, his voice quivering slightly.

"Tell us about the man with the white hair."

"You don't want to know about him. The priest is bad news. Don't mess with him."

"We know. But you seem to have helped him to hurt Blaire."

"I didn't know." He glanced at me wide eyed. "I really

didn't know. I owed the guy money. He said we'd be square if I helped him get two guys to wear some weird armbands. One of them had to be a werewolf. It seemed harmless enough."

"You stupid shit." Sebastian relaxed against the sofa.

Again, Sebastian moved too fast for me to see. Blood poured from a knife wound an inch wide across Zachary's throat. Gurgling sounds came from his mouth as red spittle drooled from his lips.

Sebastian had changed the way he was holding the knife. The handle was completely in his hand, but he now pointed the blade away from the pinky finger of his left hand.

He thrust the blade into Zachary's neck a second time.

Zachary was too slow to see it coming. The movement caught everyone off guard, and we all drew our guns and aimed them at Zachary and Sebastian.

"Where can we find this priest now?" Sebastian said.

"He should still be playing cards," Zachary said, coughing up blood.

"Take us there."

"He will know something is wrong if I show up again."

"Say you needed to fetch something."

"Let me change my clothes." Zachary carefully rose from the sofa. His chest was drenched in blood, and his jeans were blotched dark red.

When Zachary returned to the living room, he must have fed on one of his guests because the neck wound had healed and his pale cheeks were pink. He had changed into a light blue shirt with a dark blue tie, black slacks, and black boots. His long brown hair was tied back in a tight ponytail.

We followed him out into the hallway.

Ice had already started to crystallize against the walls

and from the ceiling. Zachary swore under his breath and walked at a brisk pace.

"Zachary, what is happening to the building?" I asked, trying to keep up with him.

"I don't know," he said, and broke out into a jog.

We went up three flights of stairs because the elevator was out of service due to the ice. We stopped at the end of the hallway, at the only black door. The number 119 was written in brass lettering under the peephole. Zachary fumbled with a bunch of keys and eventually found the right one to open the door.

Inside the room was a large table with six men sitting around it. At the head of the table sat a female dealer. They were all busy with their current hand, and one man had called to see the cards of the others. The man was about to put down a straight flush—all hearts—when the ace changed into an eight of clubs. His fists hit the table with a loud thump, spilling all the drinks on its surface.

"You cheated, vampire! You changed my cards for the third time today."

"Don't blame me if you can't play," said the vampire sitting directly across from him, a sly smile on his face.

The man pulled out a gun and shot the other point-blank in the chest. The other players rose from their seats and stood as far away as they could without leaving.

"Mark!" Zachary yelled, pulling the man by his arm and disarming him. "Margaret, you were supposed to take all weapons away."

A woman ran into the room from the hallway and bowed in front of Zachary.

"Sorry," she said, bowing. "Sorry," she repeated and bowed again.

Zachary gave her the weapon, and she ran back from where she had appeared.

"Lukyan, I will ban you for life, old friend."

Lukyan touched the hole in his shirt, stuck his finger in the wound, and licked the blood that coated his fingertip.

"He's been cheating all night. I had to stop him," Lukyan said in a heavy Russian accent. He stood, all eight feet looming over the poker table. "Next," — he pointed a long finger at Mark, — "I kill you." He touched his shirt again. "You make hole."

Mark stepped backward, almost into me. I touched his back, and he stopped.

"Enough. The game is over. It's time for everyone to go. Margaret!" Zachary yelled for the small woman again.

The little woman returned and stood near him. She held one hand in the other in front of her, with her shoulders slumped and her chin pointing in the floors direction; it was an odd, submissive pose.

Her straight black hair was tied in a swirly bun, and several loose strands framed her petite face. Her eyes had epicanthic folds, yet she had blue eyes and light olive skin; either her mother or father was from Asia, while the other was either Nordic or Western.

"Where is the priest?" Zachary asked.

Margaret glanced up at him. "He left a few moments before you arrived, Zachary. Did you not pass him on your way here?" Her eyes flicked to the rest of us, one at a time.

"Did he play cards?"

"He did. But then, " — she glanced at me, then back at Zachary, — "it was like something distracted him. He excused himself, cashed his tokens, and left."

"He must still be in the building, then," I said. But if that were true, why didn't we pass him? There was only one set of stairs and the elevator, which couldn't be used due to the ice.

"Margaret, do you know why there's ice outside in the hallways." Zachary asked.

"What?" she said, and opened the door. The room dropped in temperature and she slammed the door closed, rubbing her arms. "I don't know what to say, Zachary. Strange things have been happening all day. First you disappear," — she pointed a short finger at him, — "then the priest hears voices and leaves. And these two bullies have been going at each other during every game." Lukyan and Mark shrugged in unison.

"Are any of you wearing armbands?" I asked.

"No," everyone said at the same time.

There was something strange happening: the building and its weird weather; the voodoo priest disappearing; the men fighting.

Sebastian started to say something, but either he had trouble with his voice or I couldn't hear him. I glanced at the others.

It all happened slowly. Ralph and Sawyer fell to the floor, and slept. I wanted to bend down to see if they were all right, but I couldn't move my body in their direction. I frowned and then felt a tingling sensation on my face when I did.

As time lapsed, I glanced at Sebastian, but he, too, had slowly fallen to the ground.

Everything was painstakingly slow, and yet it somehow seemed to be going too fast for my mind to comprehend what was happening.

Then, I was the only one still standing. Their eyes were closed and they seemed to be sleeping, all except for Sebastian. He stared at me with wide eyes, immobile, and I saw how frustrated he was that he couldn't talk. I wanted to go to him, but I was stuck; my whole body couldn't move. Sebastian's eyes flitted to the side; to something behind me.

Someone touched my shoulder from behind. My eyes widened, and then I was able to turn slowly to see who had touched me.

The man had the weirdest color eyes; violet, like the flower. His short hair and eyebrows were as white as snow. His pale skin was smooth, like frosting. His full lips were a delicate pink.

When his hands touched my face, blackness and bright stars came.

Chapter Nineteen

There was darkness and the smell of freshly cleaned leather against my cheek. The left side of my face brushed against something soft and padded. My arms were bound above my head; I pulled on the restraints and the rope gave an inch.

I lifted my head. The dim light of the room revealed things hanging on the wall to my right: items such as chokers, a pair of handcuffs, a machete, and a single-tail bullwhip. The room was familiar. I had seen it before with Ralph.

It was the priest's pleasure room. The dark room with the black curtains. I pulled on the restraints again, and the rope gave way enough that I could come up on my elbows. I was on that torture horse that was modified for pleasure. I glanced down and relieved I still had my clothes on. My legs were pulled apart, and each had been loosely bound to a leg of the horse. Out of the corner of my eye, something moved.

"I like you on my horse, Blaire," he breathed. "It's been a while since I've had someone as beautiful as you lying on it like that." He licked his lips. "Your ass sticking out like that for me to do with as I please."

Shit!

I looked over the far right of my shoulder in the general direction of the dark figure in the corner. McNielty, the voodoo priest, stepped forward so I could see him better.

For the last four or five days, we had been trying to catch him and trying to avoid our own deaths in the process. But it was he who had been trying to catch us; taunting us with his voodoo spells, and attacked us. And, somehow, he had always been two steps ahead.

"What do you want from me?" My voice sounded hoarse. I pulled gently on the restraints.

"To finish what I started," he said, stepping closer to me.

"What does that mean?"

"You saw my lovely in the little room downstairs?"

"Yes. I also saw what you did to her?"

"It was not I who did it," he yelled. "It was those men."

"All the men you killed?"

"No, I needed them. I needed their organs to keep her whole for a short while."

"Then who are you talking about?" I asked, my frown deepening.

He stepped closer, and with two fingers caressed my face. I moved out of his unwanted touch.

"You are a tough spirit," he said, smiling. "I like it. My Ophelia could use some of that." His fingers trailed down my back, lingered as he caressed my ass, and swept down my right thigh. He made a guttural sound as he squeezed my thigh. I moved to try to get him off my body, but held on.

"Ophelia will be pleased with the body I've found for her. She would fit perfectly on my pleasure horse."

The room started to shrink, and my skin warmed. My pulse thundered in my ears, and I swallowed hard.

"What do you mean?" I said, my eyes widening.

"I have powerful spells over the dead, which I use to manipulate living souls and move them from an old body into the new. When we saw your bright light, we knew we had to have you. It put our plan into motion. Then everything fell so easily into place."

I didn't understand and it must've shown on my face.

"I am going to put Ophelia's soul into your body," he continued. "Her body was broken too badly by those men."

"Who are these men you keep saying hurt Ophelia?"

I needed to keep him talking to give me enough time to think about my next move, and how I could get out of my restraints and away from him.

"The man with the golden ring and red ruby. He was the same man who kidnapped us all those years ago. He found Ophelia and performed horrific tests on her. When I rescued her, she was broken. You saw what they did to her body. They removed her tongue and cut off her ears. They were brutal. They broke her body, and her mind was almost fractured. But we found a way to keep her mind with us until I could find the right body. Your body."

"I thought you did that to her. You have all those body parts in jars. And that shrine?"

"Those weren't her body parts," he said, the lines between his eyes deepening. "We merely acquired them to keep her alive, to keep her with us. The body parts you saw on the shrine are from a prostitute; she didn't have long to live, anyway. The organs from the eight men fed our power and gave Ophelia enough energy to stay with us."

"Why do you keep her chained up like that?" I asked. My plan was working: he was talking, but I still didn't know how to get out of my current situation.

"To keep her safe."

"Why take the private parts from the two men with the gray eyes?"

"It's part of the ritual we needed to perform."

"Why the attacks on me, on us? If all you wanted was me all along, why not just come and grab me?"

"We needed to test your strength to see what you were capable of doing. Your friend was just something for us to play with; he was sport. But when we couldn't see your white light anymore, we knew something had changed. You had changed. We realized we needed you with us sooner, before something else within you shifted. So, I grabbed you when I could."

His fingers were trailing my back again, soft as a feather, then he stopped suddenly and left the room.

I exhaled nervously, yet relieved he'd left me alone. I didn't want him touching me again. I needed to get off this thing before he started his spell.

Sounds came from below; from the secret room where he kept Ophelia.

I pulled hard on the restraints, and they loosened enough for me to lean my body away from the pleasure horse. I wasn't quite standing, but it was an improvement.

The restraints on my legs were strapped with Velcro, and they looked worn out. With my right leg, I leaned into the strap with my whole body going as far to the right as I could, and I held onto the horse's body. The Velcro started tearing apart. When I was free, I did the same on my left leg. With both legs free, I stepped off the horse and went to the other side where the rope bound my hands. Using my teeth, I pulled on the flap until it came loose.

The sounds from below stopped, then the footsteps grew louder.

My hands were free.

The steps were coming closer.

I grabbed the nearest thing off the wall, climbed back onto the horse, and leaned over it the way he had left me, holding onto the rope. My pulse thumped louder, and my clothing clung to my body.

He was near.

"This is the body I promised you, Ophelia. This is my gift to you," McNielty said as he entered the room with a woman encircled in his arms.

Dried blood trailed down her chin. Her eyes were black and filled with tiny stars like the night sky. Her hair and face were dirty, and her dress was caked with dried blood. Fresh blood trailed down her legs.

"Why is she still bleeding?"

"It's what they did to her," he said, glancing down at her. "No matter what we do, it won't stop until she has a new host."

With her restraints off, I saw Ophelia had a gold armband on each wrist. McNielty noticed what I was staring at and removed his jacket to show his matching gold armbands.

"We were once King and Queen of the red land, a country that linked northeast Africa with the Middle East. We were gods once, Blaire. Gods!"

His admission was interesting. That would mean he had been a Pharaoh in Egypt; either he was telling the truth and moved from one body to another, or he was severely delusional. I wasn't sure which was worse, but I would take delusional over powerful any day.

"Then if you can choose any body you want, why not choose someone of importance?"

"Oh, but you are important!" he said sinisterly. His face blotched red. "We chose unassuming bodies," — he pointed at his chest, — "because we cannot display our true talents to the world. We are not vain. For us to stay alive all these years, we needed to live in the shadows. And it's best if our new bodies are of the mystical type; it makes the transition seamless." He squeezed Ophelia's arms, leaving purple bruises, and she moaned. "Sorry, my love." He kissed her cheek gently.

Squeezing the handle in my left hand, hidden against the other side of the horse so they couldn't see it, was comforting; I didn't feel quite so vulnerable. It felt good to be armed, even if it was only a machete. My gun would have been better, but McNielty had removed it and hidden it somewhere.

"She's restless," McNielty said, concerned for Ophelia "We need to finish this now. The moon isn't at its fullest, but tonight will have to do." He took her by the hand and headed out of the room.

I exhaled slowly, relaxing my grip on the handle, and pushed myself up. When I heard them in the next room, I climbed off the horse.

As quietly as I could, I grabbed the handcuffs off the wall, stuck the key in the front of my pocket, and hooked the cuffs in my jeans. I also took the single-tail bullwhip and stuck the handle down my jeans to keep it in place.

Staying in the doorjamb, I listened at first, then slowly edging farther into the next room to see where they were.

Ophelia, her skin gray and losing life, lay naked on a

table as McNielty gave her a sponge bath. Deep purple marks littered her body.

Nearby were the shelves that held the jars full of body parts and the shrine. I shuddered.

There weren't many options available to me; I could sneak up on them and hope for the best, or I could find my gun and shoot him.

I suspected McNielty could sense me, considering that was how he had previously known we had been in his house. He had said he had been waiting for me, which suggested he had already known of my existence before we even entered his house. When he had first seen my light, my aura, two months ago, that was when his plan had started coming together.

I couldn't wait for him to kill me when Ophelia took over my body. I had to finish this now.

It relieved me that my sneakers were soft on the floor. I gripped the machete tightly in my right hand. In a crouching stance, I approached McNielty and Ophelia, the shelves lined with glass jars between us.

McNielty whispered under his breath as he wiped Ophelia down, cleaning her body as delicately as possible. Her eyes were closed, but tears streaked the sides of her face. McNielty went to the top of the table near her head and started wiping her face, wiping the tear stains away.

My heart thundered in my ears. McNielty glanced up. I held my breath. He wasn't looking at me, but he was looking at something. He was listening to something just above him. He whispered to himself, then continued cleaning Ophelia.

Ophelia moaned and tried to speak, but her words were incoherent. Her hands went between her legs and came back with blood.

"It will be over soon, my love. You will have a new, young, and healthy body. Then we can leave this place. Bryan is expecting us. We need to be quick." McNielty kissed her forehead, put the sponge in the bucket, and headed for the main bedroom.

Ophelia lay still, blood pooling on the table from between her legs. She seemed sad lying there, like a wilting flower. Her pale, bruised skin was smeared with her blood.

I didn't want to hurt her, but the choices were either her or me. I could turn tail and leave through the kitchen, but McNielty would just come after me again. I wanted to survive this. I had to survive them.

The thought of seeing my daughter one day was something that kept me going. The possibility of Sebastian was another.

Ophelia glanced up at me as I approached her. She tried to call out, her dark eyes searching me, but only the faint sound of her voice could be heard.

I had to be quick.

Lifting the machete above my head, I swung downward, hard and fast. The blade of the machete sliced through her neck quietly, quickly and cleanly. I caught her head before it fell to the floor.

This had to be the weapon McNielty used on his male victims when he removed their hands.

I held Ophelia's head in my hands, her eyes wide and her mouth set in a surprised 'O'. She had had no time to mutter. I placed her head back on the table and pushed it against her body so that it was positioned in line with her neck. There; she was almost whole again.

Unfortunately, there was nothing I could do about the blood on the table, and I was running out of time.

Footsteps grew louder as McNielty headed back toward

the room I was in. Not sure where to go, I ducked under the table, crouching with one knee raised and the other foot firmly on the floor.

McNielty stopped near Ophelia's head, his feet in front of me. He squeezed water out of the sponge and started cleaning her again. Her head moved above me and rolled on the table.

"NOOOO!" McNielty cried loudly, as realization of Ophelia's decapitation set in. "No, no, no, no, no! What have you done? Where are you, bitch? I'm going to fucking pull you apart before I kill you. And I'm going to make it hurt."

McNielty ran to his pleasure room in search of me. Now was my only chance. I had to kill him before he killed me. I came out from my hiding spot and stood there, waiting. He came back into the living room and froze when he saw me.

"I'm going to fucking kill you! You cost me my Ophelia!" he cried.

I switched the machete to my other hand and removed the single-tail bullwhip from my pocket. The thong of the whip was made from leather, with several braids and two bellies; this was the center of the braids, which meant it was a high-quality whip; good for me, not so great for the target. It was going to hurt.

I cracked the whip once, then twice, creating a sonic boom sound each time.

McNielty lunged at me, screaming, his hands reaching for my neck. With a quick motion of my wrist, I flicked the whip so that it wrapped around his neck and pulled hard. The momentum of him lunging at me and me pulling his body ensured he was headed directly toward me.

From reflex, I hefted the machete out in front of me and

pierced his sternum, pushing it in as deep as it could go. His chest bone crunched against the machete as it vibrated through the handle. The machete pierced his heart and exited his back.

McNielty collapsed to his knees, his eyes rolling back into his head, and he fell backward onto the floor.

A sharp pain in my ribs caught my attention. I glanced down. There was a knife handle sticking out of my left side. The handle was beautifully made; if it hadn't been embedded in my body, I would've admired it. I only felt the pain when I noticed the wound.

My chest tightened, and my heart raced. My breathing became shallow. Shit. The knife had punctured my lung.

The knife was made from gold and was adorned with intricate patterns and swirls. The detailing reminded me of the armbands. If I had to guess, the voodoo priest used the power of his gold armbands to travel from one body to the next, and had used this knife.

McNielty lay motionless on the floor. I kicked his hand for proof of life, but there was no movement; the handcuffs were no longer necessary.

He was well and truly dead.

Kneeling down, I pulled both armbands off him, but the movement pushed the golden blade deeper inside me. Bright, sparkly stars clouded my vision. I rose, holding onto the table until I could focus properly. With short shallow breaths, I could stand unaided.

I needed to stay conscious long enough to remove Ophelia's armbands and destroy them. If McNielty could swap souls, it was too powerful to leave them lying around. I had to destroy them.

Unfortunately, after a brief search, there was nothing inside the house that could truly melt gold. I settled on the microwave, set it on high, and set the timer for twenty minutes.

I grabbed the cleanest dishcloth I could find and placed it around the hilt of the knife to stop the bleeding. Mel would have to remove the blade; I wouldn't attempt to take it out myself. Until then, I had to stay alive.

I opened the gas on the stove and exited by the kitchen door. I walked away from the house, one queasy step at a time, applying pressure to the dishcloth as I ambled to the sidewalk.

After a few minutes, a loud noise erupted from the house. The microwave exploded and ignited the gas from the stove. Debris from the roof fell onto the lawn and sparks flew into the black sky. It reminded me of the Fourth of July.

Chapter Twenty

For a change, I was conscious in the hospital bed, or rather the bed in Mel's infirmary at the Labyrinth. She had stopped the bleeding and removed the knife from between my ribs without my lung collapsing or me dying.

Even though I had already started healing, I was still hooked up to an I.V. It had only been two hours after we'd arrived, but already the wound had begun to form soft pink scar tissue. Yay for vampire marks and having three strains of lycanthropy.

I'd managed to call Sebastian to inform him of my whereabouts, so when he, Ralph, and Sawyer had arrived at McNielty's house, they had found me lying on the sidewalk in a pool of blood. It was déjà vu all over again.

By the time the ambulance and police cars had started to arrive, we were already leaving the crime scene. But not before Ralph had inspected the house, making sure the flames were hot enough that no one could escape. I'd chopped Ophelia's head off and pierced McNielty's heart with a machete. I was certain they weren't going anywhere, but he checked anyway.

Luckily, the infirmary was big enough to accommodate everybody standing around as I recalled what had happened. Even Léon was there, although he and Sebastian stood on opposite sides of the room and glared at one another. I could feel their power in the air and on my skin, and it was thick enough to cut through.

The three of us needed to sit down and talk about what was happening, but the intense pull I felt for both of them wasn't something we could discuss lightly. I didn't know what was going on or why I felt this way. The whole thing left me feeling slightly sluttish, even though I hadn't bedded either of them. Yet.

Right this moment, we needed to make sure we were safe and received our money for the contract we'd fulfilled.

"Do you know who kidnapped Ophelia in the first place and why?" Sebastian asked as he reached for my hand.

"No," I said.

Devan entered the room looking paler than usual. His translucent eyes were startling; one green, one blue. He averted his eyes, standing at the back of the room.

"We went back to the house after the emergency services had doused the fire and left," Ralph said. "We found flecks of gold among the rubble, but we picked up most of it." Ralph shrugged nonchalantly. "Just in case someone went back to the house looking for it."

"Great."

"And Martin says 'thanks'," Ralph said.

"I bet he does," I replied with a hint of sarcasm. "Now tell him to pay up."

"I'll make sure of it." Ralph smiled. "Thank Christ it's

over. I was worried for a moment. It's like McNielty knew everything about us. I doubt he got all that just from sensing us in his house one time." Ralph said, taking the words right out of my mouth.

"I agree, Ralph. Someone who knows us helped him." Now we needed to find out who.

"Okay everyone, get out," Mel said when I was silent for too long. "Blaire needs to rest." She held my forearm and pushed power into me. It made me lie back on the pillows, my eyelids suddenly heavy.

"You're like a human drug. One touch, and I'm floating," I said through clouds and buttercups.

"I also opened the drip with my other hand." She giggled under her breath.

"Ah, that explains the buttercups."

"What?" She laughed.

Everyone left the room except for Mel. I did one of those slow blinks as everyone left. I think Sebastian and Léon waved at me as they exited. Another slow blink, and Mel blurred around the edges. One last blink and I slept.

There were no dreams as I slept, but I moved. No, someone was carrying or pushing me. Actually, I couldn't be sure. The only thing I could be sure of was I was moving and the aroma of disinfectant. Wherever I was, it was clean; recently scrubbed down.

I opened my eyes, but all I saw was black. The drugs were strong; I wasn't usually this groggy. I moved my arms, as heavy as they were, to touch my face. My clumsy fingers weren't my own, but I could touch my face.

Numb. Either my fingers were numb, or my face was numb. It was the same kind of weird feeling in your jaw and cheek after a Novocain injection.

I cleared my throat. The footsteps stopped. I stopped.

"Are you awake?" he whispered near the shell of my ear. His breath smelled distinctly of mouthwash, with a hint of cigarette.

My tongue and lips wouldn't move; couldn't move.

"We're almost there." His cold hands touched my cheek. We moved again. Then sleep took hold of me and I drifted away.

I woke but kept my eyes closed. The feel of the soft and fluffy duvet over me was comforting. I snuggled inside the covers, with the disinfectant smell lingering just above the surface.

I flinched and opened my eyes, pulling the duvet off, and sat up; the wound in my ribs stinging from the sudden movement. I ran my fingers over the fresh wound and felt the soft scar tissue.

I glanced around the room. It was painted teal, with a white dresser, a white chair, and a white door. I tried to climb out of bed, but I couldn't. I threw the duvet off and found restraints around my ankles.

"Morning, Blaire," someone said over a speaker, but I couldn't see where the speakers were.

"You're probably wondering who I am and what you're doing here?"

"Yeah, the thought crossed my mind," I said. My head no longer as cloudy as it was before.

The door opened, and McNielty walked in. My mouth opened in a surprised 'O'.

"I watched you die. You can't be alive."

"If I can fool you, I can fool anyone." He smirked.

"But you died at my feet!" I sounded angry, and I was. I remembered the feel of the machete as it had pierced his heart and exited his back. I had thought removing his armbands would help, but I was wrong. So wrong.

He was more powerful than I thought.

McNielty sat on the only chair in the room. He wore faded blue jeans, sneakers, a white shirt, and a white hoodie. His white clothing, hair, and eyebrows made him look ghostlike.

"What should I do to you for killing me? What should I do to you for killing Ophelia?"

"I don't know. But if you plan on killing me, just get it over and done with already. Enough shit has happened these last couple of months and teasing me is only pissing me off."

"So feisty; I love it." His mouth curved upward, making the lines at the corner of his eyes more prominent.

I crossed my arms over my chest. I exhaled slowly, opened my eyes, and glared into his green eyes. I frowned.

"I thought your eyes were a different color."

"Yeah? What color would that be?"

"Violet. It's hard to forget a unique eye color like that." I studied his face. "You're twins?"

He leaned back in the chair and crossed his arms over his chest, with one leg over the other. He pursed his lips and held his gaze on me, like he was thinking about what to say next.

"You were the one doing the killings?" I said, finally realizing how he'd done it.

He flinched, then went back to glaring at me.

"That's why the police couldn't get anything to stick on Ross, because they were focusing on the wrong person. You killed those men while your brother stayed at home and looked after Ophelia."

He tipped his head slightly.

"Very perceptive," — he touched his chest, — "my name is Bryan."

Ross had mentioned him. He and Ophelia had been planning to meet someone after they'd stolen my body.

"Bryan, you were free. No one knew about you. Why come back for me? Why didn't you just leave?"

"You took everyone I love away from me," he said sadly. "The moment you killed them, a part of me died, too. Their light forever gone. How could I leave with only my dim light shining? I'm in darkness now. I have nothing left, and you took it all away from me." Bryan raised his voice with the last sentence and pointed a finger at me.

"We can go around in circles, but you and your brother killed eight men. You tried several times to kill me, while forcing my hand to kill them in self-defense. I won't hesitate doing it again."

He nodded a few times then swallowed hard.

"Ophelia was ours. We tried to save her, but it was too late. They did too much damage to her. The same men who took us found her. They did to her what they did to us. They experimented on us, drugged us. All because we were different." He laughed. "And the best part? These weren't the bodies we were born with. We found the twins in Haiti, when they were teaching their art to students. It was easy, but it cost us so much more."

"What Ophelia was subjected to was terrible, and I'm sorry it happened. But what both of you did to those eight men was just as bad, if not worse. You removed their organs, replaced them with a voodoo doll, and dumped them like garbage. Those men had families. They provided for their families. Now, their families are in mourning, too. You took their loved ones away from them."

"It was wrong, but Ophelia was more important to us," Bryan said, closing his eyes and exhaled slowly. "I'm sorry for what we did, but she was ours." He opened his eyes and stared at me with contempt. "We have been together for centuries, moving from one country to another, one continent to the next. From one old body to a younger one. It was always the three of us. Always." His hard eyes softened and glistened with unshed tears.

"What are you going to do to me?"

"I haven't decided yet." He stood, and touched my arm. "But it will hurt."

Bryan closed his eyes, concentrated, and squeezed his fingers around my arm. His scalding hot fingertips burned deeply into my flesh. I tried to pull my arm out of his grip, but he held my arm down and pressed harder. I struggled for air. The agony was thick and suffocating. His fingertips pushed so deeply into my skin that blood pooled around his nails.

"That hurts, Bryan. Let me go. Please. Please let me go."

"You killed them, Blaire. I'm sorry, I really am, but I can't forgive you for taking them away. I am nothing without them. I would rather die than live another day without them. And I'm taking you with me." He blinked and tears fell.

The heat coming from him burned along my arm and through my veins like scalding hot water. The veins in my hands started turning black as my blood boiled.

When I screamed, so did Bryan. I struggled to breathe, and so did Bryan. We were both hyperventilating as he burned me from the inside, removing the oxygen from the air keeping us alive.

My chest rose and fell.

I closed my eyes and thought about my session with Seraphine. I needed to concentrate on the power he was using against me. I had a metaphysical picture of what he was doing to me; how he was burning me alive from the inside.

I could counteract the heat. I could use the white light that was all me, and turn Bryan's sizzling power into my weapon and thrust it back into him. I had to try or we'd both die.

I screamed again, and touched Bryan's arm with my free hand.

I held him tightly and pushed the searing fire back into him. I forced it into him as I screamed. As he screamed. The veins in his hand started turning black under his pale skin. Then the fire travelled up his arm, leaving a map of dark veins all the way up to his neck.

When the whole left side of his body was marked by his own scalding power; it crept up his neck to his jawline and near his ear. His face was mapped with dark veins as his own power burned through his blood.

His eyes turned yellow and bulged from their sockets. Bryan swayed and coughed, and spat thick, dark liquid from his mouth. His grip relaxed around my arm. He fell to his knees, his hand no longer gripping mine, but I still held onto his arm.

I pushed the last bit of blazing power back into him until there was only coldness; my cool white light coursing through my veins.

Only Bryan's arm was still on the bed. I let go of it and the rest of him slumped to the floor. I hung from the bed and dug in his pockets, pulling out a set of keys, a wallet, and a cellphone. I tried the keys on the lock that bound my ankles to the bed until I found one that clicked the locks open. Then I called Ralph. His number was the only one I remembered.

Chapter Twenty-One

"Is the money in the Ulysses account?" I asked, spooning yoghurt into my mouth.

"Yep," Ralph said, setting his plastic knife and fork on the paper plate.

"Did he shortchange us?"

"I made Martin give us a bonus, actually; twenty percent extra. It was the least he could do."

"Good." I grinned.

"How are we splitting it?"

"Three ways," Ralph said, glancing at Devan, whose smile lit the room.

"I've never seen you smile so broadly, Devan. Glad to know you're human after all," I teased.

"What about me?" Marcus said through gritted teeth.

"You deserve nothing, Marcus. Haven't you been listening to what we've been saying to you?" Ralph said, his boot on Marcus's face.

Melinda whimpered beside me.

"What are you going to do with us?" she cried, avoiding eye contact.

After I had pushed Bryan's power into him and killed him, I had called Ralph to give him my location, and I had gone through the phone while I waited for Ralph to fetch me. I had found Marcus's name and number saved in the contact list. Marcus and Bryan had exchanged many messages and phone calls over the past year, but nowhere near as many as during the past week.

It transpired that Marcus had developed a gambling problem, and he loved playing cards once a week with Zachary and Ross McNielty. Courtesy of the nervous twitch in his left eye which seemed to give his game away, Marcus had soon found himself owing large sums of money to the two men.

When Marcus hadn't been able to pay what he owed two months ago, he had taken Shane with him to one of his poker games. Shane had won a few hands, lost some, but overall, he had walked out with enough money to clear Marcus's debt and then some.

It had been Ross McNielty who had realized that Shane had been counting cards to win, and he had followed them to Marcus's house. Once there, McNielty had knocked Marcus unconscious, ripped Shane's limbs from his body, and left his torso in my car, which Shane had borrowed. Marcus had driven the car to my house and had told me that Shane would meet me at the rendezvous spot. That had been the evening I was attacked. Unbeknownst to me, I had been driving my car that night with Shane's torso in the trunk.

When McNielty had discovered my beacon of white light, he knew he had to have me, given that I would be the perfect vessel for their broken Ophelia. That was when he and Bryan had devised a plan and started exchanging messages with Marcus, forcing him to tell them more about me, along with my whereabouts. They had known that if the cops couldn't get enough evidence against Ross about the murders, Ulysses Assassins would be issued with the contract.

Zachary had been very forthcoming with all this information. He would have Alex—who was visiting on Vampire Council business—on his ass if he didn't.

In order for Bryan to reach me at the Labyrinth infirmary, he had controlled one of Léon's guards with one of the armbands. He had managed to wheel me out as if nothing was wrong and had brought me to his hideout. The guard was dismissed immediately. I felt bad for him, but he had been compromised so easily, and Léon wouldn't stand for insolence.

Fast forward to today, and Marcus had confessed to it all. He had seemed relieved to finally get it all off his chest. He cried and had begged for our forgiveness, for all that had happened because of his fuck-up.

Unfortunately, I wasn't in the forgiving mood. Even though he was our boss, there were just too many things that went wrong when we had to involve Marcus.

He was a liability.

He was a danger to all our lives.

We had asked Léon if his lawyer could draw up some paperwork for us, transferring the Ulysses Assassins business over to myself and Ralph as joint owners, and Marcus signed without reading the new contract. Marcus was very cooperative and kept glancing at Troy, his King, for approval.

We were at the Lion's Den, with Troy's blessing, to punish Marcus for all his wanton behavior. And from what Keegan had alluded to, Melinda was still tinkering with her serum, and that boy, Tommy, had passed away as a result. That was her last warning. Today was the day where both would be punished.

Ralph and I had got what we wanted. We were the new owners of Ulysses Assassins.

Ralph removed his foot off Marcus's face, but he stayed on the ground.

"What now?" Marcus said, slowly pushing himself up from the ground. He dusted sand off his face when he sat.

"What usually happens when one of your own is disobedient? What do you do?" I asked while on my haunches in front of him, my gun firmly in my hand.

Marcus swallowed hard, and it sounded like it hurt. He squeezed his eyes shut, then opened them. "We tell him to run." He glanced in the direction of the forest.

"And then what?"

"Then we chase after him."

"Go on…"

"And we make sure he doesn't make it back." His eyes shone with unshed tears.

I rose and leered at him, aiming my gun at him and staring down the sight. I went to the dark place that was mine; where it was quiet and calm. It would've been too easy to pull the trigger. I wanted him to suffer for what he had done to Shane and me. He was a selfish bastard.

"You can't kill me. I… I know too much about your past," Marcus said quickly.

"Excuse me?" I lowered my gun, and my frown deepened.

"I'm the only one who knows who you truly are; where you came from, what happened to your family, and the whereabouts of your daughter. You can't afford to kill me unless you remember."

My hand squeezed the gun until it hurt, and without thinking, I hit him in the face with the gun.

"Why are you only saying this now, Marcus? You're such an asshole! Tell me what you know, and now." Blood rushed through my veins, and I had to steady myself against a chair.

"You need me, Blaire. You kill me or Melinda and you lose everything I know." Blood trickled out the cut I had made above his eye. He looked at me with dark, empty blue eyes.

I screamed my frustration.

Keegan rose and said something to Troy which I couldn't hear. Troy nodded.

"Marcus, you are one slimy fucker," Troy said with contempt. "Blaire, has your memory returned?"

I shook my head a little too quickly. I didn't trust my voice to speak. The back of my throat hurt, and I blinked back tears. I refused to cry in front of Marcus.

"All right, we have a lock-up system downstairs—"

"No!" Melinda yelled, interrupting Troy. "Not the lock-up, Troy!" Tears streamed down her face.

"We should let you loose, Melinda, and hunt you down for what you did. But Marcus played a good hand and spoiled our fun. You can't be trusted any more than we can trust him. We need to keep you both locked up until we know what to do with you."

"My eye doesn't always twitch." A fine smile played

across Marcus's face. "I still have some good hands left to play."

I hit him in the face again, across the eye that always twitched.

The lock-up system in the Lion's Den basement had four cages strong enough to hold new were-lions during their first full moons. It was to keep them safe until they could control their animal and not shred anyone who was around them when they shifted.

They would hold Marcus and Melinda in these cages until we made a decision.

Or until my memory returned.

Whichever happened sooner.

Chapter Twenty-Two

The air had a chill to it, like drops of ice slicing through my skin. I was the only one fully clothed, wearing boots, jeans, a long-sleeved shirt, my holster and gun, a jersey, and a long coat that reached my ankles to shield me from the wind.

Most of the were-leopards wore old clothing they didn't mind shredding when they shifted. Anne, the alpha female of the leap, wore cotton shorts and a tank top. I asked if she was cold, and all she did was smile.

Kai and Lee wore matching blue jogging shorts and a stupid grin when they saw me.

Sebastian wore old jeans he had picked up at the thrift shop. They were missing the top button, so I had a great view of his inguinal crease. He was naked from the waist up, and the light hit his body on all the right places; his broad shoulders, the smooth lines across his hips, and the fine hairs that ran down into the front of his jeans.

"Blaire?" Sebastian said, standing closer and out of the light.

"Yeah," I said without blushing. It wouldn't have been

the first time he'd caught me staring, and I doubted it would be the last.

"Are you ready?" he said with a grin.

"I guess." This was to be the first time I would see him shift. I wasn't exactly sure how I felt about it, but here I was; as ready as I would ever be.

"Remember what I told you?"

"Uh, huh!"

On the way to the leap, Sebastian had gone over all the things I could expect from my first full moon with the leopards. The fact that it was a Blue Moon shouldn't change anything. I was crossing fingers that everyone behaved.

Sebastian had counted on his fingers all the points I should know.

One: Everybody would shift, and I should stand out of the way. Apparently, some shifting could get violent, as in blood violence; all it took was one moody leopard for hell to break loose.

Two: They would hunt, and at least two wild animals would be killed and brought back for the feast. Alternatively, they would feast where the animal was killed in the forest. I should expect blood, guts, and smells.

Three: They would feast on Grant's body afterward. I wasn't looking forward to that particular part of the evening, but since I had shot him, I would watch out of respect, it was the least I could do.

When I asked why they did this, Sebastian's answered as delicately as possible.

"When any of us die," he had said. "We all feast on that person to ensure they metaphysically stay with the leap forever." Again, I wasn't sure what to expect or how I'd feel watching them feed.

Four: There would be a lot of naked bodies afterward. It

was normal. It was not sexual, and I shouldn't feel jealous. I thought I might ask Rory for the car keys at this point.

Five: Sawyer and Rory would stay with me during the evening. I appreciated this point. At least I had company while the leopards were hunting.

With the meeting taking place outside, there was space for all the were-leopards to attend. The leap weren't as many in numbers as the were-wolves, but their numbers were increasing.

I stood beside Sebastian when Anne stood on the low stage at the far end of the field near her house in the mountains.

The murmurs died down when Anne lifted her hand. Her children, Greg and Ivy, stood beside her as she welcomed everyone to the Blue Moon Feast. She lowered her gaze to Sebastian and asked that he stand beside her. He squeezed my hand as he left. I stood closer to Sawyer and Rory, who stood near the fence surrounding the land.

Anne said a blessing for the Blue Moon Feast and one for Grant and welcomed me to my first full moon. She warned Sawyer and Rory that what they saw that evening was Leap business and they were only there to protect me. There were no objections to us attending, so Anne continued with other business.

My eyes scanned all the were-leopards; they were all shapes and sizes and came from different ethnic backgrounds. Lycanthropy did not discriminate, it seemed. They were all athletic, with only a handful of round tummies from fast food and beers.

"So glad you could make it, Blaire."

I flinched when I heard someone's voice and felt their breath close to my ear. I glanced over my shoulder and

Phillip grinned at me. I smiled back, but it wavered around the edges.

"Hi, Phillip, how are the sides Greg clawed you?" I said, turning my attention back to Anne.

Hands slid around my waist and pulled me closer. I hooked my fingers into his hands and pried him off my body.

"Let go of me, Phillip," I said with the full weight of my stare.

"Is there a problem?" Sawyer said, looming over us.

Phillip let go of me and I stood beside Sawyer.

"You're a big motherfucker, aren't ya, fella?"

"Blaire?"

"It's all right, Sawyer." I squeezed Sawyer's forearm. "Phillip will behave himself. Won't you, Phillip?"

"Maybe," he said, licking his lips.

Phillip stared at me with a burning need. His gaze raked up my body, painfully slowly; from my shoes, up my legs, then stopped in the general area of my breasts and, eventually, my face. The implication was very sexual, and I tried not to let it affect me; he seemed the type who enjoyed my repulsion.

"If I were Sebastian, I would look over my shoulder."

"Is that a threat, Phillip? Would you like Sebastian to knock you on your ass again?" I said, then smiled. It wasn't a friendly smile. It was the smile I reserved for the monsters.

He snorted, then grimaced, looking at something above me. I turned around and saw Sebastian stood behind me, leering at Phillip.

It was then I realized how vast Sebastian's frame really was. Despite being six foot two, he was always tender toward me, and I had always found his height to be unthreatening. But now he seemed massive and spine-chilling.

Phillip laughed, and trickles of power exploded into the air like confetti. I shuddered and rubbed my arms as his power fell over me like acid rain drops.

"Are you misbehaving again?" Sebastian asked.

"Nope," — Phillip lifted his hands, palms facing us, —"I was just welcoming Blaire. That is what you want us to do, isn't it? Welcome her into our leap?" His eyes flicked to me when he said the last part.

"Phillip, is there an issue?" Anne said loudly. The crowd turned to face us.

"Jesus!" He laughed. "Everybody just needs to calm the fuck down. I was just saying hi to Blaire, and Prince Sebastian was turning it into an issue." He edged closer to where Anne was standing. "Although I would like to challenge again, if I may, Anne? Are we still allowed to challenge in this fucking family?"

"Yes, Phillip." Anne sighed audibly. "This family doesn't rule like a monarchy; you can challenge anyone at any time. Who would you like to challenge?"

"Ivy."

Everyone gasped.

"What, me?" Ivy said, lifting her gaze to her mother. "Are you serious?" She asked with pleading eyes.

"Oh, I'm going to enjoy this," Phillip said, rubbing his hands together.

"Fuck," Sebastian muttered under his breath.

"Can she fight?" I said near Sebastian's ear.

He shook his head.

"Fine, let's get this over and done with," Ivy said.

Ivy must have had some training because she was in

defense mode, rocking back and forth on the balls of her feet.

Phillip crouched, ready to attack.

The leap crowded around them in a circle. Kai blew a whistle, and they started fighting. Phillip started the fight by punching Ivy first. The rest of the fight was a blur of speed. There were *oohs* and *aahs* from the crowd, but I couldn't see who was winning.

"Is it to the death?" I asked, leaning against Sebastian.

"Luckily not, but it may be close," he said, keeping an eye on the fight.

"I can't see the fight properly. Who's winning? Can you see anything?" I said, rambling on.

He glanced at me and smiled, lowering his face to mine for a kiss.

"You're so cute," he said, pulling away.

I frowned.

"So far, it's a tie, but Phillip fights dirty. Ivy has trained a little with us, so I'm hoping she can see through his tricks."

"I hope so."

"Step back." Kai blew the whistle. "Medic! Where's Mel?" he yelled.

Even though Mel was a were-wolf and it was a full moon, she was allowed to join any of the animal groups. Luckily, this month, she had chosen to share the moon with the leopards.

"What? What is it? I can't see," I said, standing on tiptoes.

The crowd closed in on the two fighters.

"Coming through. Out of my way," Mel said as she pushed through the crowd. "Move, dammit!"

Anne's eyes glittered in the light.

Greg's mouth gaped open.

Sebastian flinched, then froze like a marble statue.

"How is Ivy?" I said, trying to see through the wave of people.

"Sawyer!" Sebastian yelled.

"Yes, Sebastian," Sawyer said, approaching quickly.

"Keep her safe." Then he was gone. He darted through the crowd. In a speed of light, he flew into Phillip, and the two men crashed into the far side of the fence on the other side of the field.

"Sebastian, no!" Anne screamed, but they didn't hear.

The two men fought away from the crowd. I saw Phillip fly into the air as Sebastian threw him and crashed into a large tree. He started laughing, which only angered Sebastian.

"You can't hurt me, Sebastian! I won fair and square," Phillip said, yelling loud enough for everyone to hear.

Anne edged near them and stopped the fight. She was speaking to Sebastian, but I couldn't hear what she was saying.

The crowd moved toward the three, and I saw Mel kneeling beside Ivy.

Ivy was staring at me, but her body was facing in the opposite direction. There was a small spark left, but the light was fading from her eyes. That glassy look in her eyes triggered something within me.

Pain seared through my chest, and the back of my throat ached. The smell of ash and soot wafting in the air reminded me of something important, but I couldn't quite place it. That tiny spark of Ivy was worth searching for.

"Can I help?" I asked, kneeling alongside Mel.

"No, dear; it was a clean break. No matter how powerful the were-animal is, they can't heal something like this," Mel said, and closed Ivy's eyes.

I reached for Ivy's hand and it was warm in mine. I closed my eyes and allowed my metaphysical metal walls to dip just a little. I allowed the pure white of my aura to shine through. I used the white of my aura to look for that small spark inside Ivy.

I searched near her heart first and found that she was a good person. She didn't have a mean bone in her body, and the only reason she had fought Phillip was because tradition had forced it upon her. Greg and Sebastian had made her train with them in case of such eventualities.

Her heart was still beating, although the flutter was slow and losing its rhythm. I moved away from her heart and continued my search within.

When I found that tiny light, the white of my aura brushed past it until there was a flame that burned brightly. I found her snapped neck, and as I kneaded her hand in mine, I pictured her bones joining, her tissue knitting together, and her veins mending. My white aura coursed through her, straightening bones, inflating bruised organs, and smoothing out bumps.

"Jesus!" Mel said, screaming. "ANNE!"

I heard people running in the distance, but I ignored them. I held onto Ivy. I held onto the light that was her.

From the loss I felt when I saw her broken body, I knew I couldn't let Ivy die when there was still something left to save. I wanted to know if what I remembered was real or if it was only feasible in my dreams. When I opened my eyes, bright wide eyes stared back at me and a grin splashed across her face.

Ivy would be just fine.

"Holy shit! Did you know about this, Sebastian?" someone from the crowd asked.

"What about you, Mel? Did you know?" said another.

I let go of Ivy's hand, and she sat up.

I rose, blood rushed to my ears, and I grabbed the nearest arm to hold on to.

"Are you okay?" said the owner of the arm I was holding onto. I recognized his voice and turned.

Jeremiah grinned. He was naked, but it didn't bother me this time. I must have been more tired and drained than I thought.

"I'll be fine, thanks," I said, letting go of his arm, swaying slightly.

Mel stood beside me.

"Blaire, how, what, when?" she said, questioning everything without asking a specific question.

"I don't know." I laughed. "I'm not sure." I shrugged. "I wanted to find out if maybe there was a possibility that I could. That I could heal her."

"Thank you, Blaire," Anne said, hugging me. "You saved my baby." My shoulder was damp with her tears.

"Ah, Mom, please don't call me that," Ivy said in a weak voice.

Anne laughed. It was a comforting sound.

Chapter Twenty-Three

Sawyer, Rory and I huddled around a fire pit. The flames were high and warm against my face. All the were-leopards were hunting.

Phillip was pissed that I had ruined his chances of moving up the proverbial monarchy ladder, and had disappeared in the forest with a couple of human ladies who were waiting for him.

Sebastian was lost in the crowd when everyone shifted. I missed him changing into his black beast.

When I saw him, he was a beautiful large kitty-cat with grass green eyes and a gold ring around the iris. He moved toward me like liquid muscle, licked my hand, and scent-marked me before disappearing with the rest of the leap into the forest.

Sawyer had come up with a brilliant idea of making a bonfire while we waited for the leopards to return.

After about an hour, the first leopard arrived. It was Anne; I recalled her golden-gray coat. She moved with those liquid mercury muscles covered in fur to her house.

When she came out, she was human again with a gown wrapped tightly around her.

"I thought you had to stay in your leopard form until the next day?" I said with a frown.

"If you're as old as me, you don't need to." She winked.

"You can shift back so easily?" Sawyer asked.

"Yes, and as you will see, Sebastian can, too. But most of the others will stay leopards until daybreak or until after they have eaten and rested." Her smile played gently across her face, and she sat cross-legged on the grass near the fire.

"This was a lovely idea. We usually roam in darkness, eat, then sleep in a pile until daybreak." She shifted closer to the fire. "And, Blaire, thank you again for bringing my Ivy back to me. I hate Phillip for what he did, but I'm grateful she will be fine."

"I'm glad I could help, Anne."

When I remembered the dream I'd had of me trying to heal my daughter, I'd wanted to know if it was only a dream or if I really had it in me to heal injuries. And so I had tried out my theory on Ivy. She still had a spark of life left, and I couldn't let her wilt away.

Leaves rustled at the edge of the forest. Sawyer and Rory stood with their guns out, pointed in the direction of the noise. A black shadow moved, a black leopard headed toward us. The face of the black leopard changed to a familiar one, the soft black fur receded, and the animal stood upright. He was human once again.

Sebastian walked closer to me with smooth dexterity, all the muscles working together like a well oiled machine.

I forgot there were others around us. I stared at Sebastian; at his body, from his head to his toes. I glanced at all his nakedness and felt the heat flush from my chest to my head.

My pulse beat hard in my veins. My body went tight down below as he move toward me.

There was an urgent need to touch him. To run my fingers over his body. I'd waited long enough. I didn't want to wait any longer. I wanted him now more than ever.

I rose from my seat and closed the distance between us.

He picked me up, and I wrapped my arms around his neck and my legs around his waist. He grabbed my ass and pushed my body hard against his. He grinned and leaned in for a kiss that was hard and wanting so much more, and he guided me toward the house.

My clothes were off. In the heat of our kissing, everything went onto the ground except my gun, which I placed on the bedside table with my shoulder holster.

We were in a room Sebastian used whenever he stayed over at Anne's house. And we were naked. Sebastian lifted me up, my legs wrapped around his waist and pinned me against the wall.

He kissed down my neck, nibbling gently as he went. He hovered near that pulse in my neck and, for a moment, I thought he was going to take a bite. Instead he sucked gently. I moaned and arched my back, giving him access to my breasts. He stopped and stared at me, the look in his eyes typical of a man's desire for a woman.

"Are you sure?" he whispered.

"Yes, I want you. I want you now, Sebastian."

He didn't have to ask a second time. He went to the bed with me still wrapped around his waist and laid me down gently. He lay beside me and kissed each breast, sucking on my nipples until they were hard.

His hand tickled my stomach, causing all the hairs on my body to stand on end. Then he went lower, caressing my thighs and pushing my legs open. His fingers found my soft silky folds, and I gasped as he pushed in a finger, exploring my delicate depths. When two fingers entered, I bit my lip, my breathing now quick and heavy.

"God, you're so wet and tight." He whispered gruffly and kissed me.

I whimpered in pleasure as his fingers worked their magic inside me. My body tightened around his fingers as he continued to caress that spot, sending shockwaves through me.

Sebastian slowly removed his fingers, and my eyes shot open. He grinned mischievously. He moved above me, supporting himself on his arms and staring down at me. My heart raced, waiting in pleasurable anticipation. I didn't know how long it had been since I had last been with a man. But lying beneath Sebastian, our bodies touching, the intimacy made it feel like it was my first time all over again.

He positioned himself between my legs and rubbed the tip against my opening, tempting, teasing me.

"Please, Sebastian."

"Please what?"

"Stop teasing me." I swallowed hard, my throat dry.

"Only because you said please so sweetly." He grinned again, showing his fangs.

He entered me slowly, and I wasn't sure if I could take all of him. He started maneuvering slowly in and out, allowing me to adjust to his size. When he was almost all the way out, he kept just the tip inside and then, in one swift motion, thrust inside me again.

That one movement caused me to writhe from the feel of him working his way in. I glanced down the line of his body as he pushed inside me again and again, and that alone made everything tight down below.

He stared lovingly as he pushed a little harder with each thrust, but not so hard that there was pain. He continued until he found his rhythm, pushing ever so gently, yet hard enough that he hit that sweet spot every time.

I rode the wave of his body going in and out of mine. Goosebumps covered my skin as he worked his way in and out, thrusting his hips until I cried out his name in pleasure. My body tensing before the first wave hit and I climaxed around him; my body writhing beneath his.

He spasmed inside me, his body tight against mine. He flung his head backward, eyes closed as his body shuddered while orgasming. He went deeper inside one last time, buried as deep inside me as possible, I orgasmed again and dug my nails into his ass.

He slid out of me, and that made me writhe again. He collapsed onto his side to lie beside me. My pulse continued thundering in my ears, my skin tingling from Sebastian's touch, and I swallowed twice before I could find my voice.

"That was... wow," I said, and kissed him.

A *hmm* sound escaped his mouth, and his lips found mine again.

"I can't go again."

"Did I hurt you?" He chuckled.

"A little." Heat crept up my neck, and my cheeks warmed. "It's been a while."

He pecked my cheek, removed the condom, and threw it in the bin. I was not on any birth control and had asked that he use a condom. Even though the likelihood he would father a child was slim, I didn't want to take the chance.

"I could lie here with you all evening, but we should probably go. We still need to finish the feast," he said. He lay beside me again, nibbled on the breast closest to him, and caressed my waist with a fingertip, trailing lower.

I moved onto my side to face him and kissed him again. My body was still tingling with sexual satisfaction.

I'd almost forgotten about the feast.

"I would much rather stay here with you, but I suppose we should clean up and join the others." I said reluctantly.

He trailed the fine scar across my abdomen and kissed it gently.

"I'm sorry this happened to you, but if it hadn't, we wouldn't be together," he said with a hint of sadness.

I smiled and wrapped my arms around his neck for one last embrace before we climbed out of bed.

We cleaned up as best we could; Sebastian pulled on clean jeans and a shirt from a closet, and we went outside.

Sawyer and Rory stared at us suspiciously, with a look that said they knew what we had just done; we ignored them.

I sat between them with Sebastian behind me.

Everyone was back from the hunt; most were still big kitty-cats, and the more powerful ones had changed back into their human form. Some stayed naked, while others had changed into spare clothing.

Grant's body was on an offering table near the fire. There was a glass beside his head filled with dark liquid.

Greg lifted the glass and said a few words similar to a prayer. He took a sip and offered the glass to Anne, who sipped and passed it on. Greg lowered Grant's body to the ground and called the leopards in animal form to feast. There was some hesitation at first, but after one took a bite, the others soon followed.

I turned away.

I stared at the trees of the forest and felt swirls of power surround me and the leap. Whatever was happening, it was because of everyone feasting on Grant. The power it generated circled the leap and made my heart beat against my chest.

Sebastian pulled me into the circle of his arms. "Here, you need to have a sip, Blaire."

Turning in his arms, he offered me the dark liquid.

"Is this his blood?"

"You're one of us," he said, nodding. "Drink."

He pressed the glass to my lips and lifted the bottom, forcing the liquid down my throat. The liquid had no smell, but it was cold and thick. I swallowed the metallic-tasting fluid and gagged, but I didn't spit it out. I swallowed hard, leaving a rusty taste in my mouth. I passed the glass to Jeremiah, who sat behind Sebastian.

I sat in the circle of Sebastian's body and leaned against his chest with my legs to my chest.

I closed my eyes for a second. I relaxed, my head on Sebastian's chest, and felt his chest rising and falling. He was so warm and comforting. The rhythmic sounds from the forest steadied my own heartbeat.

A leopard's face come before me. Its face was furry and white, and it had ice-blue eyes. It jumped at me, and I jerked awake.

My chest ached, and I was lying on the ground with Sebastian straddling my waist. He was pinning my arms above my head.

"Blaire, can you hear me? Blaire?" he asked with a quiver in his voice. His eyes held a hint of…fear? Concern? I wasn't sure.

"Get off me, Sebastian. You're hurting me."

"Sorry," he said, letting go of my hands and sitting beside me. "We had to hold you down."

I sat up.

Sawyer and Rory let go of a leg each, while the other leopards stood at a distance.

"She smells like them," Sawyer said. "Like a leopard."

"What happened?" I glared at Sawyer.

Sebastian opened his ripped shirt, revealing deep scratches.

"Did I do that to you?" I frowned.

"You growled at me, then your eyes glowed blue and you attacked me. I had to stop you." He touched his wounds. "You were strong, Blaire. All three of us had to hold you down. You were almost as strong as Sawyer here." He thumbed behind him in Sawyers direction.

"I saw a white leopard with blue eyes, and it jumped at me. It felt so real. I can still feel it inside me, Sebastian. Like it wants to claw its way out of me." I touched my chest, feeling a heavy weight bearing down on me. "After I drank that stuff, I closed my eyes for a second, and then it came at me." I shuddered. "I want to go home."

"It could be the lycanthropy," Anne said. "Your animal could be trying to come out," she added, looking up at the Blue Moon.

"Am I really changing? Is this what happens to everyone?"

"It's not usually quite what happened to you, but it could be," Anne said. "You shouldn't go through this alone. You need to be with someone who can help you if your animal does decide to come out and you change into your leopard."

"Shit, I can't believe it. But why now? Why after two months? I don't understand it." I wiped my eyes dry.

"It's amazing you are able to hold onto three different

strains. But it seems your inner leopard has won. Let Sebastian be there for you."

I glanced at Anne; I knew the look I gave her wasn't friendly.

Whatever was happening to me, I didn't want it to happen in front of the leap. I wanted to go to my house, where I had my own things.

The voodoo priest was dead. His girlfriend and his brother were dead. It was safer now. There was nothing else trying to get to me.

Sebastian wasn't thrilled that I wanted to go to my place instead of his. He didn't want me to be alone.

"I'll be fine, Sebastian," I said, sounding angry. I crossed my arms over my chest and stared out the window of the car.

Something was happening to me I couldn't explain, and I didn't want company if I changed. If Anne was right, I was becoming a were-leopard. And my leopard was white. I'd never heard of a white leopard before, and she wanted to come out of me.

I wondered what would happen with the other two were-animals inside of me; my lion and my wolf.

Leaning against the headrest of the back seat, I closed my eyes and pictured the white leopard with the icy blue eyes I'd seen earlier. I found her; she was hiding in a cave. I scanned the area and found a lioness and a wolf, each in their stone white caves.

All three stared knowingly at me.

All three were waiting for something.

"I can still smell your leopard," Sebastian said, bringing

me out of my metaphysical realm. "We'll take you home just as soon as we're sure you'll be fine. I promise." He pleaded with his eyes.

I sighed inwardly.

"Listen to him," Rory said while driving. He glanced at me in the rear-view mirror. "Let's first find out what's happening to you. Then when things have settled, I'll drop you off wherever you want to go." His eyes flitted to Sebastian.

"Fine," I mumbled and folded my arms across my chest.

Epilogue

I stayed with Sebastian for two weeks, and during that time, my leopard didn't claw its way through me once. We decided it was a combination of the Blue Moon, Grant's blood, and everything that had happened to me with the priest that caused my white leopard to reveal herself to me. When we thought it was safe and she would not burst through me, I asked Rory to take me home.

It had almost been a month since I was last home, and the floor near the front door was littered with letters, bills, and postcards. Rory checked each room thoroughly before I chased him out. I no longer required a guard to protect me.

I scooped up all the mail and set it down on the table in my basement. I lay on my couch, focusing on the buzzing sound of the small fridge to drown out the noises from the world outside.

In my arms was the large plush teddy bear Sebastian had given me to hold when he wasn't around. He hadn't told me to throw away the hedgehog Léon had sent me, and I didn't have the heart to, either. It had a new home on top of the little fridge in the basement. Every time I glanced at the plush hedgehog from the couch, I thought of Léon. I knew it was wrong to think of my boyfriend's brother, but I couldn't help how I felt about him, either. There was definitely something there.

The two weeks with Sebastian weren't all that boring; we got to know each other's bodies pretty well. Lying on the couch and squeezing my teddy, I wished I was back in his room with his hands all over my naked body. I thought of his tender kisses and his body working its way deeper into mine, and writhed on the couch.

Sebastian laughed in the distance, and I knew he metaphysically sensed what I was thinking. It brought a smile to my face.

I was falling for the blond-haired, green-eyed were-leopard-vampire. And it scared me.

Ralph would remain human after his attack. My prayers and wishes had worked.

During those two weeks, Ralph, Devan, and I worked on a number of cases together. Some simple surveillance, two divorce cases, one minor zombie uprising, and a robbery; nothing we couldn't handle. After the voodoo priest, we all needed a breather from the scary monsters.

Marcus and Melinda were still in lock-up at the Lion's Den. Troy would hold them there until I reached a decision. I wanted them hunted and killed. But until my mind clicked into place and I remembered, I needed Marcus to provide me with information on my past.

Zachary, the little poker-playing vampire, was being kept in a cross-wrapped coffin for another two weeks. It was his punishment for aiding and abetting the voodoo priest. It was a light sentence, but if he continued to play poker in Léon's city, Alex would make an example of him, too.

Alex and Genevieve, the emissaries of the Vampire Council, had asked to stay in the city for a while. Léon had agreed.

Sebastian and his brother continued with their power struggle over my affections, but with Charlotte by his side, Léon seemed content not to press the issue. For now.

I had arranged a lunch date with Mel; there was so much we needed to discuss, and my appointments with Seraphine and Désiré were still on schedule. I couldn't wait to tell them what I'd been up to.

Each of the groups that formed the Were-Animals Alliance had heard about what I had done for Ivy and had invited me to join them; a human had never been formally invited to any of these meetings before, and I felt honored. By attending monthly, I could keep in contact with Shawn and Troy, just in case my wolf or lioness decided they, too, wanted to join my leopard and come out to play.

That was the other reason for hiding out in my basement; I was ignoring the phone calls upstairs and the letters and postcards on the table. After I opened the first one, I couldn't go through the rest of them. It was a request to visit a colony in Chicago; their King Rat was ill and needed my help; an all expenses paid trip.

I wanted to help—I knew I could—but I needed to sort my life out now that I knew what I could do.

Also, I needed time to recover.

And I still had work to do.

Next in the Blaire Thorne Series

vinci-books.com/butterflies-hurricanes

In a world of shifting loyalties—trust is the deadliest weapon.

A dying king's urgent command drags me into a deadly web of shifter murders and a mysterious serum. With my daughter's life on the line and the man I love infected, I must unravel a dark conspiracy before everything unravels.

Turn the page for a free preview…

Butterflies and Hurricanes: Chapter One

I threw my gym bag on the floor in the bathroom and emptied the dirty contents into the laundry basket. Maria, a were-rat Elena had introduced me to, started keeping my house in order for me. I had no idea what I did before someone helped with housekeeping, but I was grateful to have Maria in my life.

Maria was preparing my lunch in the kitchen while I was freshening up in the bathroom. That first day she came to work for me, she walked in on me eating butter on toast. She shook her head in disapproval, saying a woman could not survive on bread alone. Since then, she would come every day to clean and cook at least one meal for me. I didn't need her every day, as it's only me, and there wasn't much for her to do, but she said I paid her enough for her to tidy up and cook. So I let her.

She's a legal immigrant from Mexico who had been bitten by a were-rat five years ago when she was still living in Chicago. She had lost her job, her husband, and her friends. Everyone thought she was disgusting, because she turned into a were-rat when the moon pulled at her once a month. Lance, their king rat, took her in and gave her a home. I suspected it was the constant reminder that her husband, family, and friends had rejected her that prompted the move to Sterling Meadow—out of sight, out of mind. Elena had arranged with her king rat, Arturo, for Maria to join their colony in Sterling Meadow. And I had provided for her by offering her a job.

I finished showering after my hectic gym session and sat at the kitchen island with my plate of food while Maria started a load of washing when a knock came on the door. I opened the door to two men standing in front of me. The one who had knocked still had his hand up mid-knock; he lowered his hand when I opened the door.

"Can I help you?" I asked, looking from one to the other.

Both men frowned.

"It's us."

I gave them my blank expression and shrugged.

"Don't you remember us?" the one who had knocked asked. He was tall, dark, and handsome. His head was shaved; he boasted dark chocolate-colored eyes and an oval-shaped face. I could see he had once been thin, but now he sported a slight paunch. The other man was just as tall, pale, with chestnut-colored hair cut short, light brown eyes, and a Vandyke beard. I could tell he went to the gym every day; his dress shirt stretched taut against his body.

"I'm sorry. No, I don't. Who are you?"

They looked at each other then back at me with wide eyes.

"We are your neighbors, Blaire." The pale one with the Vandyke beard thumbed at the house across the street. "We rent the house over there."

I shrugged. "Sorry, but I still don't know you or what you are doing here."

"What happened?" the pale one asked.

His friend stared at me with a shocked expression.

"Were-animals attacked me six months ago, and I hit my head pretty badly. Unfortunately, I don't remember much from my life before that day. If you do know me, I would really like to know everything you know." I opened the door wider. "Would you like to come inside?"

"Perhaps you should come with us instead," the tall, dark one said. "I'm Jermaine. This is Hugh." Jermaine held onto Hugh's shoulder while Hugh held Jermaine's waist.

"You'll want to come with us, Blaire. I promise. And bring those stunning keys of yours."

"Wait, what? Are you talking about the ones with the hieroglyphics?"

They nodded as one.

"Wait here." I ran to my bedroom to grab my keys. As I closed the front door, I saw Maria shaking her head and mouthing, *No, don't go.* But I could handle myself. Plus, I'd been training with Ralph, and I was starting to do more and more. Muscle memory was working with me.

I walked behind the couple as they held hands. We crossed the street toward a single-story house with a white picket fence. Before we entered, I caught a whiff of freshly baked cookies. My mouth watered at the sweet aroma.

"Please excuse the mess," Jermaine said. "I was busy baking. Can I offer you some coffee?"

I stopped in their living room. "Yes, that would be great. Black with two sugars."

The interior resembled a show house from a catalogue for *House and Home*—modern with the latest technology, a smart television, the latest surround sound, and the electronic eyes alarm companies use for motion detection.

Jermaine activated the coffee maker, donned his navy-blue apron and removed cookies off the dry rack and into a cookie tin.

"This way." Hugh pointed to a door I assumed was the basement. "Let me show you while Jermaine gets the coffee ready."

"Uh, okay," I said reluctantly.

Hugh opened the basement door and descended the steps.

I could either go with him and trust he wouldn't hurt me, or I could bolt out the front door and call Ralph. Ever since the voodoo priest had tried to kill me, I'd started wearing my gun in the shoulder holster all day, every day. I crossed my arms and felt the hard, cold metal in my hand and followed Hugh into their basement.

"Do you want to tell me what's going on?" I asked when I reached the bottom.

Hugh stood by a door. "This is yours."

I frowned at him. "What do you mean, it's mine?"

He pointed to the lock on the door. "Where are your keys?"

I held the keychain and approached the door. The lock was ancient. I inserted the second key and turned it, and the lock shifted in place. I pulled on the handle and opened the door. I glanced at Hugh as the door swung wide. My eyes widened as my mouth opened in a surprised *O*.

Butterflies and Hurricanes:
Chapter Two

Framed black and white pictures hung on one side of the little bedroom. In these pictures, I was holding a baby in some, while, in others, I stood beside a man who looked like a young Mason. I recognized him from the photos Kit had shown me; he was Léon's private investigator.

A cot sat in the right-hand corner adorned with a neatly folded pink blanket and a plush elephant. A desk and a chair rested bedside the cot. A large corkboard with a map and thumbtacks securing notes scribbled on pieces of paper hung against that wall and above the desk. A bookshelf rested near the door. The first shelf housed children's nursery rhymes, and the others featured young-adult books. Lavender and cotton scented the room.

I blinked back tears, my body trembling and the back of my throat hurting. "What is this? And please don't lie to me. Was this my daughter's room?"

"The stuff is Scout's, yes."

"You knew her?"

"Of course, we know her. We are her godparents."

Hugh closed the distance between us, pulling me into a hug. "It's okay, Blaire. She's safe."

His shirt smelled of cookies, and I laugh-cried. It smelled like home. Drying my eyes with the palms of my hands. The edges of my smile quivered when my face and hands were wet. "I think I need a tissue."

He chuckled, letting go. He handed me a couple of tissues from the box on the bookshelf. "You always cry when you come here, so there's always tissues for you."

I laughed and more tears fell. When the tears were gone and I could trust my voice again, I said, "Why didn't you come over sooner?"

"You only pop over on birthdays, Blaire."

The back of my throat ached when I swallowed. "Who's birthday is it today?"

"Scout's." Hugh smiled, but it didn't reach his eyes. "We all miss her. We write her letters, and you send them on our behalf."

"I know where she is?"

He nodded.

"Do you know?"

"No. It was safer for her and us that we didn't know." He eyes glistened in the light.

"Do you know why she had to leave—her and Mason?" I bit my lip. I'd rather feel pain than continue crying.

"You must've hit your head very hard not to remember, Blaire."

"I'll tell you about that later. Please just tell me about Scout." I raised my voice. "What happened that she had to leave?"

"Come upstairs, have some coffee, and we'll tell you everything we know." Hugh approached the stairs. "It'll be better for you if you don't stay in this room alone for now."

I nodded too fast, and felt light on my feet. Hugh was already up the stairs while I scanned the room one last time. I touched the soft pink blanket from the cot and cradled the plush toy, the smell of fresh linen heavy in the air around it.

I locked the door behind me to join Hugh and Jermaine upstairs. I reached the top and found them sitting on their living room couch.

"Come, dear. Come sit by us." Jermaine tapped the seat beside him.

I sat beside Jermaine, my eyes flitting from one to the other. "Okay, tell me." I hugged the plush elephant close to my chest, and the faint smell of linen wafted in the air.

"Ah …" Jermaine said. "It looks like you're reliving the day she had to go."

I eyed him.

Hugh continued, "We don't know exactly what happened that day to cause all the panic. Mason picked up Scout from daycare, like he did every day. You were still working. I think it was a vampire you were tracking on that ghastly mountain. When Mason came home, he ran straight to our house instead of yours, and they stayed with Jermaine until you got home."

"Is that it?"

"Mason said he couldn't tell us anything. He didn't want us to get involved. Even though he did by staying at our house. But we never found out what he was hiding from. When you got home, you shifted into overdrive and arranged for them to leave immediately. They said their good-byes, and that was the last time we saw them. This happened over ten years ago."

This was more information than Kit could find out, and I doubted he knew to visit this couple.

"Why do I have that room in your house and not in mine?" I asked, frowning.

Jermaine replied, "You used to live here. When Mason moved in across the road, you two started dating." He pointed to my current house. "When things got serious, you moved in with him, and you rented this one to us. When they had to leave, you asked if you could use the basement, and we didn't need the space, so we agreed."

Hugh added, "I think if you didn't have the room here, we would never see you. After they left, you poured your heart and soul into your work. You were always chasing all the monsters you could find. You kept saying, *Just one more monster.*"

"Jesus, I sounded awful." I squeezed the plush elephant against my chest until it hurt. My mug of coffee on the table was already getting cold, and the plate of cookies were waiting for me to eat them, but I had no appetite. I faced the couple. "Can you tell me anything more? Anything about my life?"

"We became friends after we rented your place. When Scout was born, you and Mason asked us to be godparents. We had dinner together at least once a month. But we don't know much about your or Mason's past before then, so we don't know about your parents or if either of you had any siblings. If you did, we never met any." Hugh shrugged. "You worked for Ulysses Assassin as an assassin. Jermaine almost had a heart attack when you told him." Hugh's laugh was deep and throaty, while Jermaine squeaked. Bless his heart.

I smiled at them; they were a very cute couple.

"Oh, you hated shifters. A Lot. As in you H-A-T-E-D them."

"Do you know why?"

"No. They were your pet peeves. Not sure which shifters you hated more, but you seemed to hate them all at varying degrees. Mason didn't know either, and he suspected something must've happened in your past."

A tune I recognized sounded. I pulled my cellphone from my pocket; Ralph was calling. "Excuse me," I said and stood to answer the call. "Ralph, what's up?"

"Are you still heading out tomorrow?"

"Yeah, why?"

"You feel like coming to dinner with me and Devan?"

"I already have plans."

"With Sebastian?"

Beep ... Beep ...

"Hang on. I have another call." I put Ralph on hold, pressing the green button. "Hello?"

"Where are you?"

"At home," I retorted.

"No, you're not. Sawyer is in your house, and Maria said you left with two men."

"I'm across the road, Sebastian. Tell Sawyer to walk across, and he'll find me here." I tried to sound happier, more pleasant, but I knew I was failing.

"Please don't go anywhere without him, Blaire. *Please* ..."

"I'm sorry," I whispered into the cellphone. "I didn't think I would take so long. I see Sawyer walking toward me. Let me get him, and then I'll see you soon."

"Okay." He hung up without saying goodbye.

I opened the front door and motioned for Sawyer to enter.

"Hello ...?" I heard faintly.

"Sorry, Ralph, I forgot you were still on hold."

"I guess we won't see you until you're back in a few days' time."

"Yeah, sorry about that. Will everything be okay without me for a few days?"

"We'll be fine. Chat later."

He too hung up without saying bye. Men were so rude.

I greeted Sawyer and introduced him to Hugh and Jermaine.

"You ready?" Sawyer asked, heading for the front door.

"Yeah, just give me a sec." I faced the men still sitting on the couch. "Thank you for coming to fetch me and for showing me the room." I raised the plush elephant. "I'll hold onto this for a while."

"It's yours, Blaire. You can do with it as you please," Hugh said, standing from the couch.

Jermaine followed suit and hugged Hugh from the side. "Are you going away?"

"To Chicago for a day or two. I was wondering, can we meet again when I get back?"

"Of course. Jermaine is always at home. He's my little housewife." Hugh tickled Jermaine's neck, and they both chuckled.

"They're sweet," Sawyer said as we crossed the road to my house.

"Yeah, aren't they just?"

Sawyer stood on the porch while I packed. He was making me nervous dressed in his black bodyguard outfit with his weapons showing. I suspected he looked threatening to my neighbors. I saw a few glances our way as people passed my house.

Sebastian and I had a date night planned, and then I'd be going to Chicago for two days to meet the king rat. At first, I had avoided his letter when I had first gotten home over a month ago, but, after much convincing, I had agreed to go. I had been staying by Sebastian, so they could monitor me when we thought my were-leopard was about to go all furry on me, but nothing had happened after that blue moon when I had some of that blood.

For now, I was still a human.

Apart from the fact I now seemed to be collecting lycanthropy strains, so far I had were-wolf, were-lion, and were-leopard inside me. After that attack six months ago, the witches who had tended my wounds discovered I had a little secret—a talent of sorts. Apart from my aura that glowed white and like a beacon, I had a strong connection to the *other side*, the mystical and metaphysical world—the monster's world. I could absorb their power and use it against others. And, between all that, I had discovered I could heal others by using that white aura of mine. I still didn't understand how any of it worked, as I was trying to regain my memory.

Word of my saving Ivy had spread through the were-animal community, and they had invited me to attend the Were-Animal Alliance meeting. I had gone with Sebastian last week and had met a representative from Chicago who begged me to visit his king. Lance, the were-rat King of Chicago, had been injured during a challenge. At first, they had thought it was only a superficial injury, but he had been deteriorating, and of late, it had worsened. After trying everything, he was desperate, and I was his only hope. He would richly compensate me for my time and pay all travel expenses.

Sebastian had agreed, but only if I took Sawyer with— my very own personal bodyguard. He wanted me to have two, but that's where I drew the line and said, *No*. If I absolutely had to have a bodyguard, one would suffice.

Before we left, I told Maria she had the rest of the week off.

Her face paled. She thought I was letting her go. After twenty minutes of explaining I was just leaving town so she didn't have to come in, she was content. After she left, I locked up, and Sawyer drove me to the Labyrinth.

Grab your copy...
vinci-books.com/butterflies-hurricanes

About the Author

A Multi-genre author writing twisted endings...

N Gray is a USA Today Bestselling Author who lives in Cape Town, South Africa, with her daughter and adopted cat named Miss Beans.

During the day, she's an analyst and provider profiler for a medical insurance company. At night, she types on her curved keyboard, creating fictional characters some may love and others you want to kill yourself.

She writes in four genres: urban fantasy, thriller, horror, and paranormal romance.

She now writes under Natalie Michaels for her new thrillers and SD Syns for her new horrors.

Acknowledgments

Thank you to my readers, old and new, for taking a chance on my books.

You are the reason I write the stories I do. As long as you keep reading, I'll keep writing.

I'm truly humbled by your support and encouragement.

I write in as many genres as I love reading in. There are so many stories swarming inside my head that I could never just choose one.

Horror is my guilty pleasure. I love writing short stories filled with dark humour and the occult with a twist ending.

Urban fantasy and paranormal romance are where I love to spend my time, and I have so many books planned that I don't have enough time (*but I'll get there*).

And lastly, my thrillers. Who doesn't love sitting on the edge of their seat while reading about what goes on inside the antagonist's mind? Well, I love writing about them.

www.ingramcontent.com/pod-product-compliance
Ingram Content Group UK Ltd.
Pitfield, Milton Keynes, MK11 3LW, UK
UKHW040247291225
466476UK00003B/11